Credits:

Edited by Mollie Traver and Linda Ingmanson

Cover Design by Deranged Doctor Design

Trident
Rescue

Enemy
ZONE

ALEX LIDELL

ALSO BY ALEX LIDELL

TRIDENT RESCUE

Contemporary Romance

ENEMY ZONE

ENEMY CONTACT

POWER OF FIVE (7 books)

Reverse Harem Fantasy Romance

POWER OF FIVE (Audiobook available)

MISTAKE OF MAGIC (Audiobook available)

TRIAL OF THREE (Audiobook available)

LERA OF LUNOS (Audiobook available)

GREAT FALLS CADET (Audiobook available)

GREAT FALLS ROGUE

GREAT FALLS PROTECTOR

IMMORTALS OF TALONSWOOD (4 books)

Reverse Harem Paranormal Romance

LAST CHANCE ACADEMY (Audiobook available)

LAST CHANCE REFORM (Audiobook available)

LAST CHANCE WITCH

LAST CHANCE WORLD

Young Adult Fantasy Novels

TIDES

FIRST COMMAND (Audiobook available)

AIR AND ASH (Audiobook available)

WAR AND WIND (Audiobook available)

SEA AND SAND (Audiobook available)

SCOUT

TRACING SHADOWS (Audiobook available)

UNRAVELING DARKNESS (Audiobook available)

TILDOR

THE CADET OF TILDOR

SIGN UP FOR NEW RELEASE NOTIFICATIONS at https://links.
alexlidell.com/News

SKY

"New chick, it's your lucky day," Frank Peterson booms through *Denton Uncovered*'s messy newsroom. My new boss is loud enough to wake the dead, despite my being five feet away.

I force my face into a polite smile as Frank saunters toward me, his shoulders not quite filling in his sport jacket. I long to remind him I'm a twenty-three-year-old woman with a journalism degree, not a girl or a *chick* or whatever, but I don't. New boss. New paper. First day. *Denton Uncovered*—a tabloid in remote Denton Valley, Colorado—isn't exactly a premier paper, but after the fiasco in New York, it was the only place to give me the time of day. Part time. And I'd sent out dozens of résumés.

"My name is Skylar, Mr. Peterson," I say. "Skylar Reynolds."

Frank waves his hands in front of his face as if I'm an irritating mosquito and slaps a sheet with a scribbled address onto my desk. "Story for you!"

Here we go. My heart quickens, but I manage to keep from leaping out of my chair. "Yes, sir."

Frank nods his approval. "Car accident on the corner of Main and First."

My smile freezes on my face. Car accident. That's not a story, that's a police report.

Frank snorts. "Disappointed?"

Yes. "No, sir. I'm here for whatever *Denton Uncovered* needs."

"Excellent. Because it's not just a car accident, honey." Frank leans over me, wafting his thickly sweet bug-spray-like cologne right into my personal space. Hell, maybe it *is* bug spray. I try not to gag. The fluorescent overhead lighting makes his bald spot shine as he moves, squaring off both hands in the air as if framing a picture. "Driver's rumored to be Mr. Mason of Mason Pharmaceuticals, aka a lush, drunk more often than sober. Except you wouldn't know that from his record—money talks in this town. If you hurry, maybe you can get through before he pays off the cops and walks free."

Well, now Frank's got my attention. There's something that twists my gut at knowing that some rich asshole is paying off his DUIs. There are some things money should not be able to buy.

"On it, sir," I say, already grabbing the key to my aging Toyota Corolla and begging the car gods that it actually makes it to the scene. I won't have money to fix it until the first paycheck comes in, and that's not for a few weeks with Frank's payroll setup. Might not be enough even then. I took this job to build up field experience, but I'll need to find a second one quickly if I want to eat.

I give the office one last glance. The photographer, James Dyer, bustles out the frosted door while Frank and I are talking, so I assume whatever he's going out for has nothing to do with my story. Patrick Capaldi, the veteran sportswriter, is busy typing into his laptop behind me. I turn when the clicking of his fingers stops, and catch a smirk. Or at least I think I do. It's gone as soon as I see it.

Weird.

But maybe I'm being paranoid. Scratch that. I know I'm being paranoid. But after the shit my ex-fiancé and his marine buddies pulled in New York, I can't help it. While there are other female employees, I'm the lone female reporter. Still, I have no reason to believe that anyone here is misogynistic—for all his talk, Frank did hire me. I've had enough of that men-stick-together shit to last me a lifetime. Two lifetimes.

This is my fresh start.

My car mercifully starts on the second try, and I'm soon on Denton Valley's main throughway. Denton Valley, Colorado, is nestled—as its name suggests—in a valley, the rugged snowcapped peaks of the Southern Rocky Mountains surrounding it like a scarf. The effect is one of protection, similar to a favorite pair of thick woolen socks. Or at least that's the way I'm thinking about it. As I head toward the crash, I'm a little unsettled by the dense green—turning autumn orange—forest that encroaches from the side of the highway. This town isn't tiny, but it's nothing like my old stomping grounds in Brooklyn.

The road is curvy as hell, with the occasional deer deciding that of all the times to run across the road, doing so while I'm driving is ideal. With all my time in New York, I'm not exactly *Fast and Furious* when it comes to driving. Thankfully, it's fall, so I don't have to deal with icy road conditions. Yet. I can handle this. I can handle anything.

Exiting off the highway, I enter the more familiar-to-me urban area. The road flares and flashing lights guide me the final few hundred yards to the accident, both the red and blue ones of the ambulance as well as the amber lights of a tow truck. The vic's car —a Cadillac Escalade that seems pristine except for missing its front half—seems to have been wrapped around a tree.

At least the bastard didn't hurt anyone else.

I pull into a space a few car lengths down and pop out, notes app on my phone at the ready. But first things first. Photos.

A pair of policemen standing guard, nearly at attention.

A guy in greasy coveralls hooking the abused Caddy onto a flatbed.

A muscular paramedic wearing skintight Under Armour with *Trident Rescue* stenciled on the back looming over an annoyed-looking guy in a business suit who holds a cloth to his bleeding head, the medical Suburban's lights flickering in the background.

I swallow, my hand tightening around my phone as my camera zoom shows the medic's face in full detail. His jaw is square and clean-shaven, his cheekbones chiseled, his mouth firm. Add in the

3

mossy-green eyes full of intelligence and concern, and he's basically an Adonis. A real live Adonis. Heat rises to my face, my thighs clenching together until I can finally force away the thought of what that medic might look like shirtless and focus on the task at hand.

Making sure my press credentials are clearly visible around my neck, I come up to one of the officers. "Good afternoon, sir. Sky Reynolds, reporter with *Denton Uncovered*. Can you tell me whether you've administered a sobriety test to the driver?"

The uniformed guy looks at me incredulously. "To *Eli Mason?*"

I'll take that as a no.

"From the skid marks, it appears Mr. Mason swerved on the road before ramming a tree. Was there someone else involved in the accident? Another victim?" *Or did that tree just attack him from the roadside?*

"Single-car collision, ma'am." The guy's partner comes over with a hard expression that tells me to get the hell out if I know what's good for me.

Except that I do know what's good for me. The truth.

Ducking around the officers, I make a confident dash for Medic Adonis and his charge.

"You need stitches and might have a concussion." Adonis's voice is a rich commanding baritone that perfectly matches his chiseled body, the navy-blue cargos clinging to a taut waist. His blond buzz cut is shaved close enough that it looks like he might've used a ruler. Maybe even a protractor. Not a look I usually go for—too military, and I've had my fill of *that* mess—but on Adonis, it's perfect.

"I don't bloody need stitches." Mason sounds like a hurt animal, his British accent and bravado masking pain. Unlike Adonis's buzz cut, Eli's unruly copper hair flops onto his brow. His white button-down business shirt is spotted with blood all down his left arm. "I don't have a concussion either."

I step up to the men, extending a hand. "Good afternoon, gentlemen. I'm Skylar Reynolds, reporter with *Denton Uncovered*. Mind if I ask you a few questions?"

Mason squints at me as if his head aches, so I pivot toward Adonis. But then my eyes meet his, and I watch his gaze turn hard.

Even hateful. Nothing like the concerned look he'd had when speaking to Eli. Is Adonis on Eli Mason's payroll as well? The cops certainly seem to be.

I draw a calming breath. I've been around hateful men before, and I don't like it. In fact, I despise it. Especially when that hard gaze is immediately accompanied by a twist of his lips. A sneer. I'm standing there like an idiot with my hand stretched out, and Adonis is too busy staring me down to even notice.

"Get off my scene," Adonis snaps, his jaw flexing.

I read the name embroidered on his shirt. Hunt.

"I'm the press, and this is a story, Mr. Hunt. Which means it actually *does* concern me. If there's a reason Mr. Mason hasn't been tested for blood alcohol level? Or been given a breathalyzer test at least?"

Eli's eyes flash with fury as he twists to me and winces.

Stepping around Eli, Hunt completely blocks my access to him. He has a way of taking over all the space around him. All the air.

"I don't care if you're the queen of England, you and *Denton Uncovered...*" He gnashes his teeth, as if swallowing what he wants to say before coming up with a curt "You need to leave. Now."

I stand my ground. "The First Amendment says otherwise."

Hunt takes a step toward me, his shoulders spreading as if he's about to sprout wings like an archangel. His stance is pure trained authoritarian. This guy comes from either a law enforcement background or, more likely, a military one.

Just like my father. Just like Jaden. The thought of my ex-fiancé makes me shudder with revulsion.

"*Cullen,*" Eli says from behind the medic, the warning note in it subtle but unmistakable.

Hunt's hands curl into a fist, anger radiating from him in waves. I back up a step. A muscle in Hunt's jaw flexes, and he spins on his heel, slamming his palm against the Suburban with a loud clang—Eli saving his hand from getting crushed only by virtue of his uncannily quick reflexes.

All right, so maybe Eli Mason isn't drunk.

5

Stomping around the medical Suburban, Hunt slides behind the steering wheel.

"Mason, shotgun."

At first, I have no idea what Hunt's decree means. Did he seriously just threaten me with a shotgun? But then Eli throws me a narrowed glance before snapping to like a cadet and climbing into the passenger's side.

Ah.

I go to take another picture of the scene, my hand stilling midmotion. Not only had Eli Mason not acted intoxicated, but the way Hunt barked out orders, it was hard to imagine the medic being on his patient's payroll. The only thing Frank's lead had gotten correct, it seems, was the accident site.

The siren comes on, wailing so loudly that I clap my hands over my ears. Then the Suburban maneuvers into traffic, cutting off a sedan, and careens down Main. A couple of blocks down, it whips down a side street, the flashing lights strobing across the manicured landscaping of both buildings and residences alike.

Before I can register everything that just happened, the emergency vehicle and its surly occupant have vanished from sight.

Great. The only place willing to hire me had sent me on a story without the correct information, and I hadn't been able to obtain even the briefest of interviews from anyone involved.

What now?

2

CULLEN

"*A* dog? Seriously, Mason?" Cullen Hunt frowned at Eli Mason as the former SEAL balked at the sight of a suturing kit Cullen was pulling out. Cullen had already given up on the notion of taking the stubborn son of a bitch to a hospital to get a full concussion workup, but he wasn't about to give in on this. The laceration on Eli's arm was not bleeding much, but it was long and deep enough to develop an infection if they weren't careful. Eli got off light. Whatever else, the Caddie had one hell of a safety system.

"You can maneuver a goddamned Humvee around mortar explosions, but a dog sends you into a tree?" Cullen asked.

"It was right there in the middle of the intersection..." Eli threw up his hands, the sudden action making him wince and grab his neck. The man's British accent—which his London-born parents beat into him—was more pronounced than usual, as it always became under stress. "It was little and brown. Had floppy ears. So it was probably a puppy. I may be an arsehole, but I'm not gonna run over a *puppy*. And I don't need a nursemaid, Cullen. Or stitches. I'm—"

"Oh, let me guess," Cullen interrupted, speaking over him. "You're *fine*."

"I am." Standing, Eli paced back and forth in one of the med bays at the small Trident Rescue Medical Facility, arms crossed over his chest. At least there was no one else there to watch Eli very much *not* practice what he preached when he was the medic on duty.

Unlike Denton Valley's main emergency medical response operation, Denton EMS, Trident Rescue was a private company—one that Cullen owned. The SEALS had trained emergency medicine into his blood and Cullen brought the passion with him when he left the military.

He'd tried volunteering at Denton EMS, but the civilian service didn't scratch the right itch. However, Trident Rescue did—especially once Cullen recruited Eli Mason, Liam Rowen, and Kyan Keasley, the men Cullen had befriended at the military high school their parents had shipped them off to.

Now each volunteered a shift or two a week at the Rescue, picking up any trauma calls Denton EMS sent their way. With how shorthanded Denton EMS always was, they were more than happy for the occasional help—especially for remote mountain accidents.

It was a win-win. The Tridents kept up their skills, Denton Valley got free medical assistance, and the occasional serious accidents on the mountain got a faster response. Plus, there was only so long a man could sit behind a mahogany desk before he lost his mind, no matter how good a business he ran.

Today's traffic accident was not the usual kind of thing the Tridents responded to, but once Cullen heard the radio report of a totaled vehicle matching Eli's Escalade, he'd snatched the call. And though he'd never admit to it aloud, flashing images of Eli in a fatal crash had haunted him all the way to the scene.

Speaking of Eli, the man out and out refused to sit on one of the beds, despite being in obvious pain. Which figured. He'd behaved similarly when he'd broken his arm at sixteen. Actually, Eli's father had done the breaking for him, though Cullen and the others hadn't known it at the time. Having been wounded himself, Cullen understood. Suffering an injury in battle was one thing. To allow someone—even a brother—to hurt you when you were defenseless was an entirely different matter. Even if the hurting was for a good cause.

"*Lieutenant.*" Cullen infused the full command of his former rank into his tone, and Eli stilled immediately to focus on him. Technically, his friend didn't have to obey a word he said, but after almost a decade of conditioning, giving orders and following orders still felt as natural as breathing, though they'd been out of the navy for a couple of years now. "Get your ass over here and give me your stupid arm."

"Yes, *sir.*"

Jesus.

"So, *Denton Uncovered* has a new angle and a new face." Cullen injected lidocaine into the wound, his own shoulder twinging in sympathy.

Eli winced. "If you want to distract me, can you pick a more pleasant topic?"

Cullen snorted. The only "news" that paper *uncovered* were the rumors and sensationalist gossip it created itself. The tabloid's editor, Frank Peterson, lived for three things: power, chaos, and coming out on top. The man would do whatever it took to ensure he had all those at any given point too. And now a new low—sending in a drop-dead gorgeous reporter. Long straight strawberry-blonde hair flowing down her back like a waterfall. Fair, flawless skin. Bright blue eyes like a mountain stream. She'd been wearing a professional-looking blue pantsuit that had highlighted those eyes, and spoke with a soft and surprisingly sultry voice.

Cullen had no idea how Frank had managed to snatch Skylar Reynolds, but it likely had to do with the fact that she wasn't from around here.

Either that or she was cut from the same cloth and was eagerly following her mentor's footsteps. Who was Cullen kidding? Of course she was cut from the same cloth. She started planting lies right there at the scene. Drunk driving? Eli Mason, the head of the local pharmaceutical conglomerate?

It was a dick move. Though the girl seemed to actually believe her own words.

The sight of Sky's face flushed with exasperation and her eyes flashing with reined-in temper had turned him on. Tremendously. And the visceral way in which his cock rose to attention against the zipper of Cullen's cargos had only served to aggravate him further.

Arousal mixed with animosity proved to be an extremely uncomfortable reaction.

Besides, when it came to women and romantic entanglements, he had the worst track record imaginable. Which was probably a good thing in retrospect. Cullen had too many things fucked up with him to be fair to subject a partner to.

He'd just finished the last of Eli's sutures when the private landline lit up next to him. Since his dispatcher was on maternity leave and his office assistant had gone out suddenly with appendicitis, there was no one to route the calls to. He snatched up the receiver.

"Trident Rescue."

"Cullen, this is Suzy."

Suzy Canefield, his dispatcher, thank Christ. The past three months she'd been on maternity leave had been hell. He'd been making do with temps, but none of those people had the skill set Suzy had, and frankly, the whole point of the Rescue was to have a small tight-knit group. He needed Suzy back, and he needed her yesterday. Which meant hearing her on the other end of the line filled him with relief.

"Great to hear from you, Suz. Looking forward to being back here tomorrow?" God knew he was.

"Well, here's the thing, boss. I'm not coming back tomorrow after all."

Cullen's stomach sank to his knees. "Need more time off?" *Please say no.*

"Actually… I need to tender my resignation."

Fuck my life.

"Mind telling me why?" he asked instead, trying to keep his tone even.

"It's Bobby. His request to be stationed in Stuttgart has been honored, so all three of us will be settling in Germany for the foreseeable future. It'll get him out of the Middle East, and it's a promotion for him too. We'll be able to be together as a family now. We just received the call this morning."

"That *is* great news," Cullen said, meaning every word. No one knew better than him what horrors abounded in Afghanistan and Iraq. Bobby coming back alive and whole to be a husband and father was worth celebrating.

Not that many came back whole. Cullen sure as hell hadn't. Bar Peterson—their fifth musketeer from military school—hadn't made it back at all.

Which wasn't to say that Suzy's news didn't leave the Rescue in a lurch, because it absolutely did. Suzy was Cullen's right-hand man. Or woman. Whatever. She'd been indispensable.

"Thank you for understanding, boss. I wish I could've at least given you notice, but…" Her voice fizzled into nothing.

"Don't worry about it. I'll hold down the fort till I find a permanent replacement." He paused. "I mean it, Suz. Give my congrats to Bobby and take care of yourself. You need something, you call me from any time zone."

Hanging up, he glanced up at Eli, who'd taken it upon himself to slap a Band-Aid over Cullen's work, offer him a smart-assed salute, and traipse out of the room. Ingrate. Not that he didn't love that ingrate like a brother. He'd die for the guy and knew Eli would return the favor. So would Liam and Kyan.

What none of the assholes would do, however, was restock the supply closet or file medical reports on something other than whatever scrap of paper happened to be around when they deployed. You'd think that with all four of them now heading up major businesses, administrating something as small as Trident Rescue would be easy, but the reality proved anything but. Even Liam, who owned a security company, could barely be trusted to lock the door after himself.

"Suz isn't coming back," Cullen hollered out to Eli, and his one-time lieutenant marched back over the threshold.

"What? Not ever?"

"No. Bobby got stationed in Germany. She and the baby are going with."

Eli scratched his head. "You need to hire someone ASAP."

"Oh, you think?"

Cullen scrubbed a hand over his short hair. His assistant, Catherine, should be returning within the next few days. Unless she pulled a Suzy. Catherine Falkner, a matronly lady in her sixties, hadn't missed a single one of her workdays until she'd been rushed to the ER with a high fever and severe stomach pains that turned out to be appendicitis. So chances were she'd be back relatively soon. He hoped.

As if she'd sensed his need for her, a text bloomed across the screen of his cell.

DOCTOR SAYS *I'll need to be on half days with light duty only, but I'm released for work starting tomorrow. May I come in from eight to one?*

HE TYPED his answer to her as fast as his thick fingers would allow.

YOU CAN WORK *whenever you want. And for fuck's sake, find me a new dispatcher.*

I'LL WASH *your mouth out with soap, Cullen Hunt.*

CULLEN SNORTED.

Looking over Cullen's shoulder at the messages, Eli shook his head before swatting the back of Cullen's.

"You deserved that, asshole. But at least I trust Catherine more than I trust you to actually hire someone. I know Trident Rescue is your baby, but you need someone here. Someone who isn't you."

3

SKY

I return to *Denton Uncovered* to hear cackles of laughter as soon as I walk through the entrance. The photographer—whom I hadn't ever formally met—and the sportswriter stare at me with mirth.

"So...how'd it go?" Capaldi, the sports guy, asks.

"Did you get your story on *Eli Mason*?" Dyer plays with his camera.

I bristle. Had the bastards known Frank was sending me on a wild-goose chase? "What's so funny?"

"Ignore them, honey." As if summoned from his office by my presence, Frank materializes beside me, his tone patronizing. "Boys will be boys."

Boys will be boys. I'd heard that line before back in New York. It'd been right before my career had gone up in flames. Blood boiling, I spin to my new editor. "Why did you tell me the accident was caused by alcohol?"

"That's what my sources said, honey. And you should never believe in other people's sources." His voice hardens. "A fact you'd know if you had a shred of experience or at least some common sense. Don't like what I give you on a silver platter? Put on a short skirt and start getting your own sources. Or quit journalism. But if you're expecting to be spoon-fed stories, you're in the wrong fucking business."

"I…" I opened my mouth, then shut it again.

"Have the story on my desk tomorrow," he huffs, disappearing back into his office. When I turn back around to Capaldi and Dyer, neither of the men is laughing now. But they aren't looking at me either.

There's a huge lump in my throat, but I refuse to fall apart in front of the men. What happened at the scene with Asshole Adonis and now with my boss feels far too familiar. I'd hoped to put any chauvinistic bullshit behind me, but here I am, facing it all over again. Still, this isn't the time to show weakness.

Straightening my spine, I spend the rest of my workday shaping the actual facts I'd managed to collect into a story. Journalism is my passion. Real journalism—the kind with integrity and the power to change the world for the better. For tonight, that means writing up a traffic accident in the best way possible.

By the time I finish, everyone else has gone home. I slip my report under Frank Peterson's door, then leave. I slide into my driver's seat, finally allowing my head to fall forward. I let myself wallow for a grand total of sixty seconds, then, breathing through my nose, renew my resolve and drive to the dank basement apartment I've rented.

As I step through my door, I'm accosted by the subtle odor of mildew. My home is dark and windowless, and that may actually be real moss growing inside the crack of my door, but I'm thankful to have a roof over my head just now. If things don't change soon, that may no longer be the case. Working part-time for Frank pays nearly nothing.

I switch on a lamp and settle onto my bed to review my job hunting progress. The only other paper in town, the *Denton Valley Leader*, claimed to have no open positions, the same with the more distant publications I've talked to virtually. The details differed, but the theme stayed the same: "We're not hiring right now, but we'll keep your résumé on file."

My search outside the field is doing little better. I've got résumés out for secretarial duties, tutoring, even a few waitressing positions. Nothing.

In other words, I'm shit out of luck.

Opening my banged-up laptop, I go through the latest local offerings to send out résumés to anything that I might remotely qualify for. A paralegal offering and a dispatch/office manager post. Glancing at the name of the second business, I laugh out loud at the irony—Trident Rescue, Adonis's stomping ground.

Well, too bad. Running into the man on occasion might be awkward, but so is being homeless. I hit Send on my application and résumé. Feeling drained in every way possible, I shower, throw on my comfiest nightshirt, eat some peanut butter crackers for dinner, and fall into bed.

Which is exactly when my cell phone rings, my mother's picture flashing on the screen along with that up-and-down xylophone sound. I consider ignoring it. Conversations with my mother never leave me anything but furious—not that that stops her from starting them over and over.

Still, I can't help but wonder if something is wrong. What if this is an emergency? Not her kind of emergency, but the real kind—totally possible given the temper that some of her sugar daddies have had over the years. You'd think living with my father would have taught her the signs of dangerous men. Hell, maybe it did, and she just doesn't care.

I oscillate back and forth like a fan before finally giving in to my fears and picking up. "Mom? You okay?"

"I'm just fine. Why wouldn't I be?"

"Because you're calling me near midnight."

She giggles on the other end, dropping her voice conspiratorially. "Oh, Greg and I were caught up in Bloomy's most of the day, and then he just insisted that we visit Tiffany's. And by the time we got home, and one thing led to another... Well, I'm just now coming up for air, and I need to know my little girl is doing okay."

Translation: *I didn't want my newest sugar daddy getting distracted from buying me things, and finally, I have time alone to brag.*

"Could you please not talk about stores like they're your friends?" I rub my face, trying to remember whether Greg was the seventy-year-old doctor or the "happily" married real estate attorney. "Anyway, I'm fine. And I'm going to bed now. Good night."

"Wait! I wanted to tell you that Greg is inviting us—both of us —on a cruise! He wants to get to know you, you know, and it would be such a great opportunity to spend time together. Especially after all that's happened in New York—"

"I have a job, Mother. I can't drop it to go on a cruise."

"Don't be silly. We can talk to Greg about some positions he may help you find. But that can only happen if he knows you better."

I try not to choke on the word "positions," because I've exactly an idea of which ones he'd be looking for. "Ma, I'm going to bed now. Good night." I disconnect the line before she can answer and set the phone on silent until morning.

I'm on my way to the paper the next morning when my cell rings again. A Catherine from Trident Rescue. She sounds so competent and polite that, for a moment, I think I'm being pranked. Fortunately, I recover in time to register that I'm actually being invited to an interview.

Pulling over to the side of the road, I eagerly jot down the details. Yes, today will work. Three p.m. is perfect. I will be there.

By the time afternoon rolls around, however, I'm more confused than optimistic. Trident Rescue was described as a small rural EMS service, but the building Catherine sent me to is one of the fanciest in town—right next to the Mason Pharmaceuticals tower.

With several stories of a reflective glass façade, the place looks like a high-power office suite rather than a practicing medical facility—though the building name does have the word *Trident* in it. Grabbing my phone, I google the address to learn that I'm at Trident Medical Group headquarters. The place administers

Denton Valley Hospital and some affiliates. Perhaps Trident Rescue is just too small to be mentioned?

After circling the structure a few times, I realize I'm in danger of running late and decide to just go inside.

Stepping into the lobby with its marble columns reminds me of entering a museum, except even more opulent. My heels click loudly on the gleaming black tile floor beneath my feet as I pass two revolving glass doors and a gigantic mural of children's handprints before coming to a stop at a circular reception desk.

"Good afternoon," I tell the stunningly beautiful woman with raven-black hair and perfectly made-up features who mans the post. "My name is Skylar Reynolds. I have an appointment with Mr. Hunt." I almost cringe saying the name—an ironic match to the medic's name from the other day. "Can you point me in the right direction?"

With her chin raised, the woman peers down her pert and adorably small, straight nose at me. The placard in front of her says Rachel Arnault, and not only could she be a model, but she seems keenly aware of this. Her blouse looks silky and expensive, and her silver—or maybe platinum—necklace, earrings, and assortment of rings contrast prettily with her skin tone.

I'm reminded of what I put on this morning. While it's pressed to within an inch of its life, my belted black dress is hardly high-end. I can't afford much, so I've had to get somewhat creative when it comes to shopping for business attire. Clearance racks have long since become my best friends, and so have the occasional finds in thrift shops. I have to work not to cross my arms over my chest to cover the tide of inadequacy that washes over me.

"Of course. Ms. Richards, is it?"

"Reynolds," I correct.

"Yes. Mr. Hunt's office is located on the seventh floor, penthouse level. Just scurry to the elevator bank over there." She points. "It'll be the second door on your left. Though given that you're late, perhaps you might wish to reconsider disturbing him?"

"I'll risk it."

Rachel offers me a crimson smile that's the teeniest bit too

17

saccharine, and, doing my best not to feel cowed by it, I turn to follow her directions.

Taking some deep calming breaths on my way up, I square my shoulders and step off the elevator. My heels sink into a thick cream carpet the moment I do, and I take note of the floor-to-ceiling windows and rich dark crown molding that line the corridor. As I close in on the second door to my left, my heart pounds harder and harder. I don't belong here. People like Rachel belong here.

Stopping in front of a thick wooden door, I feel my whole body freeze as I read the nameplate: CULLEN HUNT, CEO. TRIDENT MEDICAL GROUP.

Cullen.

Obviously, it couldn't be *that* Cullen, but just the sight of the similar name sends an unwelcome tingle along my thighs. I try to knock, only to chicken out at the last instant. Closing my eyes and pulling myself together, I lift my hand determinedly. But this time, the door opens before my knuckles can even make contact. A very large—and very, very annoyed—man with an Adonis-like body and mossy-green eyes glares at me from the threshold. It's him. It's *that* damn Cullen.

My mouth dries, everything inside me simply freezing. Shit. Holy blessed shit.

For one insane moment, I consider the idea that maybe the medic from yesterday has a twin. Certainly there's something different about the man who stands before me now compared to the Cullen from yesterday. Instead of an Under Armour shirt emblazoned with the Trident Rescue insignia, this Cullen wears a tailored pinstriped suit cut from what's probably exceedingly pricey and finely woven wool. His silk tie, a mossy green that resembles his eyes, likely costs more than my entire closet.

Cullen's face darkens. "I've nothing to say to *Denton Uncovered.* Which part of that was unclear to you yesterday?"

Yep, this is definitely the same Cullen. He even wears that identical forbidding look he tossed at me yesterday. Except why is he masquerading around Denton Valley as a medic one day and a freaking CEO the next? Nothing about this makes sense. Nothing about *him* makes sense.

I open my mouth, but no sound comes out. My whole body tenses, blood pumping to my legs and lungs, my fight-or-flight instinct kicking in. But I can't fight or fly. I *need* this job. "I… I'm not here from the paper, sir." I try to swallow, but can't. "I'm here for an interview. It's for the dispatcher position? Three p.m.?"

Cullen pulls a phone from his back pocket and punches a number. "Catherine. What's the name of my three p.m.?"

"Skylar Reynolds, sir," the woman on the other end of the phone says at once. "Is she not there?"

"Oh, she's fff—she's here, all right, Catherine. Why am I talking to her?"

"Because she has the best résumé of the bunch, Cullen."

Cullen cuts off the line with a disgusted huff, then scowls at me before blading his body to let me into his office. "You're late."

"I… I had trouble finding the building."

"It's seven stories high and has a number out front. How difficult could it be?"

I curl my hand into a fist. Fine. Cullen is an asshole. I know it. He knows I know it. But still, I came here with a purpose, and I'm following through even if it kills me. The day I bend because some intimidating man says something rude to me is the day I stop being me.

I pad forward into Cullen's office, detecting his scent as I brush past him. Unlike Frank Peterson's awful bug-spray odor, Cullen Hunt's fragrance is spicy yet clean and subtle. If I'd been born a chemist and wanted to bottle the most intoxicating smell ever, it'd be this one. This exact one.

Letting the door close, Cullen goes to sit behind his massive L-shaped desk. Like the rest of the building, Cullen's office screams wealth and affluence. A state-of-the-art desktop computer sits in front of him, with an ornate wooden pen set standing off to one side. A series of maple trays sit with neat stacks of paperwork inside, and on one corner resides a foot-long wooden chest, carved into intricate abstract designs. On his wall, I spot a series of certifications and plaques, though I can't scrutinize them with him watching me. Everything feels larger than life in here, just like the man himself does. I feel like a child sent to the principal's office.

A principal's office that has a decorative case with a mounted *handgun* hanging on the wall. Bile rises up my throat. A medical office building paying homage to violence. Lovely.

"Sit," Cullen orders with all the warmth of a rattlesnake. Gathering every last smidgen of dignity I possess, I sit in the seductively comfortable chair.

Cullen taps his fingers on his desk. "The position title is dispatcher and office administrator. Denton EMS handles the actual 911 call-ins, but I like having my own person on duty to liaise when we run active shifts, which is usually four times a week. Most of the duties are administrative. What experience do you have in any of that?—By the way, I ask only because I want to honestly tell Catherine I interviewed you before showing you the door. "

Lovely. I clear my throat. "Specifically, with office administration, none. However, I—"

"What's your educational background?"

"Well, I graduated summa cum laude from NYU with a bachelors in communication and journalism. Also—"

"Also, you enjoy creating stories where there are none. Do you imagine being a dispatcher will give you some inside track? Let me save both of us the trouble and give you a radio. Our dispatch channel is easy to pick up so others know our status."

My fingers dig into the armrest of my chair. All right. I deserved a little of that. But I'm not going to let a misconception ruin my reputation for integrity. Never again.

"If you're referring to the run-in we had at Mr. Mason's accident site, sir, then I was doing my job," I say firmly. "Looking for facts. If we're on the subject, was anything incorrect printed in the paper?"

I know for a fact it wasn't, because Frank yelled at me for two hours straight about pulling defeat out of the jaws of victory before slapping the article onto the last page. I straighten my spine, sitting on the edge of the chair. "If you—"

"Why did you apply for this job?" he asks.

If he interrupts me one more time, I may not be responsible for my actions. My temperature rising, I take three deliberate deep breaths. I can't smart off to this guy. It took every cent of my savings just to provide first and last month's rent. Except for Frank Peterson —who is paying me nearly nothing—this is literally the only place that has given me the time of day.

Gathering my dignity I lean toward Cullen and place a copy of my portfolio containing samples of my past articles on his desk. Not exactly dispatch relevant, but it's all I've got to prove my worth. When the bastard doesn't react, I move the folder toward him until my hand bumps against his. The contact feels like a zap of electricity, as if I'd received a static charge.

"Mr. Hunt, I know we got off on the wrong foot yesterday. But I'm being utterly forthright in saying that my application for this job has nothing to do with my position as a reporter. I wouldn't use one to influence the other, or vice versa. It would be unprofessional and fall short of the high standards I set for myself and my work."

Cullen's eyes zero in on where our hands are still touching, but the fact that he allows me to finish my sentences is encouraging. Heart still pounding a drumbeat, I lick my lips and continue.

"May I walk you through my credentials, then?"

Cullen glances up at me, his eyes darker than I remember seeing them prior to now, before he jerks his hand away from mine as if I'd bitten him like a rabid animal.

"I've seen enough, Ms. Reynolds. You can go."

"I—"

"I said, *dismissed.*" Cullen barks the last word out as a full-on order, and I'm up on my feet before I can get control of my body.

"I was going to say, I agree," I snap back at him, the world that's been spinning around me suddenly settling with a resounding click. I know what kind of man Cullen is. He's my father. He's Jaden. All bark all the time, as if the world was invented just to scrub floors with toothbrushes on their bloody command. And this interview? I'm freaking lucky. Better end this now before his barks morph into bites. Because they always do.

I pause with my hand on the door. "You want to know why I wanted this job, you pompous ass? The same reason everyone who isn't a damn CEO playing medic for fun wants a job. Because it comes with a paycheck. But you know what? I don't need your blood money. Go find yourself someone else to abuse. Or better yet —don't."

My voice is still ringing off the walls when I storm out of his office, slamming the door as hard as I can behind me.

4

CULLEN

*C*ullen's ears rang from how hard Skylar Reynolds had slammed the door, causing a photograph from Afghanistan to fall from where it hung on the wall. The thing had survived Central Asia and the Middle East, and now one small woman nearly destroyed it. Ironically fitting.

Cullen sat there for a minute, dissecting what had just gone down between them. He didn't like Sky. She'd attempted to set up Cullen's best friend, scoured help-wanted sections for story leads, and understood nothing about why Cullen and the other Trident men served on the Rescue. She was the type of woman for whom being a colossal pain in the ass was as natural as breathing. But one thing Cullen couldn't call Skylar Reynolds was dull. She had a backbone and a will strong enough for a good drill sergeant—that much was more than evident.

Which he found, well…interesting.

And grating.

Especially when she sat there licking her lips at him. A deliberate provocation? Seeing that soft pink tongue peeking out of her delectable mouth had given Cullen's thoughts a highly inappropriate twist. It had made him hard, and when she'd shouted at him, it'd made him even harder.

What the actual *fuck*?

Cullen didn't want Reynolds making him hard. He didn't want to ever see her again.

Full of energy that had nowhere to go, Cullen stood and paced next to the framed certifications and honors he'd gained over the years, some as a SEAL and some since. The certifications were mostly tied to overseas days, like when he'd completed his Special Operations Combat Medic—SOCM—training. It'd been intense, like taking a drink from a power washer on high. By the end, though, Cullen had a competency level equal to a third-year medical student. He'd used that knowledge too. All his brothers had.

Far too often.

That was the part Reynolds didn't—probably couldn't—understand. He'd seen it in her eyes when they'd narrowed with disdain at the sight of his sidearm mounted on the wall, the backup weapon that had saved his life and taught him the value of training. Of preparedness. To the Skylar Reynoldses of the world, guns were like dangerous firecrackers, as disposable as the little green soldiers who carried them.

Cullen shook his head, not wanting to think about that.

Picking up the fallen photo, Cullen put it back beside the small accolade from Denton Valley Memorial's pediatric ward. Though he didn't spend much time there, he'd donated a substantial sum to the ward. Burns and cancer killed as efficiently as mortar rounds. He'd been unable to stop the latter. He hoped he might help fight the former.

Feeling moderately calmer now, Cullen returned to his desk—only to find Reynolds's portfolio staring right at him. Who brought a portfolio to a dispatch interview? Fuck. The woman managed to get to him without even being in the goddamned room. That took skill.

The whole interaction with Reynolds had left Cullen feeling... off. She'd traipsed in with that snug black dress hugging her curves like a glove, licking her lips and touching his hand. Again, she'd left him enraged as well as hot and bothered.

Christ.

Yet his normal defenses weren't working with this Sky woman. Somehow, she'd seeped in under his skin anyway.

Maybe it was that Skylar Reynolds was a walking contradiction. One moment she had passion for her work, the next, her passion was for a paycheck. A claim of standards and integrity against the practice of working for Frank Peterson, of all people. At first, Cullen had been certain the girl had come for a story, not a job, but maybe it was simpler than that. Maybe her principles and integrity were simply for sale to whoever was willing to pay.

Cullen didn't know. Cullen didn't care. He *didn't.*

Outside the window, a crash of thunder and lightning ripped through air with a violence that jerked Cullen around. A moment later, rain and hail mixed together in a sudden downpour that batted against the windows. *Rat-tat. Rat-tat. Rat-tat.*

Cullen's breath quickened, his eyes blinking against the darkness. *He was moving. Running. Ripping through the debris. The scent of charred flesh and copper blood filled his lungs. He opened his mouth, tasting phantom sweetness as children's screams rose on all sides around him.*

"Come with me!" he shouted, grabbing a little girl against his chest. She wasn't breathing. Snatching an ambu bag valve mask that, by some miracle, was within reach, he fit it snugly over her face, then squeezed the bag to breathe for her. The girl's chest rose.

A woman, the girl's mother, hit him with a rock. She was bleeding badly. Deadly badly. But she hit him anyway.

"You did this! You did this!" the woman shouted, trying to pull the child from Cullen's arms. He knew enough Dari to understand what she was saying, but not enough to explain that if he released the child, she would die.

"You did this. You did this!"

He breathed for the girl, moving them both toward the exit of the field hospital.

The woman somehow caught up to him, though, her hate-filled gaze cutting into him. She ripped the child away. "You."

Cullen pressed his forehead against the glass, feeling the chill seep into his skin as the destroyed field hospital evaporated. His heart pounded against his chest, mirroring the *rat-tat, rat-tat* of the hale. Fuck. Thunder didn't usually set him off, but he hadn't been expecting the storm. The sky had been clear blue the last time he checked. Maybe it had had something to do with the way Skylar Reynolds had looked at him just before leaving—like she knew he was the devil incarnate. Just as that mother in Afghanistan had.

Grabbing Reynolds's portfolio, Cullen threw the whole thing into the recycling bin and dropped himself in front of his computer screen. Skylar Reynolds threw him out of balance, and he still couldn't seem to find his center of gravity. As if she were kryptonite. In Afghanistan and Iraq, Cullen had trained himself against feeling anything. It was harder in civilian life. Too many interruptions. But it was still harder today. The thunder. The hail. The woman's eyes.

Taking a series of deep breaths, Cullen forced himself to clear his mind, beckoning the cloak of numbness back into place around him. Adding bricks to the wall that protected the rest of the world from the half-cocked grenade that Cullen Hunt would always be, no matter how many pediatric burn units he funded.

Knowing the woman wouldn't be stepping foot in his company again helped. There were advantages to being the boss, and Rachel at reception—not usually his favorite person, but a pit bull when he needed her to be—wouldn't let Reynolds even look through a window if Cullen asked.

Cullen's phone rang, interrupting his momentary peace. Rachel wanted to know whether she could tell Cullen's next interviewee to take a long walk off a short pier, given the fresh track marks along his veins.

That was…three down and five still to go for the day. There had to be someone who wouldn't make Cullen ready to shoot himself.

THREE HOURS LATER, Cullen's stomach was growling its empty displeasure when Eli knocked on the open door. Not because he actually needed an invitation, but Eli was good about making sure never to startle Cullen unnecessarily.

"I'm off to Kyan's for dinner and…" Eli trailed off, his eyes narrowing on the floor, where Reynolds's headshot had apparently slipped out of the folder and under a side table. "What the bloody hell? Is that—"

"Very much so. Just in a different costume." Getting up, Cullen pulled the photo from Eli's hands and went to stuff it back into the discarded folder. "Reynolds had the audacity to waltz in here as if she actually wanted the dispatch job."

"Oh, that's too good." Eli snatched the folder from Cullen's hands. The asshole. "Let's see, she does know that neither dispatch nor office management is customer facing, doesn't she? Unless the headshot is meant to suggest—"

"Fuck off," Cullen snapped, surprising himself as much as Eli. Eli avoided relationships, but he enjoyed women fully and made certain they enjoyed themselves too. It had been a joke, and not even a crude one. Yet Cullen's fist had tightened at his side on reflex.

Eli surveyed Cullen with too careful a gaze and held up empty palms. "Not saying anything you don't know, but if I had a dollar every time someone tried to twist my reputation, I could live off the interest alone. Fuck, I'm sure my mother hires half those reporters."

"What does that—" Cullen started.

"I'm saying I don't take that shit she pulled on Main Street personally. And I don't need you to get indignant on my behalf either. If you want to hire her—"

"I don't want to hire her." Cullen threw up his hands. Was everyone deaf today?

"Then let me see the résumé. Maybe I'll hire her."

"Asshole."

"Very true," Eli agreed companionably as he pulled out the résumé Cullen hadn't bothered reading and began to peruse the contents. "So who are you getting?"

Cullen pursed his lips. No one. A day of interviews, and he had not a single person he'd trust to color with crayons, much less run a rescue squad communications channel.

"You need to replace Suzy, Cullen." Eli's tone dropped into business mode. The man ran an international corporation and ran it bloody well, as he would say.

"I will replace Suzy, but not with Skylar Reynolds."

ALEX LIDELL

"Agreed. You need someone who won't be shy to ask direct questions. Someone who can keep track of facts, even when they get as convoluted as an NYPD corruption investigation. Perhaps someone with a degree in communications."

Cullen glared at his former lieutenant. "Seriously?"

Eli handed him the résumé and a couple of news stories he pulled from Skylar's folder. He was right. The man had a gift for zeroing in on the key information. In fact, now that Cullen looked at the résumé, Reynolds's only downfall was being overqualified.

"I'm not letting a spy from a trashy tabloid rummage through the Rescue's computer system, no matter what her résumé says."

Eli sighed. "You have me there. At the end of the day, you need to trust your people. And…" His brows pulled together as he flipped through more papers in the portfolio Skylar had left. "Wait. What's the date on the sample articles I just showed you?"

Cullen glanced down. "About a year ago. Why?"

"Look."

Pulling out the last sheet from the folder, Eli laid it onto Cullen's desk. Instead of full text, this one just listed the headlines and publication dates. Steady number from about two years ago until a couple of months back. Then, nothing. Why the gap? If Reynolds had been working a job she'd been qualified for, why had she left it? With its higher population and crime rate, the Big Apple must have a lot more opportunities for compelling stories than a place like Denton Valley. Why leave there for here? For *Denton Uncovered*, of all things?

Cullen didn't know, and for the first time, that bothered him. *Not your circus, not your monkeys,* he told himself firmly and laid the folio back on his desk. "How's the arm?"

"Fine. It would've been just as fine if you hadn't stitched it up."

Cullen grunted at him. Then paused, frowning at his friend. Eli had the best business instincts of anyone Cullen knew. "Tell me something. If Skylar Reynolds showed up at Mason Pharmaceuticals, would you offer her a position?"

He knew he'd fucked up the second the words left his mouth.

28

Eli waggled his eyebrows, grinning like the cat who ate the canary.

"Don't tell me which *positions* you could think of for her, shithead. Would you hire her or not?"

Eli's face straightened. "I would."

For some godforsaken reason, the idea of Eli getting Sky made a jolt of red-hot jealousy flare through Cullen.

5

CULLEN

*C*ullen told Eli to go to Kyan's without him, especially once he heard that Adrianna Peterson—Bar Peterson's widow— was going to stop by as well. Cullen loved Adrianna like a sister, but between her and Eli, Kyan was going to be overwhelmed by the amount of company as it was. Once a child model and actor, Kyan came back from the service with burns on a good part of his body and a big-ass gap in his soul for failing to save Bar. They'd been in the same mortar assault.

It was an absurd thing for Kyan to blame himself for, but some wounds didn't follow logic.

Plus, Cullen needed to talk to Adrianna alone about all the problems her former brother-in-law, Frank Peterson, was causing in terms of collecting Bar's benefits. Yes, that same Frank Peterson who now had Skylar Reynolds on his payroll. Cullen's gaze touched Reynolds's portfolio again. Closing the folder, he slipped it into the reject pile—neatly this time. He didn't want to hire Sky. He didn't, and though he could appreciate Eli's and Catherine's opinions, he didn't agree with them. When Catherine came in on Monday, he'd have her set up more interviews. It'd be as simple as that.

Outside the window, the evening was sliding toward darkness,

Cullen's Rolex confirming that late hour. He'd be the last one out this Friday, which was how he liked it. A commander should be the last one out.

His mind on food, Cullen stepped into the parking lot. The earlier storm had passed, but it rained still, and the long lot was empty except for his own truck and a rusted-out Toyota Corolla that looked like it'd fallen off a tow truck on the way to a junkyard. Cullen had worked on a few vehicles in his twenty-eight years—including his current Ford F-450 Super Duty Platinum Crew Cab, which he tricked out like an overzealous teenager—but the Corolla in question wasn't vintage, it was just crap. Crap that needed to get towed from his lot.

Pulling his phone out of his back pocket, Cullen searched for the tow number as he made his way to the intruding vehicle, only to realize it wasn't empty.

Walking to the driver's side window, which for some godforsaken reason was tinted, Cullen rapped hard on the glass.

"What?" The woman sounded familiar. The window lowered, and Cullen's blood pressure jumped two dozen points.

Skylar Reynolds. On a fucking stakeout in his lot.

"Which part of *get the hell out of my business* are you having trouble with, Reynolds?" Cullen's demand came out like a growl.

"The part where the key makes the car start," she snapped, her eyes flashing with a fury to match his own. Her puffy, red-rimmed eyes. She started cranking the handle to raise the window back up.

Cullen stuck his fist in the opening.

She glowered up at him. "What do you want?"

"In general, you out of my life. At the moment, you out of my parking lot. What's wrong with the car?"

Reynolds swallowed, the slight trembling of her hands betraying the effort it was taking to keep herself together. Either that, or she was a good actress. "I told you. It won't start."

"That a symptom, not a diagnosis, Skylar." It was the first time Cullen used her first name, and he wasn't sure why he did it. Didn't want to think about it either. "Open the hood."

After shaking her head and throwing up her hands, Skylar

leaned over to comply. Pulling off his Armani jacket, Cullen rolled
up his sleeves and scrutinized the inner workings of her car, the rain
battering against his shirt. The engine compartment was filthy and
appeared as if it hadn't received the proper maintenance. Then he
caught sight of the culprit—one of the clamps that attached to the
battery had come completely loose. There was obvious corrosion
there too.

Yanking out his pocket square, Cullen wiped down the terminal
and reattached the cable to the battery, then did the same to the
second terminal. Head still under the hood, Cullen yelled out, "Try
her now."

He heard Skylar turn her ignition, and the car sputtered to life.
Craning his neck, Cullen checked the girl's expression, the relief
washing over her features too open and sincere to be faked.
Something warm hit the region of his solar plexus, and disturbed by
this, Cullen ducked back under the hood for a final look. Taking his
time, he stood back, wiping his hands on the little bit of clean space
remaining on his pocket square before lowering the hood.

"You aren't maintaining your car," Cullen said, more gruffly
than he'd intended. "If you don't want this happening again, you'll
need to take it back to where you bought it." Or to the junkyard.

Skylar's smile drained away. "Yeah. I'm on that."

Cullen's brows narrowed. "Where did you get this...relic of
automotive history?"

"A farmer guy right outside New York." Skylar's nose wrinkled
as if she'd caught a whiff of some horrible smell before her face
closed again. "But I appreciate your help. How much do I owe
you?"

Cullen studied her. Not only did she have a look of distaste
wreathing her features, her posture had grown rigid, and her fingers
clutched her steering wheel so fiercely that her knuckles were white.
She had her pride, he'd give her that. Pride and no money, though
Cullen believed she'd empty her wallet to try to fill whatever bill he
came up with. Though the thought had never crossed his mind, the
fact that Skylar expected nothing from him was a rather nice change
of pace from how the rest of the world usually operated.

33

"I'm not a mechanic. And if I were, you couldn't afford me." Cullen jerked his chin toward the road. "Drive safe. And in a direction away from me, please."

"Don't." The word escaped through Skylar's clenched teeth, her nostrils flaring as she drew a slow breath before glaring at Cullen through the still-open window. Her bloodshot eyes bored into his like twin flames, her expression resentful. "I don't want your handout, Cullen. And I want to owe you anything even less. You fixed my damn car. If you don't know what to charge, have the Barbie doll at your front desk draw up a bill."

"I'll pass your compliments on to Rachel," Cullen muttered, tilting his head as he regarded the little strawberry-blonde spitfire for a long moment. Cullen was no fool, and it didn't take a genius to add up two and two and get four—even a marine could do it. Whatever else was going on with Skylar, she hadn't been kidding about needing money. And Cullen knew Frank Peterson well enough to know the bastard would do everything to ensure Skylar was barely on life support—just enough to make leaving scary and not a penny more.

When Cullen thought about it that way, loosening Frank Peterson's control over an overzealous reporter wasn't that bad an idea.

"You can work it off." Cullen raised his hand as he saw Skylar's eyes open in indignation. "At Trident Rescue, Reynolds. Office manager and glorified dispatcher. Trial basis."

"Seriously?" she asked. "You're hiring me?"

Cullen ran his hand through his hair, sending droplets of rain down his shirt. "Why not? You'll probably quit before the month is up anyway." He didn't know whether he added that last bit as a brazen challenge to the woman or a soothing prediction to himself.

6

SKY

"Fetch me some coffee before you leave, sweetheart," Frank calls from his office as I'm already reaching for the door handle.

I open my mouth to tell him off, but the image of trading my basement apartment for a cardboard box halts my tongue. More to the point—I want to be a journalist. And right now, being blackballed everywhere thanks to Jaden and the assholes at the United States Navy press office, Frank is my only chance at that. Only an idiot gives up on her dreams over a cup of coffee.

Letting go of the door handle, I go into our stinky break room— for some reason, the place reeks of onions all the time—and try to start the coffeepot. Only, that pot is some sort of weird French press contraption that's holding on to the liquid like a momma bear. By the time I work out how to coax coffee from it, I'm wearing a large stain and running late again.

Frank takes one sniff and pours it out into the trash, but at least he doesn't shout obscenities into my face.

I shake my head. Being around military vets with anger issues has plainly warped my view of acceptable behavior.

After a quick hop to my apartment to change, I set my phone's

GPS to the address Catherine sent me this morning and hope Cullen Hunt himself isn't planning on welcoming me to the office in person. My watch beeps at the late hour, and my hands tighten on the steering wheel. Bad start. Maybe I should just have come wearing coffee. It's not like anyone sees a dispatcher.

Unless Cullen *is* there today.

It doesn't help my jitters at all to remember that last night's dreams all starred Cullen Hunt. It started out with him demeaning me, then altered to some bizarre episode where we hid together beneath the hood of my Corolla. Then he stared at me with those cool green eyes until my body started to ache. My palms had grazed the light stubble along his chin and traced the lines of his muscular body, even though his gaze never softened toward me.

I woke with my breasts feeling heavy and my panties soaked through with desire. I had to take a shower just to cool down. This isn't how I really feel about him, so I don't know why my body isn't receiving that message. Cullen Hunt may be sex on a stick, but his shitty personality is more than enough to ward off any wayward cravings I might entertain about him. The bastard is antagonistic, short-tempered, and a bully.

His one moment of helpfulness notwithstanding.

Maybe that's why Cullen's image wove itself through my nighttime subconscious. When I gazed up at him, standing there with his ruined pocket handkerchief, grease all over those thick square fingers, and corded muscles filling out his once-white shirt, it'd done something to me.

It's not called something, *Sky. It's called* stupid.

I blow out a long breath. The Cullen I saw yesterday was a mirage version of him. Jaden and my father had these mirage moments too. I think it's something the military trains into them, a way of showing one thing on the outside while being anything but that in reality.

Jaden could be nice too. Flowers, fancy dinners on the Hudson River, the lights of New York City's many lit bridges right there within view. Getting me an interview—and then a job—at one of the top papers right after college. Showing me the ropes of journalism. I'd fallen for who I thought he was, hook, line, and sinker.

And then came Fleet Week, Jaden's marine buddies, and his true colors. Now I am here working for *Denton Uncovered* and being grateful for the opportunity. Yeah.

Maybe I should be grateful that Cullen has shown me his true colors already, and more than once. A lone instance of decency does not a good man make. That's not how it works.

Pulling into the parking lot of Trident Rescue's single-story brick building that reminds me of a much smaller Urgent Care unit, I shut off my car and straighten my silky blouse—even if it's made of polyester—and simple tan slacks.

Pushing through a pair of wide double doors, I find no obvious direction to go in. "Hello? Catherine? Is anybody here?"

Silence greets me.

Walking slowly through the building, I discover a collection of treatment rooms with all the customary medical paraphernalia, as well as an office with a landline, a police scanner, and a complicated-looking radio setup. The last third of the building houses a garage, with one wall dedicated to every piece of rescue gear imaginable. Being a climber myself, I only recognize the rock-climbing equipment, but given the bright orange colors over everything else, I get the general gist. Both the Suburban I saw Cullen using for fast response and a more traditional ambulance are parked inside, gleaming from a fresh wash.

For a moment, I imagine Cullen standing there with a hose, cleaning the car. The image is as delicious as it's absurd.

So the vehicles are here, but without any employees? Odd.

I'm right in front of the main double doors, about to call out again, when they whoosh open, mowing me over. I tumble to the floor, landing hard on my right side.

"What are you doing down there?" demands a familiar baritone. Cullen Hunt, of course.

"You knocked me over," I inform him.

Cullen grabs my wrist and pulls me up. I anticipate a jerk forceful enough to dislocate my shoulder—the man's muscles seem not constructed for anything but excessive force—but Cullen's surprisingly gentle as he brings me to my feet. An intangible sizzle races through me, pulsating from where our skin touches, Cullen's features a mix of concern and heat.

Then Cullen lets go, and it all vanishes. His features return to that familiar stoniness so swiftly that I wonder if the rest of it happened at all.

"Where is everybody?" I ask.

"You *are* everybody," Cullen informs me. He's wearing another business suit, this time a charcoal gray that highlights his blond hair and green eyes. "Hence, *everybody* is bloody late."

"I—"

"You're an irresponsible twenty-two-year-old who can't get herself on time to an interview, a job, or a car maintenance schedule," says Cullen.

"I'm twenty-three—"

"I stand corrected on that point."

I snap my mouth shut.

Not missing a beat, Cullen jerks his chin toward the end of the hall. "I need more coffee to deal with you. Make some. Break room's the last door on the left." Without waiting for a response, the man turns on his heel and walks in the opposite direction.

What in the ever-loving fuck is happening today?

I don't make the bastard coffee, sitting down instead at what I presume is the main dispatch desk—though the stacks of inventory, bills, and patient records piled around the computer make it seem multipurpose. Picking up the top page of a very, very neat pile, I find myself holding an overdue bill. For $15.22, with another $35 in late payment penalty.

"You know, laying your bills parallel to each other doesn't actually get them paid," I yell into the void.

"So I've been told." Cullen reappears from one of the exam rooms, this time in his Trident Rescue uniform.

I stare for a few seconds before I can stop myself, unable to make up my mind about which is better, the suit or blue Under Armour. Then I snap myself out of it. It doesn't matter which is better. It doesn't matter how hot the man is. He's an asshole, and I hate him.

"Where's the coffee?" he asks.

"I've been told it's in the break room. Last door on the left."

A corner of Cullen's mouth quirks up.

Snatching my attention back, I pull the second sheet from a stack. A paid bill for once, except what idiot buys Band-Aids at a dollar apiece? Glancing down to the bottom of the sheet, I discover the thing's been on autopayments, which is probably why no one notices. "Where is the common sense?"

"On back order." Cullen snatches the bill from my hand, frowns as he takes in the information, and puts it neatly right back on the top of the file. "Like I said earlier, most of the Rescue's 'dispatcher' duties are administrative. Denton EMS does the 911 intake. When one of the Rescue medics is on duty, Denton passes us the remote call-outs and trauma. You are our lifeline to Denton, the hospital, and any other resources. Catherine will cover the admin with you." Cullen tosses a three-ring binder onto the desk in front of me. "Procedures manual to read at your leisure. That means now. If the phone rings, answer it."

I inhale Cullen's clean, spicy scent, resenting how delicious he smells, and run my fingers over the front pages of the binder. Having expected to find a rag-tag collection of outdated internet printouts that make up most places' onboarding manuals, I'm surprised to find custom pages with dated notes, some as recent as this week. A living document. "How do I know who's on duty?"

"Email."

All righty, then. I raise my hand, and Cullen, who has now condescended to face me, rolls his eyes.

"Aren't you supposed to be in a fancy office running hospitals instead of playing medic here?" I ask.

Cullen's face darkens. "Any questions that have anything at all to do with your job?"

I hold up the binder he gave me. "I'll tell you once I'm done reading. I'm good, not telepathic."

"I take it your car is running." Cullen changes the subject, dropping into a free chair and taking out his phone.

This isn't a question, but I answer it anyway. "Yes."

"The only issue was a loose terminal cable," Cullen says, his attention on whatever he's doing on screen. "If you'd ever bothered to peek under the hood, you would've found it yourself."

His tone is accusatory, and I feel, well…accused.

"It's irresponsible to drive a car and not know how it works," Cullen continues.

"It's irresponsible to speak to humans and not know common courtesy," I snap back. "Yet I don't see that stopping you any."

Cullen lowers his phone, his attention shifting fully back to me as he weighs me with his gaze. Instead of being offended, I get a strange sensation that the man is pleased with my reply. Or rather, that he's pleased to have gotten under my skin. As if he's trying to make up for that hint of a smile he gave me earlier, to make it really, *really* clear we aren't friends and never will be.

I shake my head. "You're a horrible human being, you know that?" I say, getting to my feet in hopes of finding a better place to read. "You're rude, quick to make faulty assumptions, and you enjoy treating people like shit."

Cullen leans back in his chair, the sneer spreading over his face somehow managing to make his chiseled jaw only more unjustly beautiful. He's like one of those carnivorous flowers that look nice outside just so it can digest you more efficiently.

"Well, princess, the thing about glass houses is that you have to be careful about stone casting. From where I sit, anyone working for *Denton Uncovered* lacks either integrity or brains." Cullen stands, taking a single step toward me as his voice drops. "Which is it?"

Seriously? My heart pounds, my jaw clenching so hard, my teeth hurt as Cullen takes up all the air and space in the room. We're standing there inches apart, the world at the edge of my vision flickering with red anger. The most terrible part of his ridiculous accusation is how true the last half of his statement is. Or was. Because back in New York, I *was* a stupid, naïve girl, thinking I knew the man I thought I loved. Thinking the US Navy gave one lick about the truth.

Cullen snorts, shaking his head as he looms over me, his mossy-green gaze cold. Degrading. "As I recall, I made your probationary period a month. You won't last that long, Reynolds. Christ, I don't think you'll last the week."

"You shouldn't think so much, Cullen. You'll sprain something." I clamp my jaw shut, my lungs filling with Cullen's scent with every inhalation. Standing so close to him, I can make out each detail of his too-perfect face, from his closely shaved skin, to the small scar that cuts the underside of his square jaw, to the full lips that are near enough to me that my head spins.

"Don't bait what you can't handle." Heat radiates off Cullen's body in waves, each rushing down my skin.

My thighs clench together, my treacherous body waking to his presence.

"Tell you what, little girl." Cullen takes a step toward me, a predator claiming his territory, demanding I get the hell out of his way. When he speaks again, his baritone drips with command and challenge. "Prove me wrong. Get through a month here, and I'll give you the equivalent of a month's salary as a bonus."

I straighten my spine and hold my ground, even as my chest brushes against his, my breasts too large and achy for my bra. "Fine." The word spills from my lips, my gaze locked on the green eyes that stare down at me as if nothing else in the world exists. It's probably the kind of stare a bug gets before being squashed, but it rivets me to the floor.

Without thinking, I lift my index finger to trace along his scar, longing to feel its irregular texture.

Cullen freezes, his heart beating so hard, I can see his pulse in the soft hollow of his neck. His pupils dilate, the shifting material along his groin bulging against the zipper. My fingertip is a hair's breadth away when he moves too hastily for me to see, grabbing my wrist in midair.

"Don't," he says.

I gasp, taking a step back so quickly that I lose balance when

41

Cullen lets go and crash into the table. Radios fall from their charging cradles to the floor, a stack of papers following suit.

Holy hell. What the hell are we doing? What the hell am *I* doing?

Shaking my head to clear it, I crouch to pick up the mess on the floor and feel rather than see Cullen marching away. By the time I look up, the man's gone.

7

CULLEN

*C*ullen wasn't being a coward by avoiding Trident Rescue for a week, he assured himself as another Friday night found him inside his office. He was being a prudent CEO of a large corporation. There were calls to make. Reports to review. A board of directors to babysit. There were a lot of things Cullen needed to be doing, and one thing exactly that he needed to keep his nose—and all other body parts—away from.

Skylar Reynolds.

It was like the woman knew exactly what to do and say and wear to get his goat, so she then insisted on doing, saying, and wearing exactly that. Cullen prided himself on his laser focus, his ability to rise above distraction. Hell, he could rattle off any comms frequency in the middle of a firefight. But this woman tested every single one of his limits.

The biggest of those limits being Reynolds herself. As in, she was way off them. Not even for a one-night stand, as Eli recommended out of the blue, claiming it was the best way of getting a woman's scent out of one's system. Enticing as the notion was, Cullen did not bed subordinates on principle. There was too

ALEX LIDELL

much risk of coercion, no matter what it felt like in the moment. Period. Full stop.

Plus, Cullen didn't like the woman, who was the most infuriating combination of utter competence and just as utter ignorance. If he'd given in to the mind-numbing temptation to kiss her that night, she'd certainly have read the wrong thing into it. And if he'd taken her to bed as his cock was urging him to do with blue-ball intensity? She'd almost certainly think it was something it wasn't. Something Cullen Hunt simply wasn't capable of being.

So yes, Cullen had walked away from Reynolds with all the dignity he could muster—and then run for the first freezing shower he could find. And he *had* been busy this week, busy enough that he didn't need to add a battle with his own cock to the daily agenda. The plain reality was that Cullen's body roused to Reynold's soft scent and taut curves on sheer instinct. It was physiology and nothing more. So unless Cullen intended to gouge his eyes out with a spoon, he needed to accept it and move on.

Cullen's phone vibrated, the familiar number making him frown. Denton PD. "Hunt," he barked into the receiver.

"Yes. Um. Mr. Hunt. This is Lacy, from dispatch at Denton PD?" The young woman on the other end of the line sounded like a petrified kitten, her sentence ending with a rising, question-like inflection. "I was told we could use this number. I didn't realize—"

"Yeah." Cullen didn't care how young this Lacy was, if she couldn't form a sentence, she needed a different job. "Put the desk sergeant on."

"I'm so sorry to have bothered—"

"Hunt." A man came on the line, and Lacy disconnected with a sigh of audible relief. "What my rookie was trying to say before she forgot that the Trident gods put their pants on one leg at a time is that I've got a call I need help on. Local EMS is tied up, and frankly—"

"Roger." Cullen was already halfway to the door. Trident Rescue usually handled wilderness rescue unless the main EMS needed some help on the truly bad emergencies, but Cullen had given the PD his number directly as well. Apparently, young Lacy had expected an emergency number would be answered by a damn secretary. Somehow, Cullen didn't think Reynolds would ever make the same mistake. Hell, Reynolds would sound cock-ball certain no matter what. "Location? Disregard, I see the text."

"I know it's not your usual operating area—"

No, Hannigan's Pub on Third certainly wasn't. "I've yet to meet broken bones that cared much for maps. En route." Skipping the elevator, Cullen jogged down the stairs. The problem wasn't so much where Hannigan's was, but where Trident Rescue wasn't. Kyan—who was on call tonight—was even farther away. Fortunately, Sky was going to come in anyway to make a dent in the admin. Pushing open the exit door, Cullen stepped into the cool Colorado evening wind just as he tapped another number on the speed dial.

"Tri—"

"Reynolds." Cullen cut her off. "I need you to bring the medical Suburban to Hannigan's. Sending you the address now. Meet you on location."

His thumb was almost on End Call when she squeezed into the line. "Wait. You want me to drive that thing?"

"No, I want you to beam it over." He hovered over End Call again, the short nervous draw of air on the other end having him raise the phone back up at the last moment. "It's safer to drive than your Corolla, Reynolds."

"If you say so."

His jaw tightened. He was giving her an order, not a goddamn suggestion. "Reynolds."

"What?"

Fuck. That was fear, not defiance. Cullen sighed. "I love that truck. If I thought you could damage it, I wouldn't let you near the wheel. Hunt out." He did hang up that time.

Twenty minutes later—Hannigan's was way the hell out there, even when speeding—Cullen pulled his truck into the dirt parking lot, getting out just in time to watch Reynolds miscalculate her turn and scrape his Suburban on a corner of the retaining wall. Hiding a wince, Cullen pulled open her door.

Reynolds gripped the wheel with bone-white fingers. "I didn't run over anyone."

He stared. She didn't even *know* she'd just cut up his truck, did she? Well, he wasn't about to tell her.

Reaching behind her, Cullen grabbed the go bag and started for the pub. The lights of a police cruiser were only now appearing along the roadway, and the lack of noise as he opened the entrance door sent an uneasy feeling through him.

Inside the darkened pub room, the air hung thick with tension and spilled alcohol. The mirrored wall behind the bar reflected a rainbow assortment of liquor bottles, the cartoonish colors at odds with the anxiety pulsing through the place. The few patrons had cleared out or otherwise given a wide berth to the bar, where a bloodied bartender gripped the back of a stool to hold herself upright. A few feet away from her, a large man with a buzz cut and wild, unfocused eyes brandished a broken-off bottle, swinging his makeshift weapon at ghosts as he grunted.

"That's Charlie McTierney. He's one of our regulars." The owner, Phil Hannigan, appeared by Cullen's side. "Ileene can usually talk anyone down, but Charlie is having a bad day. He was—"

"In the army's Delta Force," Cullen finished the sentence as he caught sight of the tattoo on Charlie's left arm. Red arrowhead shape with the fighting knife inside and the word "Airborne" along the top.

"Yeah," said Phil. "You know him?"

Cullen nodded. He hadn't actually met Charlie McTierney before, but that glazed look in his eyes—he knew that well. Knew how it felt to come home, only to have the nightmares follow you across the ocean, lying in ambush in your mind.

"Charlie." The bartender, a pretty woman in her late twenties who must be Ileene, spoke calmly despite the blood trickling down her face. Cullen respected her already. "Charlie, look at me. Who am I?—Stay back."

The last, Cullen realized, was said in his direction. Or, more accurately, in the direction of Skylar Reynolds and a pair of uniforms who were now rushing forward, their timing a tribute to Murphy's Law.

Putting out his arm, Cullen caught Skylar around the waist and pushed her behind him.

Charlie shuddered. Dressed in jeans and a cut-off shirt exposing his biceps, the man was jacked—both by way of muscle and alcohol. And memories.

"That's right, Charlie." Ileene's calm, steady voice settled like a damp blanket over the tension. The woman was good. "Look at me. Look only at me."

"Get ready," one of the two uniforms behind Cullen said softly to his partner. "We take the fucker on three."

"No sudden movements," Cullen ordered over his shoulder.

"When I need advice from an ambulance driver, I'll let you know," the uniform snapped. "*Go. Now.*"

8

SKY

I gasp as the two uniformed officers rush the drunk, the man going from muttering menace to enraged bear in the space of a heartbeat. Twisting to face the oncoming cops, Charlie gets into a defensive crouch, the weapon in his hand a murderous extension of the alcohol in his gaze. My chest tightens, the absolute certainty that people are about to get hurt filling my veins.

Before Charlie's knuckles can connect with the heads of the uniformed cops rushing at him, Cullen moves in, sliding like a predator across the floor. Blading his body between Charlie and the cops, Cullen blocks the punch midswing, the muscles beneath his blue Under Armour shifting like water.

Charlie stops. Turns. Roars.

Around the bar, the patrons and even cops hold a collective breath as the full force of the madman's fury zeroes in on the lone medic. On Cullen.

Cullen holds an open palm toward the man. "Take a breath, man. Nice and—"

Charlie kicks at Cullen's knee, his boot intent on shattering the kneecap.

Cullen twists, taking the shot on his thigh. He grunts in pain, but doesn't strike back.

My heart pounds, the many ways this could end racing through my mind in flashes of blood. Pulling myself together, I slip over to the injured bartender, Ileene, and help the woman into a chair.

"No!" Ileene shouts, suddenly looking at something over my shoulder. I twist around in time to see one of the officers unsnapping the retainer on his gun. My stomach clenches. Bile rises farther up my throat as Cullen jerks at the sound of a weapon leaving its holster and—instead of getting the hell out of the way— puts himself into the damn line of fire.

Charlie swings. Again. Again.

Dancing on the balls of his feet, Cullen parries the blows as recklessly as they come. His face is emotionless. Utterly unreadable. Right up until the moment that Charlie's ham-sized fist flies directly at Cullen's temple, and his jaw flexes with grim triumph.

Ducking smoothly under the swing, Cullen uses Charlie's own momentum to twist his arm behind his back. In the next breath, Cullen slams the man's chest into the wall hard enough to crack ribs.

Holy fucking shit.

Pouring in around Cullen, the cops slam cuffs around Charlie's wrists and lead the bastard away.

Relief washes over me so forcefully that my body sways, a pair of strong hands steadying me from behind. I know it's Cullen from the musky scent filling my lungs, the heat of his body blazing like a furnace through my blouse. I turn to him, barely suppressing the urge to take a swing at the bastard myself. "Do you have a death wish, Cullen?" I demand. "What if—" I don't bother finishing. There are too many what-ifs to list, and they all end with him getting hurt.

"You shouldn't have called the police, Phil." Ileene's eyes are red rimmed as she stares after the still-swinging door through which the police just walked Charlie out. "Go tell the police I'm not pressing charges. It was an accident. I've known Charlie since first grade, and he would never hurt me on purpose."

"It looks like he *did* hurt you today," I tell Ileene gently, glancing at Cullen for support.

Instead of speaking, Cullen just takes the woman's chin in his hand to examine the gash on her cheek, his face as expressive as stone.

"You don't understand," Ileene insists. "Charlie's wife called— he'd run out of his meds. They're getting more as soon as they can. It was—"

"Ileene." I meet the bartender's eyes, which are large and blue and miserable. My heart aches. I've been here before, making explanations. For my father. For Jaden. "There's no excuse for hurting someone. None at all. If you let him get away with this, who is he going to take a swing at next? His wife? A chi— You shouldn't have to make excuses for him. There are places you can—"

"Reynolds." Cullen interrupts me midsentence, as if I were chatting about a cake recipe and not trying to make someone's life a safer one to live. "Call the ER. Make sure they know Charlie and Ileene are on their way."

I stare at him incredulously. Seriously? He wants me to go make calls on minor trauma *now*, when I'm building Ileene up to do the right thing?

Cullen's eyes meet mine, the flash of command in them leaving no room for misinterpretation. Stepping away to make the call while still keeping an eye on Ileene, I dial the ER—who puts me on hold the moment they hear their incoming patient has a pulse and an airway.

"No hospital," Ileene says. "I'm a single mom and don't have any insurance. I'm not badly off, truly. And Charlie isn't usually like this. Your assistant needn't worry."

"My assistant needs to keep her opinions to herself." Cullen's voice is meant to carry to me before it lowers a notch. "As for the hospital, I'll make sure you won't be charged. I'll have someone help you apply for benefits as well. Trident Rescue has connections to get it done."

"Trident Rescue? Isn't that the outfit of the four Trident gods —" Ileene cuts off, her eyes widening as she blinks from the insignia on Cullen's shirt to his face, something very much like gears clicking into place behind her intelligent gaze. "You're Cullen Hunt, aren't you?"

"Yes to the latter part, not so much on the divinity." Cullen's large hands deftly open packets of gauze to press against Ileene's cheek. "But I am used to getting my way. You'll let me take you to the ER, yes?"

Having bullied a reluctant but grateful Ileene into a trip to the hospital, Cullen insists on driving me to my car despite me offering to drive the mammoth Suburban back to the station myself. Neither of us speaks, the tense silence between us thickening the air. The scene from the pub keeps replaying in my head, hitting from different angles. Ileene, bloody and making excuses. Charlie, wild and assaulting the police. Cullen turning into a deadly predator, designed and honed for violence. For killing.

For the first time since coming to Denton Valley, I think I've made a terrible mistake in choosing this town. My hands tighten around the armrests, my knuckles white.

Cullen's gaze slips from the road to my hands, then back to traffic. "You're safe, Reynolds."

"It's not me I'm worried about," I snap more harshly than I intend. I'm not good at lying. I swallow. "What will happen to the asshole who attacked Ileene and the cops?"

A muscle along Cullen's jaw twitches. "The police took Charlie into custody." His words are curt. Emotionless.

"I hope Ileene presses charges."

No response. As if I didn't just state the obvious. Fine. I can do nothing about the asshole in custody, but I can certainly deal with the one sitting right beside me.

"Why did you interrupt me in the middle of encouraging Ileene to talk to the police?" I demand. "It was almost as if you wanted Charlie to get off scot-free for what he did."

Cullen's eyes stay on the road. "Don't try to get inside my mind, Reynolds. You won't like what's there."

What the hell is that supposed to mean? Wait. A new, horrible thought occurs to me. "Is that why you gave her free medical care?

So that she sweeps what happened under a rock? Did your free X-rays come with a gag order attached?"

Cullen yanks on the steering wheel, the Suburban cutting hard to the highway shoulder and stopping suddenly enough to make the seat belt dig into my flesh. When he turns to me, his green eyes flashing with icy fury, my breath stops.

"One. I don't issue fucking gag orders." Cullen's booming voice fills up the Suburban, bouncing off the closed windows. His face is dark, his nostrils flaring as he speaks. "Two. Charlie wasn't going after Ileene—he probably didn't even know it was her. And, unlike you, she's smart enough to know the fucking difference."

"Did you just actually make excuses for a man who physically injured a woman?" I shout into his face, though my hands tremble and my breath and pulse are racing each other, quick and ready. "What is this, some soldier good ole boys, closing ranks?"

I only realize that a tear has somehow escaped my eyes when it plops down on my forearm. His face a foot away from mine, Cullen is fury incarnate, his hand curling into a fist. Oh. Shit. Shit. *Shit.* My heart hammers so hard, I can't hear anything over the pounding in my head. I snatch for the door handle.

Locked. I yank it again. Again. As if I can beat the mechanism.

On the driver's side, Cullen reaches for the gearshift.

I brace myself, but instead of taking off, the Suburban settles. The red *D* on the dashboard changes to *P*, the auto locks releasing at once. Before I can move again, however, it's Cullen who gets out of the car.

"Eli," Cullen barks into the phone he just pulled from his back pocket. "I need you to pick Reynolds up. *Now.* Sending—" He slams the Suburban's door so hard that the car rocks, the rest of his words now out of my hearing range.

9

SKY

*A*fter the Hannigan's Pub incident, I decide to give Cullen a wide berth. This winds up being easy considering he doesn't show up at Trident Rescue even once during my shifts, a fact for which I'm monumentally grateful. Having finally escaped my military father and then my ex, the farther away I can keep from Cullen, the better.

I rub my shoulder, which dear old dad dislocated for me when I was seven. He got me a Barbie the next day and considered the incident closed. My gut says Cullen wouldn't even bother with the Barbie. I guess I should be glad to have finally seen the man's true colors, even if he himself doesn't see anything wrong with his paint scheme.

"So, incident log," Catherine tells me. In her early sixties, Catherine is who I want to be when I grow up. Patient, kind, competent. She has that motherly mix of no-nonsense reasoning and careful listening. And she's organized enough to run a small country by herself. To say I'm glad it's Catherine and not our boss giving me instructions now is an understatement. She opens a records program. "The guys rarely have the time to log these, so keeping track is up to you. Collect their records from this tray and log in the individual dates, times, personnel, and other details. Fair warning, they're a jumble, but it's vital to get it right."

Looking down at the "tray," I discover a wooden box heaped with loose slips of paper, including notebook sheets, sticky notes, and what seems to be a piece of an old envelope with scribbles on the back. "So they're as organized with response logs as they are with the bills, I see."

Catherine's mouth curves into a smirk, deepening the fine lines around her mouth. Her hazel eyes gleam at me conspiratorially as she leans in, making the tips of her white bob swish around her cheeks. "About. Suzy always detested digging through this mess, and now…" She picks up a piece of paper dated from six months prior.

"And now it's my problem," I finish for her.

"Well, yes."

I shake my head. "And these people run multibillion-dollar corporations?"

"If they let me hire a full suite of employees for the Rescue, it would be administratively pure. But it's Cullen's personal project. They don't want outsiders."

I let the words sink through me. No outsiders. Then what am I doing here? *Surviving a month to win a bet,* I remind myself. "Do I write the treatment notes too?"

"No. Those are confidential, so the guys are forced to do the writing themselves," she explains, and I nod. "They're actually very good about that part—that sort of information is the most vital, so that's where their focus stays. This log is important too, but since their time is so stretched, this more menial stuff often goes by the wayside. Obviously."

I grin at her, but as my mind turns to the ride I took with Cullen back from the pub, my grin slides from my face. "Can I ask you something, Catherine?" I ask, flipping through the slips of notes. None from the past week have Cullen's name. Not one thing since the pub. "Something not training related."

Her features become warier. "I can't promise to answer, but if I can, I will. Within reason."

I stare at her, noting the caution in the reply. She's loyal to

Cullen. More loyal than the man deserves. Suddenly, the question of *is Cullen Hunt always a royal asshole* doesn't seem to flow off my tongue. Wisely chickening out, I lob a softball at her instead. "Why does everyone call the men who work here the Trident gods?"

Catherine's wary features soften, amusement flashing over her face. "It's what one of their drill sergeants at Trident Academy, the military high school where they all met, accused them of acting like."

"So it's an insult?" I ask, though I'm sure that's not how I've heard it used.

"It *was* an insult when delivered by a drill sergeant to teenage boys at a military academy," Catherine clarifies. "You've no idea what they can make sound insulting. One of the boy's brothers tried to make the nickname stick in Denton Valley just to annoy them, but the plan backfired. The boys, men by then, came back so decorated from their deployments that the townsfolk mean it respectfully now, much to Frank's chagrin."

"So everyone around here looks up to them because of how well they did in the military?" I ask, careful not to let any of my feelings on the matter seep into my voice. It's not that I don't appreciate what men and women in uniform do overseas, it's that I don't think it should give them carte blanche to hurt people when they return.

"Yes, and what they accomplished since. The four who came back are all running multibillion-dollar businesses, but they all get their hands dirty too. They've all saved lives with Cullen's rescue service here. And then there's Bar."

"One of them owns a bar?" I ask, not seeing what's so noble about that. Also, this allows me to sidestep her mention of Cullen.

"Bar is short for Bartholomew. He was the one of the five who didn't make it back. Denton Valley was Bar's home town, so Cullen and the others settled here after discharge. Trident Rescue is a way they keep Bar's memory alive." She pauses while I let that sink in. "How good are you with spreadsheets?"

"I'm proficient. I'm good with Quicken as well. Not for nothing, but the Rescue nearly got the lights shut off last week because someone put a check in the envelope and never actually mailed the damn thing. I'm no you, but I can start getting this in order."

Catherine smiles, the approval radiating from her making me blush. "Let me get you logged in," she says, creating a password for me before revealing a sad shoebox of receipts that serves as accounts receivable. "This is the finale for what I call Cullen's pet projects— things that he does personally, as opposed to ones he does in his Trident CEO hat. Those, fortunately, are handled by actual accounting. I enter what I know, but when it comes to the Rescue… you need to be here."

After Catherine leaves, I fill out the incident log, mulling over what she told me. There aren't many callouts, but they're all serious ones, which, I gather, is Cullen's niche. I wonder whether each little spreadsheet row equals a life saved. Now that would make a good story. Not that Frank is interested in printing good news. Plus, I gave my word I wouldn't use the position to hunt for leads.

Log done, I start transferring the shoebox receipts into the computer, orders for gloves and rescue equipment filling in lines between what Catherine already entered—those being mostly donations Cullen has made to various local, national, and even international charitable organizations. I scroll through page upon page of money spent. The Red Cross. The March of Dimes. St. Jude's Children's Hospital. The Disabled Veterans Administration. Save the Children. Doctors Without Borders. UNICEF. The list goes on and on.

I lean back in my chair. The Cullen I know is, frankly, a brute with questionable morals, but this other version of him clearly isn't. So what's the difference? Why the Jekyll and Hyde? Does something about me in particular inspire the man's antagonism?

I've just finished roughly half of my data entry project when Eli saunters in. Like my boss, he wears a high-end suit and looks like a *GQ* model. Unlike my boss, Eli has done nothing to freak me out.

My body doesn't respond to his either. Not one bit.

"Oh, hello there, Sky," Eli says, heading to one of the four beige metal lockers the men use for personal gear. Other than my boss, Eli takes by far the most shifts at the Rescue. I've only ever met the other two men, Kyan Keasley and Liam Rowen, in passing, though I guess they live farther out and often respond without coming into the hub first. Ducking into another room for a moment, Eli exchanges the Brooks Brothers suit jacket for a tight blue Under Armour shirt, the man's unruly copper curls the opposite of Cullen's precise buzz cut.

Goddammit. Stop thinking about Cullen.

As Eli moves, I catch sight of the jagged pink line on his hand— the vestiges from the car accident where I'd all but accused him of drunk driving. My face heats at the memory, though for some reason, the incident seems to have bothered Cullen more than Eli himself. Then again, everything about me seems to bother Cullen.

Not wanting Eli to think I'm staring, I twist back around to my computer.

"Hunt around?" Eli asks.

"Uh, no," I stammer, then make it a point to shore up my voice. I refuse to let Cullen intimidate me. Especially when he's not even around. "No. He's rarely here when I am."

For the first time, Eli walks around to where he can see my face, his own tight. He looks…worried. He looks so worried, in fact, that I feel my brows pulling together. "Why? Is everything okay?"

He blows out a harsh breath. "Yeah, I'm sure it is. Hunt is one tough son of a bitch. But he hasn't been in for a while."

"In here?"

"Here or at his office." Another rough gust of air escapes as Eli sighs, and he scrubs a hand down his face. I think he's about to confide in me, but when his eyes meet mine, he shutters his expression. It's as if he just threw a wall up between us. "Mind doing me a favor?"

"Sure?"

"If he comes by or calls, tell him I need to speak to him."

"Of course."

Eli gives me a mock salute before heading out to the Suburban. Left alone, I sit mute for several long heartbeats, wondering what the hell is going on. Because I have a feeling that *something* is.

～

AFTER MY SHIFT ends at 9:00 p.m., I pull out my work folder for *Denton Uncovered*. It feels a bit strange staying at the Rescue, but working in my dim and depressing basement apartment is difficult because of the lack of a Wi-Fi signal, and going into the office to bug-spray Frank is worse. I'm working on an exposé piece about school rezoning. With all sides accusing one another of everything from fund mismanagement to incompetence, separating out the facts and verifying them is a bit of a project.

Not that Frank will appreciate the accuracy. He has one rule— sell the paper. Which means he has no intention of paying me for the time I *waste* digging through accounting ledgers when I could just as easily work on his suggested topic: a piece questioning whether the youthful female manager of the local burger joint might be responsible for the local fire chief's recent divorce.

I don't let it bother me, though. I knew rebuilding my reputation would take work, and whatever anyone can say for the rest of the paper, my stories will be legitimate. I'm not in it for the money.

I work for Cullen for the money.

Clicking on a table lamp with an adjustable neck that's also a combination pen and paperclip holder, I set to typing.

I've been hunkered down in my writing bubble for a while when the sound of a door creaking abruptly open makes me start. I jump to my feet, brandishing the first thing I can grab at the intruder, my heart sinking as I realize my impromptu weapon is a pen.

The place goes from being heavily shadowed—the overhead lights automatically go off when there's no motion to activate them —to full brightness, and I blink, nearly shrieking as a large figure lumbers through the entrance.

"*Jesus fucking Christ,*" Cullen shouts, sounding just as startled as I feel. His green eyes go from wide to narrow as they take me in. He's dressed in a muscle tee and running shorts so snug, I find myself staring, the man is carrying a heavy cardboard box with a medical symbol printed on the side. "What the hell are you doing here?"

SKY

"*I* work here." I'm actually proud of myself for not squeaking like a mouse. My voice doesn't even quaver. Unlike my insides. It's a good thing I skipped dinner. Otherwise, it might be all over this immaculately bleached floor right now.

"No, *I* work here. Your shift was supposed to be from one this afternoon until nine this evening. It's now after midnight, so I'll ask you again. What are you doing here?"

I check my watch. Sure enough, 12:37 a.m. glows happily back at me. Shit. I lost track of the time, and his tone still jangles my nerves. But before I can really get my mad on, I notice something. "What happened to your hands?"

Cullen's hands tighten around the box, the skin along his knuckles red, swollen, and scabby, as if it'd been bloodied not long ago. As if he'd beaten something or *someone* to a pulp. Oh my God.

"What did you *do*?" This last question comes out as what it is: an accusation.

I regret the words as soon as they leave my mouth. I *know* antagonizing people like Cullen is unwise. Dangerously unwise.

His face closes off, jaw tense and nostrils flaring. The kind of emotionless clampdown I've seen take over my father's features too many times. Many of those times ended with me in the emergency room.

I take a step back, my heart beating so fast, I feel like I might pass out. But I can't pass out. Can't let myself lower my guard. Men like Cullen are dangerous when angry, and the one before me is plainly none too pleased with my existence. There's no telling what he may do if I don't stay on my guard. No telling what he might do even if I *do*. I saw how he handled Charlie McTierney. Cullen Hunt is lethal when he wants to be. If he ever decides to assault me, I wouldn't stand a snowball's chance in hell.

My hands tremble at my sides, my feet rooted to the spot. Never taking my eyes off Cullen, I reach into my pocket for my phone. I might have the chance to dial 911, but not before he does his worst. Still, at least someone will come to investigate my broken skull. Right?

If I get out of here safely tonight, I'm never coming back.

It takes five more heartbeats before I absorb the fact that Cullen still hasn't moved. He's standing exactly where he was, those green eyes observing my reaction. Then his gaze drops away, sliding down to the floor.

Moving slowly, as if I'm some feral animal he's accidentally cornered, Cullen backs toward the opposite end of the room, where he puts the box on the floor against the wall. His hands come up to show empty palms. "The door is unlocked," he says evenly. "And you have a clear path to it. You're welcome to use that phone in your pocket too. If you don't have 911 tied to a side button, you should."

I swallow and try to process what's happening, my pounding heart messing with my thoughts. Cullen stands still. Waiting. Watching. Doing nothing to spook me. I rub my face, feeling stupid. The man owns this place, and all he's done upon discovering someone unexpectedly inside is raise his voice.

"I'm sorry." His words are low and soft, but not weak.

I swallow again. Did Cullen just apologize? The man I've gotten to know doesn't apologize. He's a rude, sarcastic dick with a side order of occasional violence.

"I didn't intend to frighten you," he adds.

I comprehend that he's not talking about tonight, but I don't say anything to absolve him. I do, however, feel my breathing settle. "Eli was looking for you. Said you've been MIA lately."

"Roger. I'll get back to him."

If that's not an evasion, then I don't know what is. Now that I'm calm enough to look closer, I grasp how haggard Cullen is, his piercing moss-green eyes rimmed with circles of fatigue. Sweat soaks the fabric of his shirt, which clings to chiseled muscle. It's near one in the morning, and Cullen's been working out. From the pale tint to his skin, it was punishing work too, not a light jog.

Almost against my better judgment, I find myself edging closer to him. "Are *you* all right?"

"Always."

"I'd have thought you were a better liar than that." I touch his arm, discovering the muscles coiled tightly beneath his skin. As if he hasn't relaxed in hours. Days. "When did you sleep last, exactly?"

He shrugs a shoulder, scrutinizing my hand on his arm as if it's the most fascinating spectacle he's ever witnessed.

"Why not?" I hear my tone shifting, something inside me switching from prey mode into my professional skin. Investigative journalism isn't all that different from medicine in some regard, working through layers of information to get to the truth.

"Can't."

"When's the last time you ate?" I demand, getting another shrug in return. "Today?"

"Can we go back to the version of the evening where you're scared of me and on your way out?" He is only half kidding.

I huff. Releasing Cullen's arm, I raid the mini fridge that's kept in the dispatch office, which is full of juice boxes and applesauce cups for patients. Kicking one of the wheeled chairs over to Cullen, I hand him both the items. "Drink. Eat."

"Those are for patients," he argues, but does take the offered chair. "I'm fine."

"You look like hammered dog shit, Cullen. Eat the food."

With an exasperated sigh, he pops open the apple sauce. Within two seconds, he's inhaled the small jar and accepts another two from me without protest, color returning to him with the intake of sugar. It's unexpectedly satisfying.

Grabbing the other wheeled chair, I settle myself beside him. There's a low hum of energy between us, but it's not the usual antagonism. More like camaraderie between two people who both have their demons.

"See? I'm not totally worthless, especially for a blonde," I say.

"Never said you were. And you're not a blonde."

I blink at him. "Of course I'm a blonde."

"But it's a different sort of blonde. There's like"—he makes a swirling motion with his hand over my head—"red in there too."

I huff a small chuckle, fingering my hair. Of all things for Cullen to have noticed, this isn't one I'd expected. "It's called strawberry, genius." My smile falters as I point my chin at his hands. "What did you hit, Cullen?" I really hope it's a what and not a who.

He moves his fingers around. "A few trees. A door. A wall."

"What kind of wall?"

His eyes meet mine, the green in them laced with fire and challenge. And a hint of vulnerability that's gone as soon as I see it. "Brick," he snaps.

I frown at the shift in Cullen's tone, which feels like a manufactured kind of angry. As if the man is trying to shove me away on purpose. Like an injured bear. No, a wolf. Lithe and deadly and hurting.

"Why?" I ask.

A muscle flexes in his jaw. "It was the closest one around."

"You know what I—"

"Go home, Reynolds," he says in a tone that demands—expects—obedience. The kind that I've a feeling most everyone in this Trident-god-hero-worshiping town would heed without question. I think that's how Cullen likes it, what makes it so easy for him to keep the world at arm's length. Denton Valley sees exactly what Cullen Hunt shows it: a successful CEO, a philanthropist, a rescuer. A man in constant charge of his business and himself. Now that I look closer though, I see glimmers of pain behind that curtain of perfection.

Reaching out toward him, I pull Cullen's hand into my lap, then run my thumb lightly over the injured knuckles. "I take it the brick won."

With a quick squeeze to Cullen's wrist, I get up long enough to retrieve a first aid kit and settle right back beside him, his split-knuckle hand heavy on my lap. Pulling out triple antibiotic, I debate how to spread it over the ripped-up flesh without hurting him.

Cullen chuckles without humor. "I'm not going to take your head off if the meds sting."

I nod, focusing the next few minutes of my attention entirely on his hands, the abused knuckles swollen and clearly painful. "Are you going to take my head off for any other reason?" I ask without looking up.

"Not so long as I know it's you I'm seeing." His voice is so quiet, I'm not sure he meant to say the words aloud.

He'd said something similar about Charlie. Ileene had too. *Who else would you be seeing, Cullen? Why?*

I don't press, though. Don't even acknowledge having heard the confession as I clean and spread an antibiotic ointment on the open sores while gently probing the bones beneath. Cullen was bad enough off to be hitting brick walls. What set him off, though? The bar fight? The fight between us? I shove the thought away, but I can't help noticing how the tension within his coiled muscles eases with my touch.

I bite my lip. "There may be a fracture."

"There isn't." So certain. So damn cocky.

I lift my face to call his bullshit.

"I had it X-rayed," he says, meeting my gaze. His eyes are more open than I'm used to seeing them. The pain is still there, but it's a bit softer than before. He's also sitting up straighter. Strange how I no longer consider that a threat. Still, him maintaining such intense eye contact is making me squirm. I pretend not to feel the sudden flash of heat between my legs.

"What? Why are you staring at me?" I ask, my voice higher pitched than normal.

"Why are you here so late at night, Sky?"

The question takes me by surprise, so I answer with more candor than I probably should. "It's nice here, and I needed the Wi-Fi."

A crease appears between his brows. "Your place doesn't have Wi-Fi? Is it out in the sticks?"

"No. It's..." It's a shithole. "I just didn't realize what time it'd gotten to be."

He nods as if in acceptance, but the intensity of his gaze never diminishes.

I finish tending the last of the cuts and release his hand, missing the skin contact already. "So, do you attack innocent walls often?" I mean it half in jest, only now realizing I was stretching the tentative trust between us one step too far.

Cullen's face closes off, the camaraderie we shared vanishing like a mirage. "I need to go." He stands, giving me a short nod. "Thank you for your assistance."

My chest tightens. "Cullen..."

"You may use the space as you like, but please keep the lights on the next time you're here late." His tone is polite, his gaze no longer open to me. In fact, everything about his features has gone blank. Inscrutable.

Without another word, he turns on his heel and walks silently toward the door, whooshing through before letting it fall closed with an audible clank.

CULLEN

*C*ullen stretched his arms over his head, his wrists brushing the thick rails and crossbars of his wrought iron headboard. He opened his eyes and realized a couple of things at once. It was Saturday morning. He'd managed to actually sleep, and not just sleep, but sleep deeply and late, as the sun already shining down on Pikes Peak suggested. Sure enough, the alarm clock confirmed the time. Eight thirty in the morning. Three hours later than Cullen's usual wake-up call.

Christ.

It was the first good night's sleep he'd had in days. The longest in months. Ironically, the person who'd made it possible for him to finally rest was also the one who'd set off his recent episode. No, that was unfair. Skylar Reynolds might have lit the match, but she didn't build the pyre. Cullen's fucked-up mind did that all by itself. He'd never been fit for human company, and PTSD didn't help.

Cullen yawned and sat up, the king-size mattress shifting comfortably to adjust to the change. After sleeping on bare ground for years, the bed's softness was still a small daily jolt.

For a second, he allowed himself to imagine there was a certain strawberry-blonde woman in his bed. Which was a mistake, given the sudden—and rather painful—way his cock hardened. Yes, his body was still ahead of itself. But her pouty lips, the long column of her delicate throat, and her startling blue eyes had that effect on him. Not to mention her breasts. She never exactly flaunted the goddamn things, but they called to him nonetheless. Which reminded him of how twisted up and sideways this woman had him.

Then he recalled Reynolds's desperate attempt to flee from his car, and his body cooled as if dunked into ice water. Cullen frightened her. Viscerally. Like he frightened his own family. The image of an Afghani woman flashed before him again, the one who yanked her daughter from his arms rather than let him keep the child breathing. He could still hear the fear in her voice. And the worst of it was that the woman wasn't altogether wrong. That attack *had* been his fault.

He shook his head. The smart thing to do was to keep his distance from Skylar Reynolds. More to the point, Cullen needed to pull his head out of his ass and get back in the game.

He swung himself out of bed, the movement just enough to make the shrapnel in his shoulder twinge, and took his prazosin. At least he'd kept up with his meds. Normally, Cullen went to sleep and rose at the same times. Then, an hour in his home gym, a shower, a protein shake, and work. The military had drilled a respect for routine into him, and keeping to a rigid schedule made him function better overall. Being thrown off it over these past several days made him feel as if he was crawling out of his goddamn skin.

But it was now eight thirty in the morning, and Cullen would just have to deal with it.

Pulling out his phone, he pulled up Eli's number. Since it was Saturday, the guys were likely going to make their way to Liam's club, North Vault.

Vault 7 p.m.? Cullen texted Eli. The result was predictable as hell. His cell rang within seconds.

"So you're amongst the living again?" his friend spat out, obviously pissed.

"Yeah."

"You're a fucking arsehole, you know that?" Eli half yelled into the phone, and Cullen closed his eyes. He did know that. He knew it better than anyone. But he didn't say anything in response. The silence ticked on for several tense heartbeats before his buddy broke it. "I take it you're in one piece more or less?"

"Yeah."

Eli huffed out an exasperated sigh. "See you at seven."

"Roger," Cullen replied, but his buddy had already disconnected from the line.

After walking over to his office, Cullen pulled open his laptop. Catherine had made sure the most critical calls had gotten through to him over the past few days but now he needed to catch up. Scanning through his email, he frowned at what he saw. Or, more accurately, what he didn't see.

"Adrianna," Cullen barked into the phone as soon as the line connected. "Where is my mortgage bill?"

The woman on the other end of the line huffed. "It's *my* mortgage payment, Cullen. And I'll make it tomorrow. You don't need to keep paying my bills for me, you know."

"I'm not paying your bills. I'm paying Bar's." Cullen pinched the bridge of his nose. Addie was Bar's wife and as good a woman as Cullen had ever met. Kind, responsible, strong. But she had trouble accepting help—and when dealing with Bar's family, she needed the help. Frank Peterson, Bar Peterson's brother, had launched a full-out assault on collecting all of Bar's assets before the man's body even returned from the Middle East. With the prenup Bar's family had forced him and Addie to sign and Frank Peterson's unscrupulous tactics, she was left with nothing except the house, but even that only so long as she made the payments. If the place went into foreclosure, Frank would get the proceeds of the sale.

A physical therapist, Addie had a good job—but it wasn't enough to manage everything on her own with Frank filing lawsuits left and right.

"Has Frank made any moves lately?" Cullen asked.

Addie sighed. "Filed an ordinance violation that my grass is overgrown. I swear the man must have measured it with a damn ruler. And no, I don't need help cutting it. I took care of it yesterday."

Yesterday. That would be Friday. Addie had either paid out of pocket or taken the day off work.

"Addie, I'll give you a choice," Cullen said, turning his voice hard. "You either give me the details from your bank and I'll set up automatic payments, or I'll have Liam trace it for me and you can spend the next ten years working out which Cayman Island account your mortgage payments are coming from. I promise I'll make the latter so much of a pain in your ass, you'll wish you were dealing with Frank."

Hanging up before Addie had a chance to protest, Cullen tapped his fingers on the table. There had to be an easier way of getting Addie to take the money, one that wouldn't insult her pride as well. He'd ask Liam when he saw the guys tonight. With the security company Liam ran, he had connections. And if he couldn't figure it out, Eli could.

Speaking of connections… Cullen punched Liam's number.

"Rowen," Liam answered on the first ring.

"Can you run a background on my—our—new dispatcher?" Cullen winced at his wording.

A pause. "Did she do something?"

"No. But I want to know why she might find working at the Rescue in the middle of the night more comfortable than in her own house. And she works for Frank, so—"

"So the asshole is likely doing what he can to screw with her. Got it," Liam said. "You coming today? Mason told me—"

"Mason gossips like an old woman. I'll be there. Get Keasley out too. Drag him if you need to."

"Received and understood," Liam said from the other end of the line. "And Hunt? Good to have you back."

"Fuck you." After hanging up the phone, Cullen got his protein shake and settled down to deal with the rest of the piling mess in his email.

~

CULLEN STRODE into the Vault and zeroed in on the three men sitting in a secluded alcove at the back of the club. Eli, Liam, and Kyan, the latter in his signature low-pulled baseball cap, were already there and lounging in their usual spot. Raising a hand to them in greeting, Cullen skirted the dance floor, where a sizable crowd moved in tune to the thrumming beats of the house music—Prince's "Kiss"—and stopped at the bar.

If Trident Rescue was Cullen's pet project, North Vault was Liam's. With its indirect mood lighting and blue-on-blue color scheme, the North Vault managed to be classy and seductive at the same time. Liam had designed every part of the Vault to create the sense of a world within a world, an escape for people wanting to take the edge off. The drinks were quality, the sound system the best in Denton Valley, the dance floor large, and the booths private. Drinking, dancing, general socializing, or—on specially designated days—recreation of a more specifically sexual sort were all welcome.

The aromas of freshly sliced lemon and various flavors of rum and vodka wafted over Cullen as he placed his forearm on the polished bar top, getting the bartender's attention. "Glenfiddich thirty-year, neat."

"Coming right up." The sinfully alluring brunette acknowledged the order and went to work. She wore a black blouse cut deeply at the neckline, a black miniskirt with stockings, and black stiletto heels. Sexy. Yet Cullen's mind was filled with a different set of measurements, along with a long curtain of strawberry-blonde hair that smelled like flowers.

In fact, the wall behind the bar just so happened to be the exact same blue as Reynolds's eyes. *Goddammit.* Even here, his brain seemed fixated on Sky.

Taking the drink off the bar, Cullen took a fortifying sip of scotch and made his way to where the others were sitting. In some ways, the three looked like a mismatched lot. Eli, who must have been coming directly from work, had his suit on, the tie now loosened but still screaming business. Liam looked relaxed in black jeans and a tight, equally black V-neck shirt, all showing off his honed body. With his dark brown hair curling at his nape, hazel eyes, and a dimple that came out whenever he smiled, the owner of the North Vault drew women to him like moths to a flame—and he played with them the same way: intensely and without attachment. He made as much clear going in, but that didn't slow the number of takers any more than did Eli's similar approach.

Sitting opposite Liam, Kyan Keasley never displayed much of himself nowadays, the long sleeves of his turtleneck concealing mortar round burns. They were all different, yet the same. And all of them Cullen's men.

"Ah, he deigns to make an appearance," Liam said, making an affected rolling motion with one hand as if acknowledging royalty.

"Fuck off." Sliding into a seat opposite Kyan, Cullen took another swig of scotch, savoring the smoky smooth flavor as the liquid whisked along his tongue. The drink went down his gullet like silk without even the slightest bite.

"Welcome back, arsehole," Eli said by way of greeting before frowning at Cullen's hand. "What in hell's name is that?"

Cullen examined his knuckles and Sky's Band-Aid covering the middle one. Truth be told, Cullen himself didn't know why he hadn't pulled the thing off. It wasn't actually doing any good there, but...well, he just hadn't. So there. For a moment, Cullen considered lying. He really did. He could say Catherine had done it or even Rachel. But they weren't in high school anymore. Besides, he supposed there was nothing wrong with the truth. "Reynolds wanted to play medic."

There was no need to explain what caused the injuries to begin with. The guys knew well enough.

"Takes two to play," said Liam, with such casual mildness that Cullen just rolled his eyes. Liam's games were of a distinctly kinky taste, and some of the toys he kept both in his closet and in the North Vault's private hold made Cullen cringe no matter how much Liam insisted he was missing out.

"Here you are, sir." A waitress appeared at the table, placing a Don Julio Añejo tequila before Kyan and club soda on a napkin before Liam.

"Speaking of games." Cullen toasted Liam's drink as the other men smirked at one another. If Liam was on club soda, he had a woman or few in his sights. "Evening plans, then?"

Liam waggled his eyebrows, his grin hitching up every line of his face. "Damn straight."

"Would you like another scotch?" the waitress asked Cullen.

He shook his head. Cullen usually maintained a strict two-drink limit in deference to the prazosin, which helped to keep his nightmares at bay, but he didn't today. He didn't want to go even that far. Cullen disliked tempting fate, especially where his meds were concerned. Getting the particular med and dosage just right had been enough of an ass pain.

He might be many things, but being stupid on purpose wasn't one of them.

The waitress took Eli's order and disappeared. Reclining against the high back of the booth, Cullen watched the North Vault flow through the evening around him. Liam and Eli were catching up on business and forecasting a Trident Rescue barbecue Cullen was not looking forward to. He guessed Kyan felt the same way, but it was hard to tell. Nudging the brim of his hat lower over his face, the man remained his usual circumspect self, sipping on his tequila and staying quiet. On the dance floor, the Vault's guests were dancing free, one blonde's smooth silhouette so like Skylar's that Cullen's fist clenched when a man beside her squeezed her ass.

The woman grinned. She was obviously familiar with the guy, and was just as obviously not Skylar. But it was too late. The similarity had already made Cullen picture himself blindfolding Reynolds and tying her not to one of the club's headboards, but to his own.

He immediately went hard.

Perfect, now he'd have to sit with his cock aching against his zipper and try to think of nonerotic imagery while the music thumped in the background and beautiful women traipsed by every minute or two.

To be fair, he'd had worse problems to deal with, but he didn't *want* to want Sky.

And yet he did. No, his *body* did. There was a difference. Unlike his cock, Cullen had no desire to go near her—or anyone. Cullen had always been feral, and after returning from the Middle East, well, being who he was precluded any chance of relationships.

Cullen's eyes strayed back to the strawberry-blonde on the dance floor, her face tilted back with gleeful joy. The only sensations Cullen could reliably rouse in Reynolds were terror.

"...Reynolds."

"What was that?" Cullen pulled his attention back to the men, finding Liam looking at him.

"I was saying I have the preliminary on Reynolds you asked for." Liam pulled a folder out of his bag. "No criminal record, but I don't like where she's living one bit."

Cullen flipped over the folder and felt his jaw tighten at the address. 1427-A Lincoln Drive. While Denton Valley wasn't known for being seedy or having much of a crime rate, like anywhere, there were a few locations that were subpar. And Sky's current residence was smack dab in the middle of just such a neighborhood.

"Like I said." Liam's voice hardened, his protectiveness resonating with Cullen's own rising blood pressure. The woman worked at Trident Rescue. That made her their responsibility. "I don't like it."

Flipping over the first page, Cullen examined a series of photographs showing a run-down brick house with crumbling mortar, soot-stained exterior, and debris-filled yard. The driveway held Skylar's Corolla alongside and a rusted-out vehicle up on blocks. He narrowed his eyes at it. "What am I looking at right now?"

"Our dispatcher's address. Maybe its inside is nicer than the outside."

"But you doubt it." The place was a goddamn dump.

"I doubt it. I checked past police reports, cross-referencing this specific address, and while nothing has ever happened on that plot of land, there's been lots of drug activity and vandalism up and down her street. Her neighbor from across the road reported their car stolen less than a year ago, in fact."

Cullen tapped his finger against the table. Sky's comment about the station being a comfortable place to work was finally making sense. "What haven't you told me yet?"

"That this is actually her landlord's abode. *This* is hers." Liam pulled out the final photo, this one showing a new perspective on the same cracked cement steps, now with steps leading down to a moldy-looking door. "1427-A. She lives not in the house, but in the basement."

"Not anymore she doesn't," Cullen growled, then reached for his drink, his hand stopping as something hard flickered over Kyan's face.

"Three o'clock," Kyan said in answer to Cullen's unvoiced question.

Sure enough, when Cullen cut his gaze to the right, his own jaw tightened—because one Frank Peterson had just walked into the Vault.

CULLEN

*S*waggering over to the far side of the bar, Frank Peterson planted himself beneath the big-screen television and gave the brunette barkeep a predatory smile before turning his attention to the news broadcast glowing in front of him. He wore a pale gray suit and flashy silver tie, garments intended to impress, Cullen had no doubt. While the suit looked high-end, it didn't fit Frank all that well, emphasizing his slight paunch rather than concealing it.

"Asshole," Kyan muttered under his breath. Eli nodded in solidarity.

Cullen glared at Liam, who only cocked a brow back in challenge. Liam's continuing tolerance of Frank's Vault patronage was a source of argument, but it all came down to a basic calculation: Frank regularly drank himself into loose lips—and Liam believed that keeping an ear on the bullshit Frank spilled was worth the irritation of his presence.

On most days, Cullen agreed. Today wasn't one of those.

Finishing off his drink, Cullen homed in on the images flashing across the television screen, the red "Breaking News" banner scrolling across the bottom. The footage looked too familiar. Fractured sidewalks with eroded edges. Spray-painted graffiti on stop signs. Abandoned residences. Streetlight poles. Bars on windows in residential and commercial establishments alike and there... That car up on blocks. The same one Cullen noticed in Liam's photos.

"Is that Reynolds's neighborhood?" Cullen asked, getting up for a closer look at the screens, his men falling in behind him.

"Yes," Liam answered grimly as the on-air reporter highlighted a possible burglary in progress.

It figured. By Murphy's Law or Reynolds's Law, whatever horrible thing might be happening would be there. And why fucking not? Everything about that woman tempted fate.

Yeah. Well, it wouldn't be her neighborhood much longer. Turning on his heel, Cullen pivoted toward the door—then paused as he caught a movement out of the corner of his eye.

Frank Peterson, having yanked his phone from his trouser pocket, now held the device in front of his face and spoke into the thing as if it were an old-fashioned tape recorder. "Hey, honey," Frank's eyes stayed glued to the television screen while Sky's name and photograph filled his phone screen. "Got a hot prospect for you."

Skylar Reynolds. Heat spilled into Cullen's blood.

A soft growl just behind Cullen told him the others had marked Frank's *honey* as well as he had.

A few feet away, Frank squinted at the television. "Burglary in process. Lincoln Drive. Yeah. East side of town and..."

On the live broadcast, an on-air anchorwoman went silent as she pressed a finger to her earpiece, obviously listening. Then she resumed with more intensity. "We have a new report from our on-site reporter stating that the burglary may turn into a hostage situation. We're uploading the footage as we speak."

The picture altered to a blurry video of a car pulling into a detached carport. As three occupants—two adults and a small child —got out of the vehicle, two figures with concealed faces descended upon them, forcibly pushing the victims into the house.

Cullen's concentration on the television screen was so absolute that Peterson's sudden cackle jarred him.

"Shit's getting interesting," Frank hooted, his eyes sparking with excitement. "Get over there *now*, girl!"

Before Cullen became aware he'd rushed forward, he'd grabbed Frank's elbow. "What the hell are you doing?"

"What do you want, Hunt?" Frank pulled his elbow free, his grin gone.

Heart pounding against his ribs, Cullen leaned down to stare Frank in the eye. "You're a fucking asshole," he informed Frank quietly before snatching the phone right out of his hand. "Reynolds. Don't go anywhere near that scene. That's an order."

"*Cullen?*" Sky's musical soprano came over the line, bewilderment filling every word. "Why do you have my editor's phone? And why—"

He cut her off. "It doesn't matter why. You're not going."

But before Cullen could say more, Frank Peterson pushed him. Or tried to. The man had risen to his feet in a tizzy and made a quickly aborted attempt to stand up for his property—but even Frank knew that his flabby form didn't have Cullen's staying power.

Frank slapped his hand against the bar. "That's my phone, Hunt," he snapped, spittle flying. "And if you know what's good for you, you'll—"

"I'll what?" Cullen tightened his grip on the cell so much that he heard an ominous cracking noise, his voice lowering by a whole guttural octave.

"Cullen." Eli materialized beside him, but Cullen's focus stayed on the asshole luring Skylar Reynolds into a viper pit.

"You'll be sorry," Frank said.

Cullen snorted. "Last time you and I tangled, I seem to remember my fist breaking your nose."

Frank's complexion skipped right over the color red and turned a distinctive shade of purple. "You haven't changed one bit from the violent, little, delinquent shithead you were at fourteen. Go ahead, Hunt. Take a shot. You'll find you'll get more than a spanking from the law now."

Red flashed at the fringes of Cullen's vision, his heart rate and pulse all rising, feeding an irresistible need to sink his knuckles through Frank's skull. Cullen had been fourteen the last time he'd had the pleasure, and the resulting *spanking* was a lawsuit that broke whatever relationship he'd had with his parents, snatched him out of his home, and got him marooned at Trident Academy military school.

Then again, he did meet his Tridents there, so it was more than worth it. It had been more than worth it to keep the girl Frank had been pawing from getting what the gleam in Frank's eye said he'd intended.

But Frank was right. Bashing in his skull in the middle of North Vault would tie them up in court for months. And the bastard would target Liam as the owner as well.

Frank raised his index finger and pointed it right into Cullen's face.

Cullen growled in warning.

"Peterson. *Don't.*" Kyan stepped up beside Cullen, his movement silent as a ghost's. Though Kyan kept his voice low, he emanated power with every uttered syllable and glared at the man's upraised finger until Frank wisely dropped it and took a pace backward.

Cullen went to step after him, but Kyan splayed his hand on his chest. "Not worth it, Hunt."

"Keasley's right." Eli threw Frank a foul glance before inserting himself between him and Cullen. "Are we going or not?"

There was no need to explain where. Since Skylar worked at Trident Rescue, she was one of their own.

"Reynolds," Cullen barked into Frank's phone, only to discover that the woman had disconnected. Cullen slammed the phone down on the bar, the abused screen giving a final click before shattering while its owner yelped in pathetic dismay. "Yeah," Cullen said, turning his back to Frank. "Let's move."

SKY

I stomp out of my basement apartment, trying like hell to stop seething at Cullen's audacity so I can focus on my work. Did the man seriously think it was acceptable to interfere in my journalism? To get between me and my own editor? To opine on what stories I should be covering? My hands clench into fists, my pulse rising. The next time I see Cullen, I'm going to—

Stop, Sky. I force myself to take a deep breath of the cool evening air, the breeze whipping my hair over my face. *Cullen's attempt to interfere was his fuck-up, but you letting it consume you now would be yours.*

My thoughts finally calm three breaths in, my professional mind taking over. This isn't Frank's usual drivel; this is actual news. The reason I went into journalism. It doesn't matter that I only got the lead because I'm closer than anyone else. I have it. And damn it, I will cover it.

Pulling my hair back into a bun, I adjust my shoulder bag and set a quick pace toward the unfolding scene, trying not to let the fact that it's only a few blocks from my house distract me. It's still light outside, but won't be for too much longer. Two steps later, my phone vibrates. I pull it out, expecting to see Frank's number and nearly answer on reflex before seeing the caller.

Cullen Hunt.

Yeah. Sorry, Hunt, I'm not on your clock right now.

I set the phone to silent and then, after a moment's hesitation, temporarily block the bastard's number altogether. If he can't act like a respectful professional, then into a digital time-out he goes. Slipping the phone into my back pocket for easy access and recording, I quicken my steps toward the address—and the Channel Thirteen van that's already parked at the end of the block.

Dammit. On the other hand, if rival new stations are responding as well, that underscores the relevance. Plus, Thirteen is on air and I'm print, so we go after different angles.

"Again, this is Trent Cannon, reporting for Channel Thirteen News from Denton Valley's Lincoln Drive," a well-dressed young man says into a microphone as his cameraman monitors the footage. The shot is angled to get both Cannon and a house with peeling red paint, which must be where the action is. "Here, an exclusive source reported seeing two men with faces covered removing merchandise from the residence directly behind me."

Exclusive source? I snort, willing to bet Cannon just chatted with Mrs. Frobisher, my crotchety neighbor who fancies herself the neighborhood watch and spends her day peeking through curtains and ranting about the police. Now that I think about it, she's exactly the kind of person to ring up the news instead of law enforcement should a crime happen.

"The circumstances became immediately worse," Cannon goes on, "when a vehicle evidently containing the family who lives here pulled into the carport, interrupting the burglars. Two of the criminals reacted by dragging the three family members, including a small child, inside, where they all now remain. Denton Valley authorities are expected to arrive at any moment." Cannon gives a dramatic pause, and the cameraman shuts off the footage.

"Still on burglary?" The cameraman snorts. "That's a fucking collection crew raiding a drug house. Can I help you?" The last is directed toward me.

"Skylar Reynolds," I say, my mind still reeling from what I'm hearing. "*Denton Uncovered.*" I hold out my hand, and both the men shake it.

"Welcome to the shit show," Cannon says. "Though this isn't the type of thing *Uncovered* is usually interested in. This is more…"

"Actual real news?" I supply, earning an earnest grin. Cannon has a nice-boy look about him, nothing like Cullen's dark broodiness. And he smiles a great deal more too. I stick my hands into my back pockets and peer at the screen, where the cameraman is rewinding the footage. "So why did you say burglary if you think it's a drug money collection?"

"Same reason I said the authorities were showing any time soon. Political correctness." He yawns. "This is Lincoln Drive, Reynolds. Neither the cops nor anyone else gives a flying fuck about Lincoln Drive. Now if this were happening about two miles down the road, that would be a different situation. As it is, though—we only got the airtime because it's a slow night. Plus, odds are ten to one that nothing more's happening. The bastards are going to work things out behind closed doors, and end of story."

"What about the child?" I ask. I thought he'd recorded that bit, but maybe I'm wrong.

"What about him?" Cannon shrugs. "He lives there. This is probably a weekly occurrence. Let's not drink our own Kool-Aid. A burglary claim from an annoying neighbor who calls with something every other day isn't exactly evidence. And a mom and kid? Yeah, they got ushered inside along with the baby daddy. If there was a news van outside my house, I'd be doing the same thing. No weapons, no violence. As far as a story, this is a whole lot of smoke."

I'm smart enough to give Cannon a *what are you gonna do* smile instead of arguing, no matter how much my blood is heating with outrage. Glancing at my watch, I mark the time. Whether or not this "burglary" is serious, a chronic delay in police response to a neighborhood is something that needs to come to light. Carefully. Factually. Professionally.

Making myself a mental note to pull the public records on 911 statistics and response times, I nod toward the house. "I'm going to canvass the neighbors, see if they have anything to say."

ALEX LIDELL

"Not a bad idea. A good sob story goes a long way. But...just as a matter of professional courtesy, lemme tell you, this isn't the type of street where you want to be knocking on doors and asking for testimonials on drug-dealing neighbors."

No, but it is exactly the kind of street to be asking for testimonials on police response. And not from Mrs. Frobisher.

Cannon yawns. "If we're lucky, this becomes a hostage situation and we all get the story. If not, this will die on the vine."

"Yeah, I'm sure you're right, but we don't all have a pretty camera, so..." I let my words trail off with a light little shrug. The last thing I want to do is burn professional bridges, but I'm not going to stand around, hoping for a hostage situation. If I'm working, I'm *working*.

Leaving Trent Cannon and his cameraman, who are set up a good hundred yards from the residence, I cross the street to get a better look. I've only met a few people in the neighborhood, but I think the house next door is the one with the shy tween I see flying her drone after school. I don't know the girl's name, but we wave to each other a lot. A connection. A start.

As I make my way to the tween's house, which is right behind the peeling red two-story, I catch sight of something flashing in the window. A gun. My heart stops, my chest tightening as I drop to my hands and knees, pressing myself against the house's wall. Who knows what the guy might do if he sees me out here. All right, this was a stupid idea.

Just when I manage to force a breath into my lungs, the neighbor's Rottweiler rushes to the fence, barking his head off and scaring the bejesus out of me for the second time in as many minutes. I barely keep from squawking, my heart flying into my rib cage. And it's a good thing I do, because the window beneath which I huddle opens a moment later.

"Shut your fucking dog up or I'll do it for you," a man hollers, slurring. "No respect for any goddamn person on this fucking street."

I flinch as I hear the sound of something breaking, my mind flashing back to a cheap flower vase my mom kept buying at the

84

dollar store over and over. The memories make me light-headed for a moment, but I pull myself together enough to focus. I need to get out of here. Quietly. Quickly.

Still on my hands and knees, I breathe quietly through my nose until the sounds at the window recede, then start edging away, staying close to the wall.

A thud sounds inside the house, as if something weighty has been dropped. Then the distinctive mewling cries of a child. I go motionless at once, holding my breath and lying flat in the tall unkempt weeds that pass for a lawn around here. Nausea washes over me as the sobs continue, the helplessness of the whimpers drilling a hole down to my core. Because I've been that child. Wounded and alone. Injured by a man who was supposed to keep me safe.

Despair tightens my throat as shouting rises again, the arguing adults yelling over each other while a set of little feet patters down the steps. Something that sounds frighteningly like a screen door squeaks open, and the childish sobbing becomes clearer. Outside. The child is outside. Just around the corner of the house from me.

Heart hammering in my ears, I edge around the corner toward what passes for a backyard. The child *is* there, a little boy with a bloody lip and an arm bent at a bad angle, curled into a ball by a sprawling bush. His jeans and polo shirt are ripped and stained, and he's crying into the ground as if afraid of making too much noise. Of bringing worse things down on himself.

Staying low, I rush over to the child, crouching beside him. The adrenaline pumping through my body makes my hands tremble as I touch his shoulder. "Hey there, buddy," I whisper. "My name is Sky. I'm a friend. I live just a few blocks from here. What's your name?"

The child jerks towards me, his brown eyes wide and fear filled. He looks about seven, with skinny ribs and shaking shoulders. "Zack," he whispers.

I stretch my arms out to him. "How about we go somewhere safe, Zack? Just for now. Can we do that, buddy? Can we go somewhere until the adults are done fighting?"

He nods cautiously, and I pull him toward me, my heart

ALEX LIDELL

squeezing when he holds back a whimper over his arm. He's been around long enough to know when not to attract attention. Though it technically makes me a kidnapper at this point, I hoist Zack onto my hip, murmuring some nonsense about ice cream flavors that I hope keeps both of us calm. As the boy burrows his head into my shoulder, I take my first shaky steps toward the sidewalk.

"What the fuck?"

A man in jeans and a dirty undershirt rushes out into the yard, his scruffy face looking werewolfish in the evening gloom. Throwing a beer bottle against the tree, he flashes a set of broken teeth before ripping Zack from me. Or trying to. The child cries out, but clings to me with a strength I'd not expected.

Grabbing the boy by his hair, Undershirt wrenches Zack away from me on the second try, flinging the child to the ground. Behind the bastard, a pair of other muscled thugs spills into the yard, the second one holding a baseball bat at the ready.

"Who's the bitch?" one yells as Undershirt grabs and hurls me into the wall of the house.

14

SKY

For a moment, I don't hear anything but a dull noise of impact and the cracking of the wooden siding. Then pain explodes in my face and shoulder. Before I can shout, the man pulls me back and—because slamming me once wasn't enough—he does it again. This time, the house siding separates, splinters driving into my skin.

I scream. Dizziness sweeps over me, Zack's pained crying in the background echoing my own gasps. Zack. I need to get Zack out of here. Somehow.

"Fucking bitch. Who do you think you fucking are?" Grabbing my arm, Undershirt throws me into the ground, the motion so violent that I feel something give way in my shoulder. Pain shoots through me, blazing down my arm and shoulder and back as I crash down on my injured arm.

I shriek then. I can't help it.

And someone else shrieks too. My eyes widen as four shadows spill into the yard, the one closest to the baseball-bat guy taking the weapon away from him with a single powerful jerk before driving it right into the man's gut. Another of the shadows spin kicks

Undershirt, flattening the bastard to the ground. A third kneels beside Zack, speaking to him with a deep, soft voice.

Dizziness washes over me, and for a moment, I don't know what I'm seeing. Don't understand why the shadows are so damn familiar.

"Stay still, Reynolds." Cullen's words, calm and even, cut through the pain-filled haze around me, the man himself materializing in my line of sight a moment later.

"Cullen," I say dumbly, my gaze skidding between the last man I expected to see here and Undershirt, who is stirring on the ground behind him. No, not just stirring. Reaching for his waistband. "Behind you!" I shout.

Cullen spins smoothly just as Undershirt pulls out a gun. Moving faster than I would've thought possible, Cullen rushes the thug, shoving Undershirt's gun-holding arm straight into the air. A flick of Cullen's wrist has Undershirt dropping the weapon with a scream of pain, Liam appearing beside the pair to catch the falling gun before it hits the ground. A few metallic clicks follow, and the disassembled pieces of the weapon scatter to the dirt.

Holy shit.

I try to push myself up, only to find another set of hands keeping me in place, Kyan's ocean-like scent filling my lungs.

"Easy, Skylar," Kyan murmurs to me as if I were a skittish horse. "Need to take a look at you." He flicks on a flashlight, and by its glow, I see his dark eyes concentrating on me as he pushes a lock of his glossy black hair back under his ever-present baseball cap. The burn scars touching the right side of Kyan's face manage to underscore the strong angle of his jaw, making his rare moments of connection heart-stoppingly intense.

"Scene secure." Liam strolls out of the house after switching on a security light. I don't remember seeing him enter, yet there he is, pulling zip ties from God knows where and wrapping them around the thugs' wrists. Liam rubs his hand over his face, scruffy with a five-o'clock shadow that's probably been in place since noon. "There are at least two kilos of coke they were cutting in plain sight in there. I'm calling it in."

Pulling out his cell, Liam takes a few steps away, walking as if he owns the world, menace radiating from his honed body. I don't realize I'm shrinking away until I feel Kyan squeeze my arm reassuringly. The man doesn't talk much, but he sees everything. I wouldn't underestimate any of these guys. Especially not now.

"Copy." Cullen crouches beside me for the second time. His square jaw visibly clenched, lips drawn into a harsh line. Taking out a penlight, he shines it into my eyes. Despite being small, the light is painfully bright, and I jerk my face to the side.

"No, look at it," Cullen orders. "I need to check your pupils."

I want to argue, I really do, but my shoulder chooses that moment to throb worse than ever. I go breathless at the blinding shock, my arm spasming without my control. I whimper with each involuntary movement, my vision blurring.

It hurts so much that I almost shout at him to go to hell, but I can't form the words.

"Can you move your fingers?" Cullen asks.

"Yes," I say, only then registering that I'm full-on sobbing. Great. Of all the times to have a meltdown. "How...how's the b-boy?"

"Mason's got him. He'll be okay."

"B-but what about the m-mom? Was she——"

Cullen wipes the tears from my cheeks with stunning gentleness. "Rowen's on it."

Red and blue flashes begin to strobe from somewhere down the street, and I feel immensely glad that additional help has arrived. Although it appears the famous Trident gods have things well in hand. Suddenly, the townsfolk's reverence for these men makes sense to me.

Uniformed officers flood the yard, Liam intercepting them as if he owns the place. I'm not even surprised when the cops fall in line beneath the man's curt orders.

"I had the medic unit take Zackary." Eli walks up to us, a small cut on his forehead. "It'll be a while before they can get the next rig out here." Kneeling beside Cullen, Eli softly brushes my hurt arm. "How are you doing there, soldier?"

I try to smile. My annoying sobs have ceased, but from the men's expressions, I don't think the smile's very convincing.

"Alert and oriented, lacerations, possible concussion, and dislocated shoulder," Cullen rattles off, the other man nodding along to the code. "Stable all in all."

"You want to wait or reduce it now?" asks Eli.

"Now," Cullen says firmly. "Neuro appears fully interact, and I'm not putting her through waiting a fucking hour for the ER doc."

"Wait, what?" I inject myself into a conversation that seems to have taken a turn very relevant to my well-being and am surprised when it's Kyan who replies.

"Cullen is going to put your shoulder back into place," Kyan says in his soft yet powerful voice. "It will hurt."

"No!" I pull back as Cullen reaches over and rips half my shirt open, baring a shoulder that doesn't look anything like it should. Yet, the thought of someone touching my arm makes my heart jump into a dizzy gallop. "Don't touch it." I shake my head to emphasize my point.

Cullen catches my chin between his thumb and forefinger, forcing me to meet his gaze. The man's mossy-green eyes are hard as steel, the tiny thread of empathy in them as frightening as anything. "I wasn't asking your opinion. Given where we find ourselves, I think you've done enough for one night."

"My body," I hiss through clenched teeth, "my opinion. Get away."

"What our wound-up ass of a friend is trying to say," Kyan tells me softly, "is that he thinks he can put that shoulder back into place safely now. The pain won't stop until that happens, and none of us are enjoying watching you writhe in agony."

"That's what I said," Cullen grunts.

Kyan winks at me.

I nod. "All right."

Kyan's hands brush over my body, stabilizing me from behind. "Take a deep breath, Sky," he says.

I do.

Cullen takes careful hold of my wrist.

My stomach tightens. "I changed my mind!" I jerk away, gasping as a bolt of lightning shoots down my arm. "Don't. *Don't.*"

90

To my amazement, Cullen actually pauses, though he doesn't let go. "Reynolds—Sky—look at me." His gaze grips mine again, though this time, the connection feels like a lifeline. The rise and fall of Cullen's chest shifts slightly to match mine before slowing our joint rhythm. "Don't look away," he says. Orders. "Don't look anywhere but at me."

I feel his hands moving again, Kyan's grip tightening behind me. Without ever breaking eye contact with me, Cullen wraps his hands around my elbow and wrist and begins to rotate them slowly. Gradually. Unyieldingly, no matter how much I shake from the pain. I gasp as there's a final jolt of agony before the joint slips into place with a pop, and relief floods my blood.

"You did good," Kyan whispers to me, but it's Cullen who continues to hold my gaze, a sparkle of pain flashing in his eyes.

I reach my hand toward him, and, with the next heartbeat, Cullen pulls me tightly against his chest and doesn't let go.

15

CULLEN

"*E*vening, Mr. Hunt."

Leading Sky past the double doors of Denton Valley Memorial's ER, Cullen nodded a return greeting to the security guard and then to a pair of orthopedic surgeons crossing the lobby, coffees in their hands. The key was to walk with purpose and as quickly as Sky's trembling body would allow, lest someone pull him into an administrative conversation Cullen had no appetite for just now.

Skylar had scared him. That moment when he saw her on the ground, her small body quivering, something inside Cullen had gone very, very still. Eli must have caught on, because he'd offered to drive them to the ER himself so Cullen could ride in the back with Sky.

Setting course for the treatment area, Cullen bothered with no more than a cursory nod to the check-in desk, his key card opening the sliding doors with a whispered swoosh. As they crossed the shiny linoleum floor, the familiar smell of medical-grade disinfectant masked Sky's floral fragrance, the bright overhead lights making her pallor more pronounced.

The place was busy, a typical Saturday night. A young nurse's aide blushed the color of her pink scrubs as she glanced at Cullen before returning to labeling blood samples. Behind the large square center of operations in the middle of the room, one of the docs on duty in his blue scrubs raised his hand in welcome before returning to reviewing a chart with a pair of young residents.

"Cullen," a woman called out from her station behind a computer screen. As he looked over, Michelle Mounce, the head RN who presided over the night shift, laboriously brought herself to her feet. Michelle was one of the many hospital personnel he'd worked closely with after returning from overseas. She stayed competent, cool, and more levelheaded in a crisis than most marines. She maintained an unfazed aura about her now too, soothing a hand over her hugely pregnant belly.

"Michelle. I've a trauma for you. Sky here had some help running into a wall. Possible concussion, left shoulder dislocation reduced at scene, multiple lacerations." He reached out for the individual patient clipboards and a pen. "Notes coming."

"Nice to know she's already been in your extremely capable hands," Michelle told him before addressing Sky. "Hi, sweetie. Let's get you looked at."

The nurse's warm and caring personality was the polar opposite of Cullen's, and he could see Sky's tenseness lower by a noticeable fraction. In other words, Michelle had done in one moment what he had failed at for two hours straight.

"When's your baby due?" Sky asked her, and the nurse pushed her coppery-red braid behind her shoulder.

Michelle snorted. "Monday."

Cullen paused, his pen stilling on the clipboard. "Monday is two days from now, Michelle."

"Oh, I meant *last* Monday."

"Christ," Cullen muttered under his breath.

"No kidding." Michelle smirked at him.

"What the hell are you doing here, then?" Cullen barked, regretting it a moment later when Sky flinched.

Michelle, unfazed, looked right back at him. "This is my third child, and I know what to expect. Besides, if I do go into labor, I'm already here, aren't I?" She cocked a brow. "Stop looking at me like that, Cullen. You're perfectly safe standing next to me—pregnancy isn't contagious."

As they'd been speaking, Michelle shuffled toward one of the curtained-off treatment alcoves lining the perimeter of the ER and took a hospital gown from the shelf.

"Is your baby a boy or a girl?" Sky asked.

Michelle patted the exam table, and Sky shifted onto it, wincing with the motion.

Cullen stepped up behind the raised bed at once, stopping within arm's reach. Michelle glanced at him briefly before returning her attention to Sky.

"Boy. Our first two were girls, so this should be fun. We're naming him Henry after my husband's father."

Every molecule in Cullen's body froze like ice. Henry had been *his* father's name too, and that man, along with his mother, had thrown Cullen into military school just to get rid of an embarrassment. His father had died still thinking of Cullen as a grenade with the pin half pulled.

Not that it mattered. None of that mattered. It was all ancient history.

Shaking off the thoughts, Cullen forced himself to back up a step while Michelle helped Sky into a gown, took her vitals, and yielded the spot to the doc, Ricky Yarborough.

"No allergies, no medications, no preexisting conditions?" Dr. Yarborough asked, holding out his hand for the medical file in Cullen's hands. Yarborough—who had patched up Cullen more than once—was not usually in the ER, and Cullen would bet his bank account that Michelle had given him a ring. "Loss of consciousness?"

"Unknown," said Cullen.

"No," said Sky.

"Unknown," said Cullen, his tone hardening.

"I was there." Sky whipped her head around, only to groan when this jostled her injured shoulder. "And why do you have my medical file, Cullen? Isn't it confidential?"

"Not to the man who owns this hospital," Cullen shot back. If Sky thought she was going to downplay what happened, she had another damn think coming. "Listen, Ricky—"

Yarborough held up his palm. "What Cullen is trying to say, Ms. Reynolds, is that you're unlikely to know whether or not you lost consciousness. And given your other injuries, it suggests the mechanism of injury was forceful enough that we can't rule out a head injury."

"Very well." Sky nodded at the doc, then shot Cullen a narrow-eyed look, which told him their other discussion was far from over.

Cullen crossed his arms, not budging one step while Yarborough finished his exam, ordered a CT scan for Sky's head, and X-rays to check the reduction, and promised that if the imaging came back clean, she could go home with some stitches and ibuprofen.

"Cullen, a word?" Yarborough said, holding the curtain to the exam room open for Cullen to precede him into the hallway. There was something about the doc's tone that made Cullen's chest tight around his ribs.

"What's wrong with Reynolds?" Cullen asked, stepping in front of Yarborough the moment the pair of them entered one of the empty enclosed treatment rooms. "Is she—"

"Why the hell are you reducing a dislocation in the field when you're thirty minutes away from an ER?" Yarborough demanded. "This is Denton Valley, Colorado, Cullen. Not Afghanistan. It isn't even a back country where you'll be hiking a patient out."

Cullen's jaw tightened. "She was in pain when she didn't need to be. Is there a problem with the shoulder?"

"I don't think so, but even I won't know until I see an X-ray. And I'm saying that after a full exam in a treatment room, not a field assessment in the dark with her fully clothed." Yarborough put his hands on his hips and leveled him with a hard gaze. "There's a reason we don't treat people we care about, Cullen. Because sometimes letting a patient be in pain is the right call."

"I—" He rubbed his face, swallowing the lie from the tip of his tongue. "Fine. Message received and understood." He sighed, glancing at the door.

"Not yet." Yarborough forced Cullen into meeting his gaze. "Take off your shirt."

"You aren't my type, Ricky."

Yarborough didn't even blink. "I would usually simply charge some extraordinary penalty for someone who missed three appointments, but given your bank account, I'm going to resort to more underhanded measures. Take off your shirt and get on the exam table, or I'll leave a copy of your X-rays with Liam, Eli, Kyan, Ms. Reynolds over there, *and* Catherine."

Cullen had been right. Yarborough was not in the ER by chance.

"I'm going to fucking fire Michelle," Cullen muttered, pulling his shirt off in a smooth motion, his only further protest limited to refusing to wince when Yarborough palpated the shoulder and the shrapnel embedded in it.

"The longer you put this off, the more difficult the surgery is going to be," Yarborough said. "And yes, I said it is, not *may*. I know the notion scares you shitless, but——"

"It doesn't bother me much, Ricky," Cullen said. "The shoulder. It really isn't much trouble."

"No shooting pains?" the doc prodded. "No numbness or tingling? No stiffness or achy joints?"

"I didn't say I have no pain, but it's nothing I can't handle. I need to stay on task at the Rescue. It's important work."

"Which is all the more reason to take care of this." Yarborough sighed, his tone softening as he handed Cullen's shirt back. "How are the nightmares?"

His jaw tightened. They were going over all the fun things tonight. "Rare."

"How rare is rare?"

"Every other night." Cullen sighed. "And I had a flashback a couple of weeks back."

"The field hospital?" Yarborough asked.

"In full color."

Yarborough nodded, unsurprised. "Are you still taking your prazosin?"

"Yes, Doc. Every day."

"All right. You're free for now. But listen to me—you can't keep ignoring the shrapnel. You've been lucky that it hasn't migrated too drastically, but luck isn't what I want to rely on, especially not with how physical you get."

The sound of a bed being wheeled across the floor echoed from the hallway. Sky being taken to CT? "I hear you," Cullen said, his attention on the door.

"Do you?" The doctor's tone dropped low and harsh, snapping Cullen's attention right back to him. Yarborough was in the med corps and had a way of putting any SEAL in his place.

"Yes, sir," he answered, this time with more fidelity, and tried not to look like he was escaping as Yarborough bladed his body to let Cullen out of the room.

Returning to Sky's bed, Cullen was relieved to find her still there and looking as comfortable as someone could in the ER. Pulling up a chair, he heard Yarborough's words echo in his mind. Ricky was wrong, though—Cullen cared about Sky because she worked at the Rescue. The reduction decision was a risk benefit analysis, not a judgment impaired by emotion. It wasn't.

"Why did you go to that house alone?" Cullen asked Sky, more harshly than he'd intended. "I told you not to."

Her brilliant blue eyes zeroed back in on his. "I'm not going to dignify the latter part with a response. As for the former, I was given an assignment. As you very well know."

"You have to be smarter than that. Frank doesn't give a damn about you. He'd send you into a burning building if he thought he could get more newspaper subscribers out of it." In deference to their location, Cullen kept his voice low, but his aggravation twisted his words into a rough growl. "Hell, you dying would just make that issue sell even faster."

"I'm not an idiot."

"Could've fooled me today."

Eyes flashing, Sky grabbed Cullen's shirt with her good hand. "You might be my boss when I'm at Trident Rescue, Cullen Hunt, but what I do as a professional journalist is *not* up to you. Are we clear on that?"

Cullen's breath caught as a zap of energy shot from Skylar's tight grip right to his cock, her fire-filled eyes heating his blood, her sweet floral scent grabbing his chest. For a heartbeat, he could do nothing but scrutinize that mouth of hers, the way it hung open just a little in her indignation, her lips soft and supple and goddamn kissable.

"My job is to get the story. The end," Skylar went on, chest heaving.

Cullen's chest was heaving too, though fury at Sky's stubbornness was only half responsible. The rest had to do with how the top of her gown exposed a lacy white bra. Lace that was, for all intents and purposes, transparent.

"And only I get to decide for myself how much risk I'm going to take," Sky finished, scowling as she let go of his shirt. Her voice softened. "Besides, I hadn't actually meant to get so close to the house. But once I saw Zack..." She shook her head, her face changing to a distant pain-filled look. "They hurt a child. I couldn't leave him. And no matter how much you growl, I'm willing to bet you wouldn't have left him either."

"No, I wouldn't have," he agreed quietly. "But you aren't me. And I promise you, that's a very good thing."

16

SKY

I meet Cullen's gaze. His face is inches away from mine, his breathing accelerated. His eyes—typically a gorgeous mossy green—have darkened to near blackness, and I can feel the heat pouring off him. His firm lips are so tight that they've basically disappeared, and the smooth expanse of his wide forehead is creased. I want to slap that perfectly formed face of his for insulting me, and I want to pound my fist into the bastard's massive, muscular chest. And damn it, I want to crush my lips to his mouth all at the same time.

I fight against the magnetic force drawing my face closer to Cullen's. Everything about the man, including the pull he has on me, is wrong. Insane. Unwanted. And yet the distance between us still closes, our mouths millimeters apart. I can feel Cullen's breath mixing with mine, tickling my skin—when there's an expulsion of breath from someone else.

Cullen and I freeze.

"Excuse me." The woman who appears in my peripheral vision clears her throat nervously. "I'm here to take Ms. Reynolds for some scans."

I peer over my shoulder to find a tech with a white lab coat and turquoise hair hovering by the door.

"I'll have her back to you as soon as I can, Mr. Hunt," she promises, her face coloring as Cullen swings his gaze to her. I get the feeling that she'd ask him for an autograph if she could.

"Of course, Summer. Thank you," Cullen says politely, and I swear the tech's blush deepens another two shades. What is it with these people treating Cullen like a celebrity?

What is it with me that I care?

After I've endured X-rays and a scan in a big donut-shaped machine, Summer of the turquoise hair returns me to my alcove. We're almost there when I hear Cullen's voice mixing with several others. Eli's, Liam's, and Kyan's deep masculine tones I recognize immediately, but the fifth—a bubbly musical soprano—is something new.

"Lovely to see you again, Jazzy-girl," Eli says with a warm chuckle. "When did you get in?"

"My question exactly." Kyan sounds much less amused.

"A few hours ago, and don't you dare look at me that way, Kyan. If you'd read any one of my emails, you wouldn't be standing here with your mouth hanging open like a fish now, would you?"

"I might be somewhat behind," Kyan grumbles.

"Might be?" Jazzy-girl's voice rises, the rich notes filled with incredulity. "I sent you *five*. And I sent you the first one a month ago."

I come up to the threshold to see five people crammed into one miniscule space, the hulky size of the men making the room feel even more cramped than it did to begin with. Now also with them is a young woman with rich tanned skin, flowing black hair, and beautiful dark eyes. Despite Kyan's scars, the resemblance is obvious.

"Sky." Cullen steps forward, taking the bed away from the tech and locking the wheels into place. "The imaging came back clean. How are you feeling?"

"Like I want to know how you know my imaging results before I do."

Eli snorts. "She seems fine to me."

Jazzy-girl clears her throat, and Kyan throws her an irritated look.

"Jazmine, meet Sky, the Rescue's new administrator and dispatcher," Kyan says solemnly. "Sky, meet Jazmine, an impossibly irritating human being who was just leaving."

"I go by Jaz." She grins at me. "And if Kyan calls me Jazmine one more time, I'm going to get this whole town to start calling him... What was the name of Jafar's parrot in Aladdin?"

"Iago?" I say.

"Right. Iago." Jaz's smile broadens, Kyan's resulting eye roll seeming like something from an alternate universe. Customarily, the man is the most closed-off of the Trident gods, and considering Cullen is part of that group, that's saying something. Jaz's attention returns to me, open and infectiously friendly. "I hear you were Wonder Woman today, busting up drug rings and saving children."

"She busted something, all right," Cullen mutters under his breath.

My mood sobers, my attention turning to the guys. "Does anyone know what happened to Zach? And everyone else?"

"The boy's been admitted," Liam answers. "Child protective services will take him once he's discharged. Dad—that's the drunk asshole who attacked you—was charged with aggravated assault, felon in possession of a gun, and drug possession. The two others, his business partners, are in custody as well."

I shudder. "What about Zach's mom?"

"Methhead," Cullen answers for Liam, butting his way into the conversation. "She was high the entire time—and apparently is still confused as to what's happened. The social worker is trying to get her to rehab, but... It wasn't a good house to go near, Sky."

"Well, somebody had to," I shoot back, regretting it a moment later as pain sings up my arm in protest.

Cullen opens his mouth, but Jaz plants her hands on her hips and glares up at him. "How about you broody bunch go get us some Frappuccinos," she says, herding the men out of the curtained-off room. Liam and Cullen scowl, though Eli snorts in amazement. And Kyan… Kyan digs his car keys out of his pocket and walks away.

Jaz swallows, her eyes sad as she watches her brother's back. I want to ask what's going on, but it's beyond none of my business. Plus, I owe Jaz for getting me some breathing room.

"So what brings you to Denton Valley?" I ask.

"School." Forcing her gaze back toward me, Jaz conjures a smile and sits cross-legged on one of the chairs. She has a small, strong physique, which makes even the sweats hanging off her hips look like a designer outfit. "I'm getting my masters in exercise science at University of Colorado at Denton Valley. I'm not gonna lie, the rock climbing here might have snagged me as much as the program."

"Oh my God, you climb too?" My spirits lift despite the night. I've always loved the outdoors, from camping and hiking to climbing, but it's rare to find another woman who likes the rocks as much as I do. I haven't rock climbed once since the Jaden fiasco. "Actually, I don't know why I'm surprised. You look like you should be modeling climbing gear."

"Oh, I do." Jaz shrugs. "Well, did. Kyan and I did a whole bunch of that type of work as kids. Now I have to stick to the brands who sponsor me and stuff."

From someone else, the words might have sounded like bragging, but the way Jaz's jaw tightens when she mentions Kyan tells me her thoughts are solidly on her brother. Her scar-covered brother who used to be a model. Shit. Kyan…

As if having read my thoughts in my face, Jaz shakes her head. "Our whole family in California is in the acting and modeling circuit. I've a suspicion that's part of the reason Kyan hasn't stepped foot in LA since coming back. Which is just stupid because all we care about is that he came home alive, you know?" Jaz winces. "I'm sorry, I just kicked the guys out for spoiling the mood, and now I'm doing the same thing. So, it's decided—the moment you're cleared to go climbing, we're going to the cliffs."

I smile. "Deal."

Jaz holds up a finger. "Though I highly recommend you don't

share those particular plan details with Cullen until we're well on our way."

My chest tightens at the sound of Cullen's name, the phantom feeling of his mouth so close to mine washing over my memories. I clear my throat quickly. "Why do you think Cullen would care if we go climbing?"

Jaz shrugs one pretty shoulder. "Oh, just a hunch."

17

CULLEN

"*I*'m going to kill Frank Peterson," Cullen told Eli and Liam as the three dutifully waited for the demanded Frappuccino.

"An appealing solution," Eli agreed. "Did I tell you the wanker has been down at Harvest Bank a bloody lot lately? Visiting with Norwich?"

Cullen's eyes narrowed. Darrell Norwich was that bank's mortgage loan officer. Typically, mortgages were sold to big-name national companies or banking institutions, but according to Addie Peterson, Darrell had kept her and Bar's mortgage loan local so far. This seemed a nonissue to Cullen before now, but if Frank was rubbing shoulders with the man in charge of Addie's loan, there could be something to it.

"Tell me again how a guy like Bar managed to grow up in a viper pit of Frank and company without losing his shit?" Cullen shook his head. Addie was Bar's widow, for Christ's sake. And all Frank cared about was getting his hands on every penny his dead brother left. "All right. We all know Frank wants the money from the house, and that he can't get it unless Addie's loan goes into foreclosure. And I've got the payments on lockdown now, so he has very limited room to maneuver."

Seeing the Frappuccinos come out, Cullen grabbed the pair and headed back to Sky's room. The more he thought about Sky working for that piece of shit, the more he hated it.

"Speaking of getting back," said Eli, directing his words to Liam. "Given that Kyan took off, do you want to give Jaz a ride, or should I?"

A muscle ticked at the side of Liam's jaw. "If she's getting into my car, she's getting out at the damn airport."

"Very mature, mate," said Eli.

"If Kyan wants to be alone, she should leave him the fuck alone," said Liam.

Eli cocked his head, everything about his posture seeming calculated to most get under Liam's skin. "Aren't you always going on about giving people what they need, not what they want?"

Liam pulled his shoulders back, his chest out as if the man was spreading wings. In his regular uniform of black jeans and tight V-neck tee, he tended to draw the eyes of every single female around.

Not for the first time, Cullen found himself utterly unsurprised at the number of women who dreamt of a chance to throw themselves at Liam's feet. Literally. "Subs, asshole. Not friends."

Without waiting for Eli's reply, Liam turned on his heels and headed for the door. Which was probably a good thing since a brawl in the middle of the hospital atrium, while stress relieving, was undoubtedly not going to be good for anyone's public relations department.

In typical Eli fashion, the man merely turned his attention to Cullen. "You lost your Band-Aids."

Cullen shook his head. "Christ, you're a prick."

"That's already been established." Eli stuck his hands into his back pockets, his long strides easily keeping up with Cullen's double-time pace. "But just to point out the perfect little storm you've got going. Swooping in to rescue a damsel in distress, one who was kind enough to patch you up, just—"

Stepping in front of Eli, Cullen smacked the Frappuccino hard enough into the man's chest that the icy crystals spilled over his shirt. Cullen might've enjoyed it more if he could've splashed it on one of his pristine suits instead, but Eli had removed his jacket before the tussle on Lincoln. "What's with you today? First Liam, now me? Why are you baiting everyone?"

Eli glanced down at the Frappuccino, then extracted the cup from Cullen's fist and sipped the whipped cream. "Liam, that was just for fun. You... I've not seen you like a girl before, Cullen—Betsy Delmata of ninth grade notwithstanding. I just want to make sure you aren't so blinded by your own idiocy that you don't see what's right in front of you."

"What are we, in high school?" said Cullen. "Reynolds works at the Rescue. That makes her my responsibility. And she's too close to Frank Peterson, which puts her in harm's way. The rest... It doesn't matter."

And that *was* the truth. It didn't matter what Cullen did or did not feel for Skylar Reynolds, because he couldn't have her.

"I beg to differ, Commander." The humor seeped from Eli's voice. "I'm not claiming to be any kind of expert, but I remember how good Addie was for Bar."

Bar was the only one of the five of them who'd had a girlfriend, then a wife. And though they'd given him nothing but shit over it at first, Bar's contentment far outweighed any of their teasing. Of all of them, Bar had been the most at peace with everything that had gone down overseas, and he'd come right out and said the reason for it was Adrianna.

"I remember watching Bar's widow sob at his funeral," Cullen said. Besides, from everything he'd seen about Sky, Cullen knew he was a bad match for her. Sky pretty much disdained everything he held in high regard, and God knew Cullen had his own baggage. It would be a bad mix.

Not that Cullen planned to ever mix permanently with any woman. He couldn't inflict himself on someone. It'd be a nightmare. Not to mention unfair. He wasn't fit for a relationship and never would be.

"I scare her." The words escaped Cullen before he could stop

109

them. "When I ran into her at the Rescue yesterday, I hadn't expected anyone to be there. She surprised me, and I…yelled at her. She gaped at me like I was a knife-wielding serial killer."

Eli cocked a brow. "But she patched you up anyway," he said, letting the words settle for a heartbeat before stepping away to release the tension and starting them back to Sky's room at too peppy a pace.

A tech carrying a suture kit appeared at Sky's door just as Cullen and Eli did. As Eli—who'd efficiently had someone bring his car over to the hospital for him—called Jaz out to take her home, Cullen placed the Frappuccino on a shelf and walked up to stand beside Sky while the tech laid out his tools.

"We can go home after this," Cullen said, laying a hand on Sky's shoulder to feel tension vibrating through her whole body—and flowing directly into his. Stitches. It was just a few stitches, not a blown-off limb. And yet…it bothered him in a way he wished it didn't.

"Right." She tried and failed to sound peppy.

"Let's get you numbed up," the tech told Sky. In dark blue scrubs, the man seemed competent enough—but he wasn't one of the staff Cullen knew personally. Glancing at the name tag, Cullen saw *Denver ER* stamped into the plastic. A recent transfer, then. That explained the new face. "Small stick."

Sky gasped as Denver slid the needle in, her eyes glistening. It hurt. Of course it hurt. But it didn't *have to* hurt so much.

"Slow up pushing the lido," Cullen said. "And I mean by a fucking factor of ten."

Denver glanced up at him wearily, but did slow the injection, giving the tissue more time to absorb the liquid.

"Did you buffer it?" Cullen demanded.

Denver sighed. "Buffer it?"

"Sodium bicarbonate. It—"

"Buffers the pH to mitigate the sting. We do that for pediatrics," Denver finished for him. "Sir, can you step back, please? You're blocking the light."

"You should do it for everyone," Cullen snapped, reaching overhead to adjust the light for the tech's convenience.

Sky hissed as Denver finished up the injection, Cullen leaning down so low toward her that his chest nearly rested on her strawberry hair. With his hands braced on either side of Sky, he watched Denver lay the first suture, go to start the second, then push himself away from Sky altogether.

"Sir? Sir, would you like to take over?" Denver asked, meeting Cullen's gaze without flinching. "Because right now, your choices are to suture Ms. Reynolds yourself or get out of the room so I can work."

"Sorry," Sky told the tech before Cullen could respond to *that*. "Cullen has issues with letting people do their own jobs. It's a personal quirk of his."

Stiffening, Cullen took a full pace backward and leaned against the wall behind him. A more than just compromise, as far as he was concerned. Denver, apparently knowing better than to snatch defeat from the jaws of victory, grunted and went back to his work. Admittedly, the man was competent, but the gash would likely leave a scar anyway.

The problem was that this whole situation had been unnecessary. Feeling his hands curl into fists, Cullen strode out of the treatment room before his suddenly flashing memories of seeing Sky being thrown into a wall made him do something foolish. Breathing deeply through his nose, Cullen tried and failed to slow his heart's pounding against his ribs. How could someone as intelligent as Sky think sprinting headfirst into danger to get Frank tabloid fodder was a good idea? Goddamn it, if—

"It's all right." Waddling over, Michelle patted Cullen's shoulder. "My husband passed out cold when I was having my first one. And I don't mean the birth—he only made it long enough to see them start the IV. We never like to see those—"

"One more word out of your mouth, Michelle"—Cullen's voice dropped menacingly low—"and I will make sure HR stretches your maternity leave to a full six months starting yesterday."

18

SKY

ullen opens the door to his truck for me, his hand warm on my back as he helps me inside. For all the prickliness he works so hard to show the world, the moments when he lets his guard down show a different side of him altogether. One that Cullen seems determined to hide most of the time. The man has been oddly quiet since walking out of the room in the middle of my getting stitched up, but if the wave of exhaustion now hitting me is anything like what's rolling over him, this isn't the time to ask what happened. Actually, I don't even have the energy to ask. Or to buckle my seat belt.

Reaching across me, Cullen slides the belt into place, his clean, spicy scent washing over me.

"I could have done that," I mutter.

"And I'm a Disney princess," says Cullen. Walking over to the driver's side, the man pulls a bottle of water from his pocket, opens the cap, and hands it over, along with a dose of 800 mg ibuprofen.

I swallow the pain meds, leaning back against the comfortable leather seat of the car as Cullen sets us quietly into motion. My eyes drift closed to the silence, the white noise of the motor, and the feeling of Cullen beside me lulling me into an exhausted sleep.

I open my eyes to the sound of a garage door opening, Cullen's truck climbing nimbly into a massive three-car garage that is most certainly not on Lincoln Drive. I sit up quickly, rubbing my face. "Where are we?"

"My garage." After getting out of the driver's seat, Cullen walks around to open my door.

"You said you were taking me home."

"I never said whose home," says Cullen. Unbuckling my seat belt for me, the man starts to slide his hands beneath me. Another second, and I know I'll be in his arms—the thought of which is too tempting for comfort.

"I want to walk on my own," I mutter.

He stops, his face tight as he watches me climb out of the passenger's seat, as if it hurts him to watch me struggle. Strange. I would have thought he wouldn't miss the chance to needle me with another variation of *I told you so*, but for some reason, just this moment seems to be a line not to cross for him.

I swallow. "You could have taken me to my place."

"I didn't want to," says Cullen.

My gaze snaps to him.

The man crosses his arms over a broad, muscular chest. "*Your place* is a shit hole not fit for the mice who live there," he says, back to being his smug self. "It's also about three blocks away from where you just got four people arrested. So how about you don't show your face on Lincoln Drive for a bit?"

He has a point, but then again—he also has a bank account. I'm not living on Lincoln Drive because I choose to. I'm renting what I can afford. But that's a conversation for a different day. At this point, I'll happily curl up on a doormat if I can just go to sleep in peace.

I follow him through a minimalist-looking foyer painted in soothing bluish tones and decorated only by a series of stainless-steel coat hooks and past a massive open living space with a fireplace I could probably curl up and sleep in. Walking down a well-lit hallway with a single piece of abstract black-and-white artwork, we finally stop at what Cullen tells me is the guest bedroom.

I eye the tall queen-size bed while Cullen pulls out a set of towels and a large gray shirt he says I can sleep in. Given how massive the man is, the shirt is bound to come to midthigh.

"That door right there is the bathroom," he says, resting a muscled forearm against the doorframe. "My room is at the end of the hall if you need anything. I'll leave the hallway light on."

Whatever reservations I had about staying the night disappear as I settle onto the highest-end mattress I've ever felt and dissolve into sleep without bothering to change or take off my shoes.

The next time I open my eyes, my shoes are no longer on my feet, and the cool cotton sheets beneath me brush against my bare thighs. Sitting up with a start, I pat myself down to discover I'm wearing that gray shirt Cullen had brought, my clothing nowhere in the room. My heart pauses for a beat, then jumps into a gallop as I feel around in the dark for my phone.

It's there. On the bedstead. Plugged into a charger, 3:23 a.m. glowing in big white numerals on the screen. All right. So Cullen had actually undressed me sometime after I fell asleep. Which was overstepping things, but somehow nice anyway. Pulling off the thick down comforter, I swing my legs over the edge of the bed and wince at my aching body. Still, I'm lucky to be alive. A tremor runs through me, starting at the base of my stomach and running up my shoulders.

Get it together, Sky. Slipping onto the floor, I walk over to the bathroom—which is larger than my bedroom on Lincoln Drive—and wash my face, the sound of the running water as soothing as its coolness. When I turn off the faucet, however, a grunting sound, like a bitten-back scream, catches my ear from down the hall.

I walk gingerly to my door, the hardwood floor cool beneath my bare feet. Peering into the hallway, I see a long stretch of parquet floor and a tall white table displaying a pewter chess set, ending with a door at the very end. Cullen's bedroom. The bitten-back scream comes again, escaping from beneath the door. My breathing quickens as I head toward the sound, my hand hesitating on the round door handle.

"Cullen?" I call, pushing the door open slowly to behold a battle scene. In the light streaming from the hallway, I see sheets and tossed pillows crumpled on the floor. The blanket, which I imagine started its evening atop Cullen's grand king bed, is now a balled-up mass in the corner. And in the middle of a luxurious mattress, Cullen's whole body is tense as if curling protectively over something while invisible blows rain onto his shoulders.

With him dressed only in boxer shorts, I can see every muscle coiled beneath taut skin as he thrashes, grunting and fighting whatever nightmare is holding him in its grip. My chest tightens, my mouth dry as I approach the bed. I don't know what Cullen might do if I wake him now, but I don't know that I can bear to walk away either.

As the man recoils from an invisible blow, my stomach clenches.

"Cullen." I reach for his shoulder, ready to jump away if he wakes swinging. "Cullen. *Cullen,* wake up! Please."

His eyes snap open just as his hand closes into a fist, the man pulling the blow as he jerks awake. Sweat mats his short-cropped hair and slides along the groove of his back. He twists to me, his chest heaving from the unseen battle, his eyes sweeping the room before finally focusing on my face. "Skylar." His voice is gruff. "What's wrong?"

"I…" *I heard you in pain, and I couldn't bear it.* "I had a nightmare."

His eyes narrow on me. "Did you?"

Wishing I was a better liar, I bite my lip and shrug. "A lot happened."

He rubs his face, his head shaking. "Do me a favor, Reynolds. Never play poker."

I give him a half-hearted chuckle, but the truth of it is that I was only half lying before. With the worst of the fatigue behind me, I fear what awaits me the next time I close my eyes as much as I fear hearing Cullen scream again. "I don't want to be alone tonight," I say softly.

For a moment, he says nothing, studying my face as my pulse continues to pound. Then slowly, he extends a honed arm toward me. "Come here."

An invitation. An order. Whatever it is, my treacherous body responds to it with a wave of relief. Climbing up onto the bed, the mattress yielding gently beneath my knees, I let Cullen draw me up against him. As he settles onto his back, tucking my head securely under his chin, his clean male musk washes over me like a security blanket.

Closing my eyes, I brace myself for flashes of Undershirt throwing me into the house siding, but instead only feel the rise and fall of Cullen's chest. With my face resting against him, the slowing steady beat of his heart chases my thoughts away. Putting my arm on his chest, I find myself slipping into unconsciousness, Cullen's body slowly relaxing beside mine.

19

SKY

I wake to a mix of blissful softness urging me to slip back into unconsciousness pitted against the ache in every damn muscle in my body. The aches win, bringing me back to the surface against my will. I blink my eyes open, expecting to see my dingy, dark apartment, and instead catch sight of the opposite.

Sunlight pours in through windows so clean, it's like there's no pane, the brilliant snow-capped summit of Pikes Peak visible in the distance. God, what a view.

Cullen's view.

Cullen's house. Cullen's *bed*.

I remember his hot, tense body easing into sleep around me, the feeling of being cocooned in safety settling around me as securely as the down comforter. Then the rest of the night rushes back as well. Falling asleep in Cullen's bedroom. Waking. Finding him in the midst of one hell of a nightmare, his muscles coiled and flinching from invisible attack.

The investigative journalist inside me itches to know what can possibly haunt a man as strong as Cullen, but my heart just aches over the bitter helplessness of watching him thrash in pain. *What do you see when you close your eyes, Cullen? What—or who—are you trying to shield in that nightmare of yours?*

If he were anyone else—if he were a normal sane person—I'd just ask. But with Cullen, my gut tells me that what I saw last night wasn't ever meant to be witnessed. If I go about figuring this out the wrong way, if I press too hard or open too wide, Cullen will ensure he is never *ever* vulnerable around me again. And for some reason, the thought of that happening bothers me.

A lot.

I know without having to look that Cullen is no longer there. The bed feels too large and empty. I wonder how much of his leaving while I still slept was to keep away the awkward moment of us staring at each other across the sheets. It's for the best, of course, and yet a jolt of regret still shoots through my chest.

Blocking my eyes from the streaming sun, I swing my feet over the side of the bed and discover a clear garment bag hanging on the wrought iron railing of the headboard. A bright orange sticky label on the parcel declares Express Delivery: Overnight. Frowning at the clear film, I see a pair of feminine jeans, a long-sleeve top, and several other items that are most certainly not meant for Cullen's body. And just in case that isn't clear enough, a second—roughly scribbled—note attached to the bed reads: *Reynolds*.

My heart quickens slightly as I pull out the clothes to discover that they're not just jeans, but Gucci's, and in my exact size. Shit. I don't know whether to be impressed or appalled. But given that I came home in borrowed hospital scrubs last night, I'm not above pulling on the clothes—carefully hiding the tags instead of taking them off altogether. If Cullen can give me a ride back to my place, I can change, and he can return these.

Walking past a walk-in closet that rivals my basement apartment in size, I engage all my self-control not to give myself a tour of Cullen's wardrobe, and instead veer off into the master bathroom. One step into the giant space and I'm barraged by a sea of gray-and-navy-blue tile. In the corner, a shower with a waterfall nozzle beckons me inside, especially since the cabinet above the toilet is full of white towels. Stopping first by the long ceramic vanity, I cringe at my reflection. I look how I feel—and I hurt.

Opening Cullen's medicine cabinet, I pray the man has a stash of ibuprofen within reach. Instead, I'm presented with a bottle of aftershave, razor refills, deodorant, and, uh...an extra-large box of condoms. The one and only medication in sight is a bottle of prazosin. I pause, my gaze hovering on the typed prescription lettering. Yeah. I know prazosin. My father had the same damn prescription, and it did nothing to stop him from smacking me and my mom around.

Slowly closing the cabinet, I rub my face, the pieces of Cullen's puzzle coming together. The nightmares. The short fuse. The way he'd reacted to the drunk at Hannigan's. PTSD. The realization squeezes my chest, everything inside me simultaneously longing to wrap my arms comfortingly around him and run the hell away.

My mother always said my father's mental health issues weren't his fault. But they weren't the fault of the seven-year-old me either, yet I was the one in the ER.

I shake myself free of my memories, really not wanting to think about all that right now. No, what I need right now is to shower and seek out the owner of my temporary accommodation.

Trekking through the hallway ten minutes later, I pass the living area with its awesome fireplace, but don't see Cullen anywhere. I find a nice-size kitchen with a copper pot rack and gleaming stainless-steel appliances, but the room looks so immaculate that I wonder if it goes mostly unused. Finally, I follow a series of thumps and grunts to an exercise room overlooking a sunny terrace and find my host in the middle of walloping the crap out of a punching bag.

In a pair of loose gray shorts and a sweat-soaked sleeveless tee, Cullen dances around the punching bag with a predator's deadly grace. Each time he moves, his coiled muscles shift smoothly beneath slick skin, the speed and force coming from each blow sending vibrations through the room. *Thump. Thump. Thump.*

For the first time, I notice Cullen's ink—an emblem just below his left shoulder of an eagle perched on a shield with two anchors coming out of the bottom, plus a spiky tribal pattern that wraps his

ALEX LIDELL

left bicep. With Cullen's smooth motions and glistening sweat, the inked predator seems alive. Shit. Everything about him seems alive and potent and too damn beautiful for fairness. Watching a light dew of perspiration glisten over his forehead, I feel my panties dampen.

And knowing I slept with him in his bed last night?

I press my thighs together, taking several deep breaths to calm my body. *Not good, Sky. Very not good.*

Cullen jumps and turns in the air, landing a back kick that knocks the punching bag clear off the rafters above. "Fuck," he mutters, walking over and heaving the punching bag up onto its hook as if the massive thing was just a potato sack. "How are you feeling, Reynolds?" he asks without turning around.

I swallow. Of course he knew I was there watching. "Fine." Except for the fact the temperature feels like a hundred degrees just now. At least my voice didn't come out all sultry like some Mae West knockoff. "You?"

He turns toward me, breathing hard from exertion as he wipes his face with his shirt. "Good."

Well, nice to know we're both being open and honest about everything.

He glances at his watch. "Your timing is impeccable. I just ordered some breakfast. It'll be here in fifteen. Let me go hop in the shower."

I nod, stepping out of his way as he sets course for the door, his scent filling my nose as he passes. God, how is it even possible that the man smells good enough to eat even after working out?

I close my eyes, reminding myself to stop going there. What is up with me today, anyway?

"Thank you for the damsel-in-distress recue last night," I call after him. I know I'm tempting another reprimand, but I owe him the acknowledgment. I owe him a lot more than that. "To you and to the guys. I know you didn't want me going forward, and it put all of you in danger to come after me. That certainly wasn't my intention."

He stops and turns, his face serious. "No thanks necessary.

122

You're one of ours, Reynolds. We have each other's back no matter how the problem starts."

I tip my head up. "Does that mean you *aren't* upset anymore over my going to that house?"

Cullen leans his arms against the doorframe, his brow furrowed. I hadn't expected him to give quite that much thought to the answer, but I'm discovering there are many things about Cullen that I didn't expect. "Oh, I'm furious as hell. At Frank Peterson and you both," he says matter-of-factly. "I just haven't worked out what to do about it. But to my previous point, I don't need to like what you're doing to have your back."

Stepping forward, I lay my hand on his chest, his heart beating hard against my palm. "Thank you," I whisper, rising up on my toes to kiss his cheek.

Cullen blows out a breath. "You're going to be the death of me."

"On the bright side, I'm pretty sure we saved Zack's life. He'd have gotten seriously hurt sooner or later in that place. So all in all, it was a win."

He snorts, unimpressed. "Bad decisions can lead to good outcomes," he says, his gaze going distant for a moment. "And good decisions can end badly too."

I'm fairly certain he doesn't realize that he's said the latter aloud, but my breath stills anyway, my journalistic instinct scenting an opening. "Is that what your nightmares are about?" I ask. "A good decision gone badly?"

Cullen tenses, his gaze narrowing. "What?"

I step back carefully, just in case.

"Damn it, I'm not going to attack you," he says, then sighs and shakes his head—probably realizing what had happened. What I was asking and why. "Yes," he says curtly, as if reading from a military report. "I stood up a field hospital in Afghanistan for civilians unable to get medical care. The plan backfired." He shakes himself, a shift in his eyes and shoulders warning me against pressing further. Now, or ever. "I need a shower. Please try to stay out of drug dens, gang wars, or anything that's likely to get you shot while I'm looking for my shampoo."

With Cullen gone, I spend a few minutes trying to absorb everything he just told me before forcing myself to shelf the thoughts until I have the time to examine them in full detail. Shrugging myself back into the here and now, I set a course for the kitchen in search of coffee.

For an investigative journalist, I'm a hell of a terrible pantry searcher, though, given that I'm still at it when the doorbell rings a few minutes later. I start toward the door, hesitating at the thought of letting anyone into Cullen's house, even though it's most likely the delivery guy coming early. Still, after yesterday…

The doorbell rings again, followed by a pounding on the door that makes me flinch. Before I need to shore up courage, however, Cullen emerges from his bedroom, a towel around his otherwise bare, wet body. My adrenaline skyrockets as I take in his flawlessly shaped pectorals, abdominals, and obliques. The man could easily be on the cover of *Men's Fitness*. I'm studying his six…no, *eight-pack* of abs when he jogs down to the living room and barks at the delivery guy to stop the racket even as he opens the door.

Except it's not the delivery guy. It's Frank Peterson.

20

SKY

"Why, Hunt, if I knew that's how you felt, I'd have brought lube." Snorting at his own jest, Frank steps inside, his beady eyes taking in the place. Before I can step behind something, the man's gaze lands on me, his eyes widening as color rises along his neck. "Never mind. I see your cock is taken care of."

Heat rushes to my face, though at this point, anything I do to get out of sight would only make things worse.

Shifting his weight to put himself more firmly between me and Frank, Cullen crosses his arms over his wide chest. "What do you want, Peterson?"

Frank reaches into his jacket and pulls out a sheet of paper. "This is the replacement bill for my personal property, which you damaged in your temper."

Cullen looks impassively at the paper. "Two thousand dollars? There isn't an iPhone on the market with that price tag."

I keep my face schooled, though if Cullen destroyed Frank's phone, I finally understand the lack of messages from my editor. Wait, what the hell am I even thinking? Cullen broke Frank's phone? What are we, in middle school?

"It wasn't from the mass market. It was customized," says Frank, reaching for the bill in Cullen's hand. My editor runs a hand down his suit lapels—a forest-green number with too-wide pinstripes that might work on the golf course, but not so much in real life, no matter how expensive it is. The man shrugs. "If you prefer to contest the damage, I'll be happy to file a police report instead. This was simply a courtesy to settle things outside legal channels, one I extended only because I know your *condition* makes impulse control a challenge. Plus, my brother was fond of you."

Cullen's jaw tenses at Frank's mention of his brother, his very unclothed body radiating menace. "File whatever you like; so long as you get out of my sight. You know my attorney's contact information, I believe."

Frank sighs. "This is stupid, Cullen. You're going to pay more in attorney's fees than you would for the phone. Look, how about we split—" Frank cuts off as Cullen advances on him, encroaching on his personal space until the smaller man retreats back out the open door, which Cullen shuts in his face.

Right. I let out a breath I forgot I held as Cullen's shoulders rise and fall with a heavy sigh, the man plainly trying to get hold of himself. Being the smart person that I am, I disappear back into the kitchen before he looks up.

By the time Cullen joins me in the kitchen a few minutes later, his face is schooled back to his usual granite. Though my lower regions miss the sight of his glistening half-naked form, the mossy-green sweater that matches his eyes and a pair of dark jeans he's put on is a rather pleasing consolation prize.

I pull my gaze away, needing to get a grip. Of course, getting a grip on him would be nice as well.

"Thank you for..." I wave my hand over my body to show the jeans and shirt I'm wearing thanks to Cullen's good graces. "Next time I get into a fight with a drunk drug dealer, I'll be sure to have a change of clothes ready."

"Yeah." A corner of his mouth actually twitches at the joke, which for Cullen must be like laughing aloud. "Oh, before I forget." Ducking out into the hallway, Cullen returns with another garment bag, the now-familiar orange overnight delivery tag stuck to its side. "It came late."

Tentatively taking the bag from Cullen's hand, I reach inside it to pull out a gorgeous pale yellow dress, its wraparound design promising to accentuate my body without being too snug or uncomfortable. A matching set of pumps and—holy crap, an Arc'teryx jacket that is a climber's dream and perfect for the Colorado autumn weather—completes the set. The price tags have been taken off, but I can tell the stuff in here is worth at least a month's salary.

Unsure exactly how to handle this, I revert to our familiar-to-us dynamic and go on the offensive. "Cullen, you can't keep getting me clothes. I…" I can't afford these. "This isn't my style."

"It should be." Cullen stretches his back and heads toward the ringing doorbell again. "Your other choices are anything that I have in my closet or the scrubs the hospital let you come home in," the man calls over his shoulder.

Actually, my other option is to go home and pick up my own things, but that would require a ride from Cullen, which puts me back into the same boat of owing him something. I hesitate another moment, then decide to put the dilemma on hold for now, given the smell of fresh-baked crepes that's sneaking from the delivery the man just accepted.

For the next quarter hour, we enjoy raspberry crepes with some of Cullen's espresso, which was stationed in the one place I hadn't looked. I only realize how starved I am two portions into my breakfast—but by that point, it's too late to worry about appearances. Fortunately, Cullen tucks in with the same companionable vigor.

"I have some admin to catch up on," Cullen says once we've devoured our breakfast like a couple of vultures. He frowns at the word *admin*, and, based on what I've seen him leave for me to do at the Rescue, the attitude is unsurprising. "But I'll be back around four to pick you up for Eli's damn barbecue."

I blink at the presumptuousness. "Why do you think I'm going to this barbecue?"

"Because it's a Rescue thing and you're an employee," Cullen informs me. "And because if I have to go, you have to go."

I roll my eyes. "Can you drop me off at either my place or the Rescue on the way? I've got work to do and no laptop to do it on." At least I hope I still have work to do, if Frank's little visit this morning isn't leading to me getting fired.

"Use mine." Beckoning me to follow him into his office, Cullen pulls out a laptop and taps a few keystrokes where I can't see his screen.

"If you're deleting porn from your history, don't bother," I tell him.

"Don't worry, the porn is bookmarked for your convenience," he replies without pause, then turns the computer toward me. "Password is pipe hitter five zero five, all one word."

"Speaking of porn..." I mutter.

Cullen snorts. "Pipe hitter is a special forces term SEALS use a lot to refer to themselves, not whatever it is you were thinking."

"Right." Despite being the one to have started this line of conversation, I feel my skin heat. Nonetheless, I pull myself back to the one elephant in the room we'd not touched on. "What's with you and my boss? I didn't know you two even knew each other."

Cullen's eyes darken dangerously. "I grew up in Denton Valley," he says curtly. "We know each other." There's a finality to his words that makes it clear we're done with this line of questioning. But just in case I need further clarification, Cullen turns on his heel and walks out the door.

Very mature.

I spend the rest of the day on the computer, typing up my hard-won story along with my initial research into police response times, interspersed with bursts of checking email. There's one from my mom, asking me to call her, several from climbing stores promising to sell me the best gear at rock-bottom prices I can't afford, and a note from Frank informing me that he expects my extracurricular activities with my boss at the Rescue will not interfere with my deadlines. I reply to none of them, though Mother, being Mother, keeps sending me notes as if I might have just overlooked the first five.

Finally, when my achy body no longer agrees to typing, I set up my phone on FaceTime while I scour Cullen's kitchen for crepe leftovers.

"Lary, darling." My mother's face appears on the screen, her makeup as perfect as her face-lifted visage. In the background, the ocean waves lap each other in little curls—she must be on that cruise with Greg. "I've been trying to get through to you since last night. What's so important you can't call your mother back?"

I rub my temple. When all else fails, try the truth. "I was in the ER. A man came after me, an—"

"No!" My mother's hand covers her mouth, her eyes wide and the Tiffany diamond tennis bracelet on her wrist catching the light.

Realizing what I inadvertently said, I shake my head. "No, no. He just shoved me around a bit. A dislocated shoulder and some bruises. Nothing broken."

Relief floods my mother's face, and for a moment, I want to reach through the screen and hug her. Then she speaks. "Oh, thank the Lord—nothing that a little makeup can't fix, then."

I swallow a sigh. Right. "Makeup doesn't actually fix anything, Mother," I say on reflex, though I'm not sure why I bother. In her world, it likely does.

My mother leans closer to the screen. "Where is it that you're talking to me from, Lary? That looks like a man's house. Is it a man's house?" Her eyes narrow, and I swear to God I see a flash of jealousy sparkle beneath the heavy makeup. "If you turned down an invitation to a family event to trollop around with a—"

"Ma. Stop." I rub my temples and count to five before my anger settles. "One, Greg is not family. Two, I'm staying with a friend because I was assaulted last night."

"Mmm. And did this *friend* get you the Gabbana tee you're currently wearing?"

I look down at my chest, realizing that, holy crap, she's right. I knew the jeans were designer, but I hadn't looked closely at the top before pulling it on this morning.

"Now listen to me, Lary honey. This friend might seem nice at the moment, but I'm telling you right now the gravy train will not last. We need someone stable. Someone with values. And I must tell you, Greg's feelings were quite wounded at you not coming with us. I do think it's important to make it up to him. I'll have a plane ticket sent to you to join us at the next port of call and—"

I hang up the phone and send Mother's three subsequent attempts to reach me to voicemail. Cullen went overboard with the clothes, but he probably just tapped whatever ad showed up on his phone. At least I hope that's what happened.

Putting both the conversation with my mother and my phone out of my thoughts, I dive back into my work.

IN THE LATE AFTERNOON, I'm back in Cullen's truck, watching the still-unfamiliar roads go by as we head to Eli's. Making a sharp turn, Cullen enters what I think is the best-paved Colorado street ever, but turns out to be a long-ass driveway. It's lined on both sides with such thick Douglas firs that it feels as though we're driving through a tunnel. As we pass the obscuring evergreens, I finally catch sight of a large bed-and-breakfast-like building.

Cullen pulls up in front of a wide iron gate, the vast fence looking like it surrounds the property.

"Where are you taking us?"

Cullen shoots me a quizzical glance. "To Eli's barbecue."

"I thought you said it'd be at his house."

"It is at his house. This is it."

I whistle softly. I saw a number of high-end homes in New York, but everything there is stacked up on each other. With the space available in Colorado, Eli's mansion has the room to sprawl and unfurl its wings. The bottom two stories are built with what appears to be the native red sandstone, the reddish-orange hue going beautifully with the upper story's cedarwood finish. Two sections on either side of the house rise into octagonal structures, almost like castle towers, with the middle and largest part elevating into a peaked roof with floor-to-ceiling windows. My favorite part, though, is how the house backs up into one of the lower hills before they become steep Colorado mountains.

As Cullen punches something on his phone to open Eli's gate, I shake my head. I knew the Trident gods were all well-off, but I never connected the tailored suits to quite *this* level of affluence. Not in someone as good-natured and laid-back as Eli. Granted, beside Cullen, a cactus would come off as good-natured and laid-back. Still, I'd never have guessed that after checking and wiping down the Rescue's equipment at evening's end, this is where Eli heads home every night.

"So is Eli related to the Rockefellers or something?" I mutter as Cullen leaves the car on the semicircular driveway and cuts the engine.

"Something like the British version of that. But don't bring it up," says Cullen. "They're not close."

I can relate.

"Cullen. Sky. Glad you could make it." Walking around the corner of the mansion, Eli is dressed down in a pair of jeans and a long-sleeved button-down, a beer in his hand. "We're all out back. How are you feeling? Do you like your new place?"

For a moment, I just stare at Eli in utter confusion, wondering if he somehow found out that I spent my night in Cullen's bed. Whether this offhand jab is a shot in the dark or...

"You did tell her." Eli's gaze narrows, cutting to Cullen. "I mean—"

Cullen rubs the back of his neck, a tell of his that I'm beginning to catch on to. "Of course I told her." He turns his head toward me. "The guys moved you into a new apartment, Reynolds." He turns back to Eli. "See. Told her."

"But... I don't... How could... When?" I stutter out, a million thoughts bubbling through me, not one of them making any sense.

"This morning." Cullen starts toward the back of the house as if the conversation was over instead of just starting.

Quickening my step, I get in front of him and turn, cutting off his path. If possible, he's somehow even more beautiful than usual now, the light playing off his fitted sweater to sculpt the muscles beneath. Looking at that strong jaw and those mossy-green eyes, I can't help feeling my thighs tingle even as I really, *really* want to put my fist through that perfect mouth.

"Eli, could you please go host somewhere else for a moment?" I ask, my eyes gripping Cullen's like iron spikes. My pulse quickens, my hands opening and closing at my sides. This morning, after we held each other in the night and had a companionable breakfast, the man had gone and upended my life. And he'd lied to me to boot. "So now I know the truth about your bogus admin stuff. How did you even get inside my apartment?"

"Liam owns a security company," says Cullen, not flinching one bit from my ire.

Seriously?

"And that somehow gives you the right to break in?"

Cullen sighs and shifts his weight as if *his* patience is running low. "No one broke in. Liam handed the landlord a hundred dollar bill, and the ass was more than happy to open up the place. The movers packed you out carefully and brought everything to a safer location just down the street from the Rescue. There's no sense in you living in a drug den when it's unnecessary. If you're really that nostalgic, I'll go back and get the mice for you and bring them over. Should I grab the cockroaches while I'm at it?"

My hands curl into fists, which I place squarely on my hipbones. "How do you know whether I can even afford this so-called better and safer location?"

"It's rent controlled. It'll cost you about the same as your current monthly payment."

"And how the fuck do you know what my current rent is, Cullen?" The swearing, which I usually try to keep in check when I'm talking directly to someone, escapes in a possibly Freudian slip. Before this moment, I would have sworn that being murderously furious and ridiculously horny were two utterly conflicting sensations, but my body is proving that wrong.

Up above, the clouds shift, letting a new ray of sunlight play across Cullen's much-too-old-for-twenty-eight face. "Security and background checks were run when Catherine employed you. You signed the forms."

"Yes, I signed some forms, but not one of those forms said anything about digging so deeply into my financials that you can recite my bank account number. I also never authorized you or your Trident gods to go through my personal effects. What is wrong with you? What gives you the right to ride roughshod over all my boundaries?"

For the first time since I cut him off, Cullen's eyes flash, his voice changing from indulgent to machine gun fire that sends a jolt of energy down every single one of my nerves. Suddenly, the man standing before me isn't a business executive or even a rowdy paramedic, but a predator in a man's skin. The kind that could give an order and have hundreds of men follow. And now the whole of that power is turned on me. "When you decided to risk your life."

"That's my decision," I snap right back at him, my heart pounding so hard that it must be bruising my ribs.

"Welcome to the world of consequence."

I swing my hand at his face, all my common sense rushing from me.

Cullen catches my wrist in midflight, his strong fingers going easily around my wrist. Something primal and predatory flashes in his eyes, turning the moss green to a dark, dark brown just as he presses his mouth against mine, the heat of him rushing through my whole core.

21

CULLEN

*C*ullen felt Sky's mouth yield to him and pressed onward with all the frustration and need that was ripping him apart inside. His tongue raked over her mouth, deep and rough and punishing, even as his cock grew so hard, he was ready to scream from the pressure. Sky's mouth gave so beautifully, so generously as her small body vibrated in his arms, that Cullen felt absolutely drunk on the taste of her.

Inside his grip, Sky's wrist was pulsing hard enough that he felt the rapid rhythm of her heart. Pinning her wrist against her body, he wrapped his other arm around her back, his mouth devouring her softness. Live currents of electricity sang through his veins, as if Sky's passion and determination and everything that made her unlike him now flowed through his blood, mixing with the fury that woman sparked with such damn efficiency.

And when Sky's mouth returned the kiss, her own body pressing against Cullen's, the sensation seared a path from his mouth right to his full, full cock.

His heart was hammering as he pulled away, his chest heaving with harsh deep breaths. The realization of what he'd just done washed over him with a mix of ice and flame that was as disorienting as a flashbang grenade.

Her head tipped back, Sky stared up at him, her perfect mouth soft and slightly open and so tempting that it was all Cullen could do to stop himself from taking her right then and there.

"Cullen," she breathed, her eyes dropping to where he was still holding her wrist tightly enough to cut off circulation.

He couldn't have let go quicker if he'd touched molten lead. "I —" He stopped, words failing him, together with his common sense. Cullen didn't know what to say, and was slightly afraid that his pulsing erection would make anything he did try to utter sound high-pitched.

Sky bit her lip, her beautiful and all-too-intelligent eyes seeming to see right through any shield Cullen put up. The tip of her tongue flicked out to moisten her now-swollen lips.

"Everything all right?" Eli stuck his head out the backyard gate fence. "You lot coming in?"

"Yes," Sky and Cullen said at the same time.

Eli raised a brow and quickly retreated.

By the time Cullen had found his voice again, Sky was straightening out the material of her pale yellow dress and walking with purpose toward the party. Hanging back a moment, he couldn't stop himself from watching how the fabric hugged her curves, gliding over the kind of ass that made a man hard from one glance. He shuddered, took one step to follow, and then turned on his heel and marched himself into Eli's house instead.

He needed an ice-cold shower.

When he rejoined the party fifteen minutes later, he surveyed Eli's backyard to find his Tridents gathered together at one end, while Jaz, Catherine, and Sky chatted inside a gazebo. With its octagonal cedar construction, the building complemented the other structures on the property. The evergreen scrubs and flowering trees along the perimeter of the backyard were as well designed as everything else in the mansion—all perfectly calculated as a fuck-you from Eli's mother to the son she never wanted.

"What the hell happened to you?" Eli asked as Cullen grabbed a local craft beer and joined the group, positioning himself with his back toward Sky. "Did our new recruit rip you a new one like I told you she would?"

"It's fine." Cullen took a sip of his beer to buy himself another moment. He still couldn't explain the kiss to himself, so he sure as hell wasn't going to be able to explain it to the Tridents. All he knew was that somewhere in the middle of his fury, an irresistible pull from Sky made him lose all common sense. "We're fine."

"Famous last words," said Liam.

Cullen flipped him off.

Liam rubbed the back of his neck, studying Cullen with an intrusive gaze he usually reserved for play partners. Liam was the only one of the Tridents who came from poverty, and he'd learned to read everything about body language at a young age. That type of scrutiny made Liam invaluable in interrogations and, from what Cullen gathered, in his recreational activities. But it made him damn uncomfortable as a friend.

"What?" Cullen demanded.

"You're allowed to like Reynolds," Liam said.

"I don't like Reynolds."

Liam shrugged one shoulder. "Fine. You're allowed to be sexually attracted to Reynolds. She may not be my type, but the woman is smoking hot. Look me in the eye and tell me you've not noticed."

"I've noticed that Jaz is at the Rescue barbecue," said Cullen, knowing it was a weaselly way to avoid the subject. "Did someone hire her and forget to tell me?"

"Eli invited her," Kyan said, flashing their host a venom-filled gaze that set the conversation off in a new direction that Cullen pretended to follow.

After half an hour separated by gender groups, Eli declared his party wasn't a middle school dance and lured everyone together with a promise of burgers. Jaz, who was in the middle of describing her adventures backpacking through Europe the summer prior when Cullen and the others came up to join them, stepped back to widen the circle.

"I've climbed in Frankenjura, Germany; Finale Ligure, Italy; Osp, Slovenia; and on the sea cliffs of the Formentor Peninsula in Spain," Jaz's eyes sparkled with each memory. "Looking down to watch the waves crashing below is like nothing else."

"I'm adding that to my bucket list." Sky's musical voice shot straight into Cullen's chest. "In fact, I'm earmarking my savings for it now."

"Do you travel a bit for journalism?" Jaz asked.

"Not yet, but I'm on track for investigative reporting, so I hope to in the future."

Investigative reporting? Cullen filed away the thought, remembering Sky's original line of questioning when she'd first come up on him and Eli.

"Why Denton Valley? I can't imagine there's much here. Is there?" Jaz dropped her voice, leaning closer; Cullen fighting the urge to do the same.

"Actually, there is something," Sky told Jaz. "Or *might* be. Yesterday, when I went to the scene, Channel Thirteen was already there, but the cops weren't. It's come to my attention since that Denton's emergency assistance comes much more quickly to those who live in these types of neighborhoods..." She gestured around Eli's opulent abode, "than to the Lincoln Drive-type dwellings. If that's true, it's *not* okay."

"Agreed." Jaz nodded vehemently, and Cullen made a mental note to check in with the chief of police to see if there was something to the claim.

"The first part, though, is actually checking the facts and the environment, both in terms of records and local sentiment. Seeing whether things match. It could be a self-fulling prophecy. For example, Lincoln Drive residents might be so demoralized with prior police response that they no longer call. So the police don't know to come, and it all reinforces the neighborhood's belief that cops never show up. Point is, a problem can't be solved unless its causes are fully understood. And that's what I'm going to do, starting with interviewing Lincoln Drive residents."

"Like hell you are." The words slipped from Cullen's mouth

before he could even consider putting them in more diplomatic terms. Hell, fuck diplomacy. The woman was less than twenty-four hours out of the ER and she was already talking about going back into a drug den.

"Opining on my business *again*, Cullen?" Sky shot him a fire-filled gaze that made him go hard all over again. "This is becoming a really bad habit of yours."

"What part of 'stay out of danger, Sky' don't you understand?" he demanded.

"Likely the same part that confuses you in 'stay out of my decisions.'" Sky's jaw tightened, and, though she was much smaller than Cullen, she met the whole storm of his wrath without backing away one step. Most SEALs couldn't do that. And yet here she was. "You don't own me."

"Never said I did." Cullen felt the air around them heat several degrees, the others staying quiet as he and Sky faced each other in a duel. Cullen's pulse quickened, and he had to remind himself to breathe several times before trying for a reasonable tone. "But it seems Frank Peterson does. If you want to be an investigative journalist, why are you working for a piece of shit of a human running a glorified tabloid?"

Sky swallowed, vulnerability flashing in her gaze for a heartbeat before her fists clenched at her sides. "I'll write the story in such a way that he can't refuse to publish it."

Liam, who stood behind Sky, frowned. This was the second time in the conversation Sky had avoided the *why here* question, and Cullen's security operations friend had caught on as well. Cullen's gut tightened. Maybe he was going about this all the wrong way. Maybe—no, certainly—he was a blind, bullheaded asshole. "I have a win-win solution," he said, capturing all Sky's attention and savoring its intensity. "Work at the Rescue full-time. You have the skills we need, and I'll make it worth your while. Cut Frank out of the picture completely—he's not a man you want to be dependent on for *anything*. Trust me on that."

To his utter bewilderment, Sky shook her head. "You don't get it, Cullen. This isn't about Frank. This is about my career.

Journalism is in my blood. And the free press? It isn't a paycheck, it's what makes a free society stay free. Just like your work at the Rescue—"

"You want to know the first goddamn rule of rescuing?" Cullen's blood, which had cooled to a reasonable simmer, shot right back up to his head. "Dead rescuers help no one. And I am not okay with you—"

"*You're* not okay with—" Sky shouted over him.

"Stop." Liam's low, powerful voice cracked through the conversation. Striding forward as if he owned the very air between Sky and Cullen, Liam looked between them and—for once—Cullen shut his mouth in deference while his chest heaved. Liam nodded as if he expected nothing less from both parties. "My line of work exists because too many people need to go into dangerous situations that they, in a perfect world, should not be going near. But this isn't a perfect world. If a doctor or a diplomat is needed, you can't send a marine instead. So we mitigate. We use trained security. And we target harden."

He twisted toward Sky. "You want to go into danger? Learn to defend yourself. Or take someone who can do it for you. Preferably both."

Sky's spine straightened. "No one is coming on my interviews with me."

"Then I'll see you on the mat at six a.m. tomorrow morning," Liam told her.

Sky, whose mouth was hanging slightly open, shut it with a resounding click. Liam was very hard to argue against when he got persuasive. There was just one last point to address.

"She can't do tomorrow morning," he told Liam. "She's just been through hell and—"

"And if you can't stand watching, Hunt, stay the fuck home," Liam shot back. And that was that.

22

FRANK

rank Peterson ran a hand through his thinning hair, frustrated beyond belief. One would think that between owning the whole damn medical industry in Denton Valley and being worshipped by everything with two eyes and a pussy, Cullen Hunt would have better things to do than insist on ruining Frank's life at every turn. But no. No, not at all.

After failing in his scheme to block the Peterson family from collecting the military's death benefit for Bar—Frank's own little brother—Hunt got busy conspiring with the gold digger who'd tricked Bar into marriage. And now... Now Hunt was going after Frank's piece of ass.

Frank's hand tightened around his beer, the tinted glass reflecting the dark granite countertop of his kitchen island. It had been bad enough to discover that Reynolds never reported back on her assignment yesterday. It was worse to learn *why* she hadn't called in her story. Because she was busy fucking Cullen goddamn Hunt.

After everything Frank had done to secure the little journalist, to give the bitch a job when no one else would, to fucking spoon-feed her leads while she teased her way around the newsroom and never *put* out—after all that, the skank dove for Cullen's cock the first chance she got. Did Sky imagine Frank wouldn't find out? That he'd just keep waiting for her indefinitely while she sampled the whole damn town?

Well, at least Frank now understood why Hunt had thrown such a temper tantrum at the Vault. The asshole thought he had some sort of claim on Skylar and had been acting in accordance. Because, as usual, Hunt had wanted what Frank already had.

Fucker.

Frank threw his empty beer bottle into his kitchen sink, feeling the slightest bit of relief at the sound of the glass shattering into hundreds of pieces. He imagined taking one of the sharpest shards and slitting Cullen's throat with it, just to be rid of him once and for all. But then Frank leaned on his granite counter, taking some labored breaths. He had to be careful. The fucking Trident gods were beloved by many in Denton Valley, especially by members of the powers that be. If Frank crossed any of them in too direct a manner, he'd end up with more trouble than he could shake a stick at.

One tenet Frank lived by above all else was the value of plausible deniability.

Ironically, that lesson Hunt himself had taught Frank back in adolescence. And of course, it all started with a skank. Not any skank, however, but one Frank was taking to the eighth grade dance. Sick of being a virgin, Frank had chosen a girl he knew longed to spread her legs for him—and would most certainly have done so had Hunt not interfered. Reaching up, Frank rubbed the bump on his nose, which had never healed right from Hunt's knuckles.

The worst part was that Hunt's only punishment had been a fancy new school and a shiny uniform—but Frank had realized something important over that incident. If he'd gone through with what he (and secretly she) had wanted that evening, the whore might have twisted things into making Frank the villain. And since Frank had never been as lucky as the town's precious Trident gods, there might have been a good dose of nastiness poured on his head.

In other words: distance was key.

Frank pursed his lips as he contemplated the broken glass. His housekeeper would come in and take care of it, so that didn't concern him. The pattern of the shards was giving him an idea, which solidified as he looked again at the bright orange sticky tag he'd ripped off Hunt's mailbox while storming away that morning. It'd been a small, impulsive movement, and the tag was nothing more than a reminder from Overnight Express on an upcoming shipment to be delivered Wednesday between ten and noon.

But now that Frank was looking at it more closely, he knew his instincts had been spot-on—because the upcoming shipment was from Trident pharmacy, and it had a drug reference number on it to boot. Prazosin, the same shit Bartholomew had been on to keep him from rushing about like a rabid dog and destroying the furniture between deployments.

Pulling out the throwaway phone he used when he needed to re-up his roofies order, Frank ordered some sugar-pill placebos from his bewildered contact, then dug through his address book for the right person.

Timothy Browning, one of the underlings in Liam Rowen's security firm, picked up on the third ring and grunted into the receiver.

"I need Hunt's outside security to come down for emergency maintenance Wednesday, ten to noon."

Browning's response was clipped. "*Cullen* Hunt? Jesus Christ, Frank, I'm not comfortable with that. Plus, that's just down the street from Arnie and Phylicia. "

"Would you be more comfortable if I went public?" Like any good journalist, Frank had things stored for later reference—one of them being a recording of Browning banging the wife of the chief of police, who also happened to be Browning's best buddy. The unfortunate couple were the aforementioned Arnie and Phylicia.

"It's not that I'm refusing, Frank. I'm telling you it's impossible. All those homes have state-of-the-art systems."

"You mean the same systems you install? Don't patronize me, Timothy. You'll do it, and you'll do it right."

Frank heard a huff of exasperated breath. "Fine. But it will be only the outside system. I can't touch anything inside the house without Liam noticing. So unless you're planning to spray-paint his front door, I'm not sure what good it's going to do you at all."

"Maybe I do want to spray-paint the front door," said Frank, reaching for the button to end the call. "Not that it's any of your business."

Leaning back in his chair, Frank interlaced his fingers behind his head and grinned. Replacing Hunt's chemical muzzle with sugar pills had a poetic justice to it, like journalism. All Frank was truly doing was stripping away the fraud to let the truth bubble to the surface. And when that happened, when the real animal hiding beneath Cullen Hunt's expensive suits came to light, Frank and *Denton Uncovered* would be there to document it all.

Hell, maybe he'd even have Skylar Reynolds do it, and then take her fine ass atop the printed news sheets.

23

SKY

The next morning, we don't go to Liam's on account of him getting called away for work. When I express my disappointment to Cullen over breakfast, he looks at me for so long that I shift uncomfortably in my seat.

"What?" I demand.

"The training. It isn't going to be fun, Reynolds. It will be months before you enjoy it—if you ever do."

I raise a brow at him over my morning coffee. "How exactly do you know what I will and won't enjoy? For all you know, I've always wanted to be an MMA fighter."

Cullen snorts. "And yet, you aren't one."

Touché. I stick my tongue out at him. Not that I'm not still mad at him over the apartment thing, but it's hard to resist the moments when Cullen is being almost funny. Plus, the memory of having slept with his arm wrapped around me again makes me moist. We hadn't talked about it last night, not even one word. Cullen had just left the door to his bedroom wide open, and when I went to pick up my—his—sleeping shirt, he'd moved over to make space. I never left.

"You want to see your new place?" he asks, putting away his

coffee cup, and I try not to think about how much like an eviction that sounds. Though it isn't as if I thought I'd be staying here to begin with.

Putting on the brightest smile I can, I nod quickly. "Absolutely. I'm more than ready to have my own space. Not that I don't appreciate staying here but…you know."

"Yeah." His jaw tightens for a moment, then he turns decidedly and strides out of the kitchen. "I'll be ready in ten," he calls over his shoulder.

Not just an eviction; more like an emergency evacuation.

Cullen drives me over to my new place in awkward silence, pulling up to the Pine apartment complex at the same time as another car pulls into an empty visitor spot next to us. Not only is this location leaps and bounds better than my former abode—sadly, Cullen had been right about the mice and roaches—the complex itself looks gorgeous and nothing like the rent-controlled places I'd need in New York. With elongated log-style buildings, the garden apartment's knotted pine exterior matches the real pines dotting the property. Like Eli's home, the Pine has that rustic Colorado feel, but without the over-the-top luxury.

The place has a bicycle stand and individually assigned covered parking spaces. Making a mental note to double-check the lease for any hidden provisions, I'm halfway out of Cullen's truck when Jaz pops out of the other vehicle. There's an Uber sticker flashing at me before it pulls back out of the space.

"Jaz?" I turn toward Cullen. "Is this your doing?"

"I texted her just before we left and told her to meet us here."

Told her? As in ordered her? Great. That's about as helpful as when my mom walked into my kindergarten class and demanded the first three kids she saw invite me to their next birthday party.

"Something wrong?" Cullen asks.

He truly doesn't even know. "No. Thank you." Waiting until he can't see me wince, I work out a mental apology to Jaz—only to find myself enveloped in an enthusiastic hug.

"Look at this place!" The girl spins around, her wide grin genuine enough to evaporate any guilt I might feel. Cullen may have asked her to come, but she plainly doesn't mind. "This is perfect."

"You could move here too," says Cullen, stepping out from behind me and earning himself a glare from Jaz.

"I could," Jaz says a little too sweetly. "However—"

"There's a trail in the back that takes you right to several climbing routes," Cullen continues. "If you were going to—"

"If I were going to be so crude as to tell you where to shove your meddling ideas, I'd do that just now. But given that I'm a sweet little thing, I'll just politely tell you to fuck off. Tell Kyan that I'm staying right on at his ranch whether he likes it or not. And Cullen—if I were you, I'd not try to get in the middle of that. Hmm?"

Cullen's glare is enough to chill hot coals, but rolls off Jaz so easily that I can't help wonder how she does it. The man clears his throat. "All right. Then I shall leave you two ladies too. The movers should have your things in the apartment already and you'll find the paperwork in the office."

"Excellent." Hooking her arm through mine, Jaz steers me past a little kidney-shaped pool to the administrative building, her chin held high enough that she seems part cat.

"What was that?" I ask.

She gives me a sly look. "Cullen likes to fix everybody's problems, but we disagree on just how much space Kyan needs. Tough love and all. Anyway, *look* at this place! I may not live here, but girl, I hope there's a couch, because you're having visitors."

Inside the office, a young girl at the desk goes over some pamphlets about apartment rules, mailboxes, and so forth before handing me the keys. "Apartment 222," she says, grinning with a mouth full of metal. Braces? How old is this girl? "The furniture delivery was last night—please let me know if you find anything damaged."

Clearly, she hasn't seen my furniture.

And just as clearly—I realize as Jaz and I cross the threshold a few minutes later—neither have I. In place of my Goodwill-acquired basics, the living room is furnished in butter-soft leather furniture, its delicate off-pink hue looking inviting instead of tacky.

Topping it off, there's a quaint little breakfast nook, and a lovely red brick gas fireplace with wooden logs set beside it for decor. The rest of the place is fairly standard for a one bedroom, one bath with the usual appliances in a galley kitchen, and a regular tub and shower combo, but it's all new, like it's been built in the last year. And that's not all.

"Sky, come out here," Jaz calls to me, and for the first time, I step into my bedroom. My friend is there waving to me from a lovely balcony that looks out onto a tree line filled with a mixture of evergreens, mostly, of course, pines. But it's stunning. And all my belongings—at least the ones that seem to have passed the Trident gods' inspection—are already here: laptop, clothes, personal things.

"I can't believe Cullen did this," I say, still unable to make up my mind on whether to be upset over this or grateful. The place, the furniture, everything is beyond reason. Also beyond asking my opinion.

Jaz laughs. "Listen, that's Cullen for you. He's not going to come out and say something nice, and he definitely isn't a hugger, but seeing a problem and solving it for someone—that's who he is. Now, let's go check out your kitchen."

"He backed off from your wrath," I point out, following Jaz to admire the fully stocked refrigerator and pantry. Expecting another chuckle, I'm taken aback when the girl turns, her face serious.

"He's different with you, Sky. It's… You're good for him."

I'm still trying to work out what I think about Jaz's observation and my new life at the Pine when, Monday evening, I get a text message from Liam. He's back, the message declares, and he expects me at his studio by 6:30 a.m. the following day. Provided I'm not going to wuss out.

Not wussing out, Tuesday morning I pull up to the address fifteen minutes early—to discover all the Tridents' cars already there. My gaze lingers on Cullen's vehicle, my stomach tightening despite myself.

Dressed in my spandex shirt and yoga pants, I'm not sure what I expect to find inside as I approach the door, but my heart is pumping in readiness to kick some ass. I might never have done martial arts before, but my body is still toned from when I used to rock climb regularly. Add to that a morning helping of prophylactic ibuprofen, and I can honestly say I feel good. Strong. Even my shoulder, which I tested out with a pull-up on my doorframe molding this morning, feels stable.

Or maybe I'm just running on adrenaline and nerves.

Slipping through a door that emits a musical *ding* when I open it, I walk past the still-empty reception desk and locker rooms toward the sounds of male grunting in the back. Here the corridor opens into a kind of gym that probably makes Olympians salivate.

In addition to the usual open space with a hell of a good floor mat, the school-gymnasium-size room has a boxing ring, a free weight corner, several punching bags, three racks with training targets and weapons, and, last but not least, a station with a climbing rope and various pull-up bars that the climber in me can't wait to try. A back door in the corner of the room has a big sign depicting the running trails in the woods behind the complex, as well as a set of bright yellow reflective vests for joggers.

And then there are the men themselves, all gathered beside the ring, their sweat-soaked clothing betraying how long they've all been here already. It's my first time seeing Kyan in short sleeves, and I can't help staring at the roughened flesh snaking down his chiseled biceps. I wonder if he knows that his scars somehow make him more beautiful. No, I know that he doesn't—and wouldn't believe me if I told him. I hope he finds someone he will believe, though.

Turning my gaze to Liam, I see him standing with his arms crossed over his chest while Cullen and Eli square off against each other. Liam nods to me in quick greeting and jerks his chin toward the empty mat space. Translating his curt gesture to mean something like *Good morning, Sky! Please make yourself comfortable and stretch while we finish up,* I lower myself to the mat.

Every one of the Tridents is a sight to behold, but it's Cullen my eyes never lose sight of as he and Eli circle each other like predators. In another sleeveless tee and a loose pair of workout shorts, Cullen's muscles are again on full display. So are his tattoos, the ink making my fingers long to trace those distinctive patterns, to feel the warmth of his skin beneath them.

"Go," Liam barks so hard that I flinch at the sudden sound. Then I flinch again when Cullen shoots his fist right into Eli's head. The headgear the men wear seems very unlikely to offer much protection against the blow.

Lankier than the larger Cullen, Eli dances away from the blow, his bare foot cracking against Cullen's ribs. Cullen blocks the next kick with his forearm, retaliating with unrestrained brutality that takes my breath away. The merciless exchange continues, each blow filled with power and coiled muscles, each impact sending a feeling of shuddering force through the gym.

"Get your goddamn hands up," Liam bellows at Eli as Cullen's fist clips the man's face and draws blood from the corner of his mouth. When Cullen lands another shot right on Eli's jaw, Liam explodes with expletives in a booming voice I've never heard from the man. And never, ever, want to hear again.

For the first time since waking up this morning, I think I've made a mistake coming here, my heart picking up speed.

Meanwhile, in the ring, Eli gets his blows on Cullen's muscular frame, the men's glistening muscles coiling and exploding with power that saturates the air with intensity. *Thump. Thump. Thump.* The blows come with deadly speed, landing with no mercy for the punishment they inflict. It's no longer beautiful. It's brutal and cruel and so harrowing that my bile rises up my throat, my moist hands clenching my yoga pants.

Cullen grunts in pain, the sound low and quiet. And potent enough to wrap an iron band around my heart. Moving slowly, I inch my way to the exit, the pristine mat no longer welcoming or comfortable beneath me.

I somehow hear it before I see it, Eli's gasps of pain as Liam inserts himself into the fight and knocks the man all the way to ground. "You like your goddamn brains splattered?" Liam yells into Eli's face as the man gathers himself painfully to his knees, his muscular shoulders heaving with panting breaths. "Let me do it for you and save us the fucking trouble. What the goddamn fuck—"

I draw a sharp breath, my hand over my mouth as Liam's dark face lifts toward me.

"Shit," says Liam again, but more quietly this time, while Cullen —who now marks my presence—scrubs his hands over his face.

Before I can move, Liam hops over the rope barrier and slowly walks toward me, his palms up while I try to remember how to move. How to run.

"Look at me, Sky," he says, capturing my gaze with that unyielding command. "I'm not going to hurt you."

Accepting Cullen's outstretched hand, Eli pops gracefully to his feet and hops the ropes with the same ease Liam had. "I'm quite all right, soldier," he says, the nonbloodied side of his mouth coming up in a half grin. "These blokes were just working with me on something."

"I... I don't want to do this anymore," I say, taking a step back.

Liam crouches, balancing easily on the balls of his feet as he makes himself shorter than me. "No one is going to be doing full-contact sparring with you for a long, long time, Sky. You're not remotely ready for that. You must know that, right?"

I nod slowly.

Liam mirrors my movement. "All right. So what scared you?"

"You," I blurt out, blood draining from my face as I realize what I said.

Eli laughs.

Shooting Eli a dark glare, Liam turns to Cullen. "I'm going to need you to get her started, Hunt. She doesn't need to be working with me yet."

"No," says Cullen.

I try and fail not to flinch. "It's all right. No one needs to train me. I'm fine. I never should have come."

"That's not... Jesus Christ." Hopping the ropes, Cullen strides over to me. Taking hold of my shoulders, he twists me around to face him, his eyes capturing my gaze until the whole rest of the world slips away. Carefully, so carefully, Cullen's thumb traces the line of my cheekbone, his calloused finger sliding over my skin and sending zings of energy through every nerve in my body. "I didn't think you'd *want* to work with me, Sky."

"I don't know what I want," I whisper, my gaze darting toward Liam, who seems genuinely troubled. Disappointment races through me, weighing down my limbs. I was supposed to learn to defend myself today. For the first time in my life, someone was going to teach me to fight back. But... "I can't... I mean if you—"

"Liam hit Eli because Eli was working on something," Cullen says, his gaze too perceptive of my thoughts for comfort. "I've no intention of hitting you that way. None of us do. But if you do want to learn self-defense, there's gonna be a good deal of suffering involved."

In my side vision, Liam nods. "Nothing you can't handle, Sky. But this isn't water aerobics."

"Do you trust me to walk you through it?" Cullen asks, drawing my attention back. "Through the early conditioning? I want you to think carefully before you answer. Eli or Kyan or—"

"You," I say before I can change my mind. "I'm in. With you."

24

SKY

*P*ulling on a pair of sneakers, Cullen motions me toward the back door with that running trail sign. Not what I expected, but going on the trail seems safer than staying anywhere close to the boxing ring, where, I swear to God, the other Tridents are busy trying to choke each other unconscious. Liam is no longer yelling obscenities, though I suspect that will change the moment I step out the door.

"The military has its own language," Cullen says, following my line of sight.

I shrug one shoulder. I'm not sure how any of that makes it okay to be disrespectful to your friends, but this isn't the time to discuss it. Especially not with the serious face that Cullen turns toward me.

"Understand me, Reynolds. There is no gray zone in training with me. You do what I tell you, when I tell you, for however long I tell you. Or you tell me you're done with this endeavor and we go home and never do this again. There is no in-between. You can say stop any time you want, but that's about the only opinion you get to have. Got it?"

Sounds like being engaged to Jaden. "Got it."

I follow Cullen out onto the trail, the SEAL setting a brisk pace uphill that has my muscles going from warming up to burning within minutes, though the calm of nature offsets the discomfort as it always does. Gambel oaks, spruces, and cottonwood trees streak by on either side, filling my nose with clean wilderness freshness. A pair of squirrels keep pace with us for a bit before losing interest. By the time we're two miles into the run however, and still heading away from the studio, I begin to worry.

Another mile and I no longer care for the beauty of the oaks, spruces, or cottonwood trees, my breaths coming in painful, ragged bursts, my lungs aching from the exertion that seems to bypass Cullen completely. When the man comes to a stop atop another hill, I fall unceremoniously down to my knees and gasp for breath.

"On your back, legs six inches from the ground," Cullen orders harshly. "If you want to roll in the dirt, we might as well use it."

I grit my teeth but do as I'm told without complaint—a fact that Cullen neither notices nor acknowledges. By the time he's had me do thirty burpees, bear crawl through a puddle, and sprint up the next two hills, however, my good humor has reached its limit.

"Move, Reynolds," Cullen shouts as I trip over a root, barely recovering without falling flat on my face. At the edges of my vision, the trail seems to shrink into darkness, my eyes unable to focus on anything not right in front of my nose. Cullen comes up behind me like a wolf herding his prey. "*Move.*"

"I *am* moving," I snap back at him, my silent endurance at its blazing end.

Something dark flashes across Cullen's face. A warning to keep my mouth shut and...and what? Throw up? Fall down in exhaustion? We'd agreed for me to learn self-defense, not join Cullen's do-it-yourself boot camp.

My head comes up, my body not backing away an inch even as ragged breaths threaten to rip my lungs to pieces. "Why are you being an asshole?"

Cullen cuts in front of me, blocking my path, his muscular body silhouetted against the glorious sky. "You think *that* was being an asshole? You know what I think? That you aren't even trying. Work or quit." He bares his teeth. "And I think you should quit."

Fury, a burning inferno of fury, rushes through my blood. My feet hurt. My lungs feel like someone has taken a knife to them. My muscles tremble from the effort of keeping me upright. And after all that, now the asshole wants me to quit?

Or is that what he'd wanted all along? To punish me for arrogantly pursuing my dreams instead of following his orders like some mindless soldier?

My jaw clenches, my eyes flashing as they meet Cullen's moss-green gaze. He never liked the idea of me training, of me doing what investigative journalism requires, and has finally found a perfect way out. Make me turn back. Run me into the ground until I've no choice but to crumple and admit I'm not good enough.

Shows how much he knows. In my mind, I picture Lincoln Drive again. Imagine holding Zack in my arms. Tell myself I must run to keep him alive. And so I do. I put one foot in front of the other and push on, pouring everything I have into keeping ahead of the bastard who has a foot of height and years of training on me.

For a while, it works, my body moving even as I can no longer keep track of where I am. Twigs crack underfoot, my breaths filling my ears. I'm on another muddy uphill slope as I stumble again, landing on my shoulder, searing pain taking what little breath I have.

"Get up," Cullen hollers. "Get up, get up, get *up*."

I don't know if it's the extreme fatigue of my joints and muscles, the damage done to my shoulder and arm, or just the fact that Cullen is being so unfathomably cruel, but I lose it. Without warning, tears well in my eyes and stream down my cheeks. Climbing painfully to my feet, I pull back my fist and jab my knuckles into Cullen's chin.

To my utter surprise, the man takes the shot.

Ironically, the force of the impact sends me backward, my foot slipping on the muddy slope. My precarious balance gives way, and I have half a heartbeat to realize that I'm going down. That the pain I felt moments ago will be nothing compared to a full tumble down the rocky slope. Half a heartbeat, and then I fall.

A large, muscular body wraps around me, Cullen twisting us so

155

he takes the brunt of the impact, his powerful arm securing my injured shoulder like a splint. As we come to the bottom of the mudslide, to the point where I expect Cullen to shove me off him, I feel his arms tightening around me instead.

"I'm...not...quitting," I try to yell at him, my sobs punctuating the vowels. "I'm—"

"Done for the day," Cullen responds gently. Shifting me in his lap, he settles my head into the groove of his shoulder, his free hand rubbing a quiet circle along my trembling back. "You did good, Reynolds. We're going to make a warrior of you yet."

"What?" I scrub my face, but the treacherous hiccupping breaths won't stop coming. Cullen's words wash over me, the potent mix of relief and confusion making my head spin, his praise filling me like a drug. "But you... Is this what you wanted from me? Tears?"

"I don't care one way or the other about tears." Cullen brushes my sweat-soaked hair away from my face, his large hand stroking my head. "Or about how far you can run just now, or how many pushups you can do. This was about fighting."

I shake my head, not understanding him at all.

Cullen sighs. "From what I saw in that Lincoln Drive yard, when you get hit, your only instinct is to shield yourself from more punishment. No one wins a fight that way. I needed you to learn what your body can do, to keep your wits about you, to know that a bit of pain is not a reason to surrender. And you didn't." Cullen leans down, his forehead touching mine. "You *didn't* stop, Reynolds. Didn't surrender. Hell, a week ago, you cowered when I raised my voice—and now you took a shot at me instead. And I'm more proud of you than you can imagine."

"I'm not sure about the wits part," I whisper, savoring the heat of Cullen's body as he holds me against him, his spicy scent mixing with the fresh scent of earth.

A corner of his mouth twitches, which makes his severe face soften into something rare and vulnerable. "Well, can't lose what you don't have. There is that."

My lips part, Cullen's mouth lowering to cover mine softly, his tongue slipping between my teeth as if seeking permission. Pleasure and warmth spider through me, my mouth yielding to Cullen's just as my body sinks fully into the kiss.

The tension magnifies, the kiss morphing from gentleness to something more primal. More needy. More wild. My breath catches, my hips rocking against Cullen's to register his erection expanding beneath me, my panties dampening at once.

I shift my position, directing the friction between us to where I long for it most, as Cullen lowers his head to nip the side of my throat. Tiny prickles of pain spice the pleasure, and it feels so good that I moan.

The noise seems to excite him. The nips morph to long delicious suckles that snake down my skin to the hollow beneath my left ear.

"Yes," I pant, my eyes closing so I can absorb all these sensations at once.

Adjusting my legs so I'm straddling him fully, Cullen lets his hands knead down my back, his strong fingers digging into sore muscles beneath my shoulder blades. Each press sends a rush of pleasure through me, making my thighs clench around the man's taut, hard waist.

Running my hands through Cullen's short blond hair, I find the thick strands much silkier than I would've imagined. So much about this man is a dichotomy. A set of Jekyll-and-Hyde contrasts that defy logic and reality.

Just like what we're doing now, in the middle of the vast Colorado forest. Holy hell. What *are* we doing? The sobering thought sends a shiver through me, even as my body keeps rhythm with his, refusing to break the tantalizing sensations. A mistake. I know this is a mistake. But it's a mistake I really, really want to make.

Cullen's fingers weave deeper into my hair, removing the elastic band to set the strawberry strands free. For a moment, he buries his nose in its waves, inhaling my scent with primal urgency, before his palms lower to my waist. In the next second, his thumbs have worked their way beneath the hem of my yoga shirt, peeling the snug spandex right off my body. I feel the air on my newly exposed skin, but the uncontrolled shiver is from far more than the chill. In fact, with how desperately my sex clenches over the emptiness inside it, I'm certain I'm about to combust.

Laying me down on a nearby patch of grass, Cullen buries his face in my cleavage, nuzzling along the zipper of my sports bra before closing his mouth around my straining nipple and sucking it through the cotton. Hard.

"Oh God." I buck beneath him as arousal rushes through me, making my breasts and back and thighs ache with need. Wrapping my legs around Cullen's waist, I feel his own desire iron hard between my legs. My brain engages just long enough to wonder if I'll survive this, before deciding that it doesn't much care.

Grasping Cullen's wet shirt, I struggle to yank it from him, the promise of inked skin beneath my touch turning my movements into desperate jerks. Everything inside me suddenly aches to explore the expanse of man I've seen and slept beside, yet never, ever touched.

Removing his shirt obligingly—because it's clear to us both that I lack the coordination and strength to wrestle anything off Cullen —the man snakes the delicious cotton beneath my head. As soon as that's done, he unzips my bra, flinging it away with predatory intent.

My breasts fall free, the nipples peaked in the chill, my breaths coming fast and shallow as my legs tighten around him.

Taking each of my breasts in his hands, the pressure just enough to ride the edge of pain to make it transform into molten pleasure, Cullen leans his upper body toward mine. The contradictions of cool air and warm flesh, hard muscles and soft earth assault my body, playing off each other in a dangerous cascade of sensation.

My breasts ache. My sex and thighs need more more more as I press myself against his throbbing erection.

With his chest bare, I see his rapid pulse beating in the soft hollow of his neck, just a hand width above the collarbone. Raising my head, I run my tongue over the spot, savoring its spicy, clean scent as Cullen flinches but holds still. I feel as much as hear the man's breath quicken as I pursue the sensitive artery, scraping my teeth along the delicate skin.

"You'll pay for that," he promises, his voice as strained as his cock, his arms trembling as he braces himself on either side of me.

"Mmm," I murmur, feeling all the pent-up fury I've ever felt for the bastard transform into heady passion. Into a craving that must be sated. Catching sight of Cullen's tattoo, I do what I've longed for since first seeing it—trace one finger along the tribal ink that swirls around his arm and up to his shoulder, pausing to outline the eagle before dragging the edges of my teeth across the top of the shield. And then I bite into him, not bothering to be nice.

Cullen jerks beneath me, a groan escaping his mouth.

I lean up to whisper in his ear, "You deserved that."

"Agreed," Cullen sounds low and dangerous and so damn seductive that my arousal soaks through my yoga pants. "But you'll pay for it anyway."

CULLEN

*C*ullen was losing his mind, the fierce meeting of lips and skin and bodies driving him beyond logic. The floral smell and the sweet honey-like taste of the woman in his arms made him want to devour her in a single gulp. He ground against her, savoring the way her hips swiveled, pressing up against his stone-hard cock. Cullen's vision narrowed, the damn world narrowed, until all he could see was the single pinpoint that was Skylar Reynolds.

His seeking hand found a tender spot just on the inside of her hipbone, and he tugged her skintight yoga pants down enough to suck that skin into his mouth.

She cried out at this, her musical voice catching with arousal even as she squirmed. Sliding his hands under Sky's backside, Cullen gripped her hips and kept her in place as he continued pulling on her flesh until a raspberrylike mark blushed over the milky skin.

"*Cullen...*" Sky gasped, her hips trying to undulate beneath his unyielding hold.

The sound of his name on her lips lit a new blaze inside him, the flame searing his skin. She liked being held down, and fuck, Cullen loved doing it. Loved watching Sky's blue eyes glaze with desire as he stroked her over the juncture between her thighs, the pads of his fingers detecting a noticeable wetness soaking through the stretchy black material.

Whatever thin thread of restraint he'd been holding onto snapped. Sliding his thumbs into her waistline, Cullen seized both the pants and the panties beneath them off her in one swift motion, exposing her to his view. She'd shaved herself utterly smooth and, as he opened her legs wider to put her pink and glistening center on display, he nearly came without any further provocation.

Sky's thighs pressed against his hands, her face turning the same pink shade as her sex. A sweet, innocent embarrassment that begged to be conquered. Holding her open, Cullen dropped his mouth to her center to stroke his tongue between her folds until the woman vibrated deliciously beneath him. A moan escaped as he traced the tip around her hood, brushing her clit just enough to make her buck in his hold.

"Cullen! Please!" Sky's words melded together, her sex dripping thicker and thicker the more she struggled against Cullen's tight grip, her attempts to hide her sex from him fully forgotten. "I can't... I need—"

"Wasn't I going to make you pay for something?" Cullen murmured right at the level of Sky's clit, his breath tickling the swollen bud. "Ah, yes. That bite."

Enjoying her distressed whimper, Cullen lowered his face toward Sky's deliciousness once more, this time flicking the tip of his tongue all around that sensitive swell until the whimpers gave way to uncontrolled moans and then a desperate, needy keen. Ah, there it was. Smiling to himself, he put his mouth over Sky's apex and *sucked*.

The woman's back arched as she screamed into the forest's stillness, her muscles tightening over and over through a desperate climax. Christ, she came beautifully. Gorgeously. Releasing his iron hold on Sky's thighs, Cullen gathered the woman in his arms, savoring her softness and warmth as he held her through the final grips of orgasm.

For several moments, she lay limp and blessedly bare in Cullen's arms, the most intimate parts of her moist from his attention and his tongue. He could get used to seeing her like this, her glossy reddish-blonde hair sex tousled and flying freely around her shoulders, her lips kiss swollen, and her skin glowing with a satisfied flush.

His cock agreed, twitching so painfully that he nearly gasped. Shifting Sky to relieve some of the pressure, he studied every line of her face before reaching impertinently between her thighs. She yelped in indignation, but the moisture flowing from her gave him all the information he needed.

She wanted more. Was ready for more. And holy hell, so was he.

A feral and animalistic craving seized Cullen at once. His blood rushed south until any other thought became impossible. He had to have her. Now. Setting her down on the mossy ground, he struggled free of his shorts and hauled himself on top of her.

She softened beneath him, open and welcoming, the feel of her making everything inside him demand more. Dropping openmouthed kisses along her neck and shoulders, he tasted the heady saltiness coating her skin as the head of his cock lined up at her slick entrance.

Fuck, she felt good. Too good. It took every remaining brain cell Cullen still had functioning to shift off her long enough to find his shorts again. Digging almost frantically through his back pocket for his wallet, he secured the foil packet.

Sky, meanwhile, had recovered enough to skim one sharp fingernail along his pectoral muscles.

Cullen growled a warning.

Sky smirked right back at him, and it was all he could do to keep from slipping her onto her belly and slapping that cheeky ass a time or two before burying himself inside her.

Tossing the packet to her instead, Cullen gripped the woman's eyes with his own. "Put it on me."

Sky sat up, her chest heaving, her swinging breasts pointing their nipples right at him. After tearing the packet with her teeth, Sky removed the latex and then… And then, instead of rolling it down his length, the little minx leaned down and swirled her tongue all around the head of him.

"Sky," Cullen warned, his voice low and full of gravel.

Grinning slyly, Sky swallowed him down in one fell swoop.

Cullen groaned, the sound shifting to a stream of profanity that would make any sailor proud. Pushing her head back right before he hit the point of no return, he snatched the foil packet from her fingers and sheathed himself, yanking her beneath him the moment that was finished. Shoving her thighs apart, he pinned her wrists to the ground in a way he knew would make her eyes widen and her channel slicken, and slid his way home.

Christ, she was tight. And hot. And perfect. Using all his hard-won restraint, he paused above her, letting her body adjust to the intrusion before starting to move. Slowly at first, then faster and faster, plunging himself in Sky's heat with a desperate *thrust thrust thrust* of his pulsing cock. Beneath his hold, Sky's body undulated, taking him deeper and deeper, while their heaving breaths formed a low rumble beneath the songs of morning birds.

Thrust. Thrust. Thrust.

Sky's hips rose to meet Cullen's assault, her channel clenching around him. Shifting her wrists until he could hold them with one hand, he dropped his other to her clit, savoring the sudden hint of anxiety crossing her features.

"I can't," she breathed. "Not again, not—"

Gripping her wrists more tightly, Cullen found that swollen clit he'd become intimately familiar with, and he stroked the sensitive flesh with merciless flicks. Right side. Left. Left again. Now.

"Cullen!" Sky howled as her body cinched around him in uncontrolled pleasure, her second climax forcing her hips off the ground with its intensity.

Dropping his lips atop Sky's open mouth, Cullen swallowed her moans as he came, pouring everything he had inside her.

26

SKY

Several ragged breaths later, Cullen pulls himself out of me, my body mourning the loss of him even as my mind tries to catch up to what's just happened. I had sex with Cullen Hunt. Mind-blowing, panty-wetting sex. With my boss.

Pushing himself up on an elbow, Cullen looms over me, his heart galloping as forcefully as mine is. His beautiful hard face watches me intently, a thin sheen of sweat making every ridge of his muscled abdomen sparkle in the sunlight.

Reaching up, I run my finger along the small, jagged scar under his chin. "Well." I puff, my breathing still too fast for propriety. "That was…"

"Yeah," he agrees.

"Yeah."

Silence settles over us, shifting from companionable to uncomfortable as the chill seeps back into my skin. Beneath Cullen's intent gaze, I feel as vulnerable as ever, his slow caresses along my hair making me long for him all over again. Clearing my throat, I reach for my clothes. Cullen takes the hint to get his own self dressed.

"Do you mind if I…" I wave toward my car as we return to

Liam's gym, the thought of facing the other Tridents just now making my skin heat.

Turning me toward him, Cullen takes my chin into his strong hand. "We'll be here again Friday morning. Are you coming back?" he asks, his voice controlled despite the pulse beating hard against the side of his neck. "To train, I mean. Are you coming back Friday to train?"

I bite my lip, willing myself to *not* look at his mouth. To not think about his large, large cock pounding through my channel. "Unless I learned everything today, I guess I'd better," I whisper.

"Good." Releasing me with a suddenness that I don't know how to interpret, Cullen opens my car door for me, staying still with his hands draped behind his back until he disappears from my rearview mirror.

Blowing out a slow deliberate breath, I shake my head. How is it even possible for a man to make my body come alive one moment and shut me out a few breaths later, retreating completely into his stony self? More to the point, how much pain am I setting myself up for by letting any part of me want someone who I know I will never truly reach?

I TRY and fail to get Cullen out of my head for the next two days and have just settled myself enough to do my work by Thursday morning when Jaz shows up with climbing gear and undoes all my righteous effort.

"All right, spill," she says, zipping a windbreaker over her climbing jacket. We're doing a last gear check before shouldering our packs, the call of the Pikes Peak mountains already singing through me. I'm not surprised the WorldROCK, the nationwide climbing tournament that's coming in shortly, has chosen this area for this year. Up above, the sun is out and the sky is an almost iridescent blue, but any time the wind picks up, it's cutting. Jaz pulls her hair back into a ponytail, tucking it under a fleece cap. "All Kyan would tell me is that you came to training Tuesday, and Cullen worked with you. I want details."

My face heats despite the chill, and I turn away, quickly putting on my pack. I can't help wondering exactly how much Kyan told her. Hell, I can't help wondering how much he and the other Tridents know about what happened. The guys don't seem to have secrets between them, but Cullen isn't the talkative kind either and—

"Sky?"

Shit. Realizing I've been quiet too long to now veer off topic without raising suspicion, I clear my throat and start us into motion. "It was intense. Have you ever seen them train?"

"Oh yeah. They are competitive as shit—have been since high school. Screaming into each other's faces and pushing buttons. It's like part of their toughness depends on who can be the biggest asshole, you know?" She frowns and suddenly gets in front of me, cutting off my path. With her fists planted on her hips and the mountain rising high behind her, Jaz looks like a girl on a postcard. "If the bastards hurt you, I'm going to put poison ivy in Kyan's sheets."

"No. Nothing like that," I assure her quickly. "Well, Cullen wasn't exactly gentle putting me through my paces"—*or through other things*—"but—"

"Oh. My. God." Jaz's face transforms into impish delight, the girl bouncing on her toes once before grabbing my arm and pulling me along on the trail. "Never play poker, Sky. I've seen sunsets dimmer than that blush. *Spill.* I love new developments."

I scowl, but Jaz has me pretty well nailed down. Plus, I'm so confused that I wouldn't mind her bit of common sense given that I'm pretty sure I've lost all mine somewhere. "We had…a one-off. An intense and very pleasurable one-off. Which is going to make for some awkward-as-hell moments when I see him next, but it is what it is."

"So…you aren't the least bit interested?" Jaz clarifies. "Beyond the mind-blowing exercise."

"It's more that we don't actually really know each other."

"Let's see, what do we know of Cullen?" says Jaz, pulling a pair of granola bars out of her side pocket and handing one to me.

"He's gorgeous. Buff. A billionaire. A philanthropist. He saves lives on a daily basis. I mean, if you spot major drawbacks to any of that, let me know."

"The part about him being an overprotective jerk who thinks he has a say over how my life should go might be one." I bite into the bar, the sweet and salty taste reminding me too much of the man we're discussing. "Oh, and he's my boss."

"*And* his eyes follow you everywhere you go. When we were at the barbecue, every time I peeked up, he was staring at you." Jaz grins conspiratorially. "I'm telling you, he watches you like a starved man eyeing prime rib laid out on a plate for him."

Well, I'd definitely been laid out for him...

I think of how his hands felt on me as we lay on that spongy forest ground, his groan reverberating through my body, and feel myself getting wet all over again. But... But there's also the other side of the man. The Hyde to the Jekyll. "Looks aside, what do you know about Cullen?" I ask.

"Not as much as you'd think. I'm six years younger, and Kyan was always devoted to keeping me out of the loop—but I know Cullen is from Denton Valley originally, just like Bar was. There was some issue at Cullen's middle school, and his folks carted him off to military school as a punishment. Then he took to it, went to Annapolis with the guys, and then tried out for the SEALs. He didn't wash out, obviously. None of them did. Then he got out after Bar died and came here."

"To his family?" I ask. He's never mentioned them. Actually, Cullen has never mentioned anything about himself, which makes me unreasonably curious. Curious and discouraged. With how intensely closed off Cullen is, a relationship beyond sex might not be possible even if I wanted it. Not that I do.

"Nope. His mom got remarried and moved away after his father died. He came back here because of Addie. Bar's Addie. They all go way back. Anyway, none of the guys re-upped after that, and within a few months of the funeral, they were all here for good. And don't ask what happened to Bar—none of them talk about it, though Kyan was nearby. He got hurt in the same op."

"Wait, seriously? You don't even know what happened to Kyan?"

"That's right," she confirms. "You know how closed-off Cullen is—well, they're all like that. Don't get me wrong, it drives me flipping *crazy*. But I've learned the hard way that maintaining any sort of relationship with my brother means letting that sort of thing go."

I chew on Jaz's words as the ascent becomes too steep to continue the conversation. The small glimpse Cullen had given me into his nightmares is probably a great deal more than most people will ever learn about the man. I wonder what Jaz would say if she knew I'd found Cullen's PTSD meds. That I've seen him flinch in the middle of the night. That instead of telling me to leave when he relived his horrors, he'd tucked me close and let my presence settle him to sleep.

For the next ninety minutes, the cliff swallows all my concentration—which is what I've always loved about rock climbing. It requires all your physical and mental strength at once. No room for problems or outside worries when you're on the side of a mountain. I find it incredibly freeing.

For the first time since arriving in Colorado, hell, for the first time since the whole Fleet Week-and-Jaden debacle, one hundred percent of my focus is on my inhales, my exhales, my next handhold, the next bit of stone to which I entrust my weight. They're the only things that exist. And it feels great.

Pulling up onto our horizontal target, I clip myself into an anchor Jaz has set up and sit on the ledge, my legs dangling over the abyss. Below us, the Garden of the Gods spreads out like a bumpy tapestry, the sharp protrusions of sandy rock mixing with the adjacent reddish columns. Adding to the breathtaking texture, the pointed tops of the evergreens draw designs over the patches of white snowcaps, underscoring the whole awesomeness of nature.

"It's like looking at an alien planet," Jaz says quietly.

Nodding, I lean back on my outstretched arms and let the pine-scented wind kiss my face. Between Cullen's training and now this, my body is going to be hating me the rest of the week. But it's more than worth it. Plus, I need to increase my stamina.

This thought, of course, makes my mind wander to Cullen's level of stamina, and then I'm all tangled up in my thoughts again. Except it's not Cullen's stamina that worries me. Between first my father and then Jaden, I've brushed up against military types enough that I know what happens when tempers snap—and there's nothing to suggest that Cullen is any different. There's an aggression there, lurking behind those moss-green eyes. Couple that with ability and an internal compass that says that sometimes, hurting people is okay, and you get a not very good cocktail. What happens if a Lincoln Drive-type situation arises again, with Cullen believing I shouldn't go after a story—except this time, he's close enough to physically stop me? Would he? Would that fall under the military's code of measured response and acceptable loss?

Fool me once, shame on you. Fool me twice, shame on me. Considering going for number three is insane.

I run my gloved fingertips over the rough material of the stone we're sitting on. "Hey, Jaz? Do you think it's strange how none of the Tridents are in a relationship?"

"Nah. I mean, they've always been like that. They're basically just a pack of wolves on the prowl all the time. Although it sounds like Cullen may be trying to mend his ways." She gazes out at the vastness surrounding us, her expression turning wistful, and we both fall quiet for a moment. "Give him a chance," she says finally. "Don't put up with any shit, but give him a chance."

"I don't think Cullen wants to date me," I say finally, picking up the threads of conversation. "Though I can't say I haven't enjoyed our other pursuits. Except... When I came to train with them Tuesday, Cullen and Liam were going after Eli. *Hard.* Whatever Eli said about not minding, what kind of assholes hurt someone they care about?"

Jaz turns to me, her brows lifted. "You're kidding me, right? Liam has a whole kink for hurting people."

I stare at her blankly. "What?"

"You really don't know?" She chuckles. "He likes to take

charge…with a crop and shit. I mean, it's consensual and all, and the women absolutely throw themselves at his feet to be walloped, but at the end of the day, it says a lot about him. Namely that any suspicions you may have about him being an asshole are well-founded." The last comes out with more force than necessary, and Jaz screws her lips to one side in consternation. "You ready for the descent?"

As we rappel back down—my favorite part—Jaz's words mix with my own thoughts. While I don't share my friend's indignation over Liam's sexual preferences, the fact that I had no idea of what's apparently common knowledge shows how little the guys have shared with me. How little Cullen has shared with me. Hell, I learned more about the man in these few hours with Jaz than I had in our entire time knowing each other.

If the two of us are going to be nothing but occasional sex buddies, that's fine. But that's the extent to which it could ever go. Jaz called him closed-off and private, but what that truly equates to is secretive. I know more than most about him, and that's still near nothing.

I've already been with someone I'd believed I could trust and had been dead wrong. Being with someone who actively hides everything? If that's not a definition of foolishness, I don't know what is.

Cullen is closed-off. Controlling. Obstinate. He's big enough to do damage and very possibly volatile enough to do it.

Good thing I'm not looking for a relationship with anything but journalism, because digging too deeply into Cullen is a way to disaster.

SKY

*F*riday morning, I stride back into Liam's gym like a warrior wearing chain mail, determined not to let the naked time I shared with Cullen derail my learning plans. Unlike on my previous visit here, the guys are busy with calisthenics instead of beating the shit out of each other—though the sweat-soaked shirts and a fresh bruise on Kyan's chin suggest that was done earlier this morning. Fortunate happenstance of schedule or a catering to my tender sensibilities? And is it bad that I'm glad for it?

Before I can spiral down into a puddle of self-doubt, Liam waves me over for a tour of the training circuit setup today around the gym. Everything from jump ropes and push-ups, which the guys are doing upside down, to rope climbs.

I listen with too much attention, the effort of *not* thinking about Liam's North Vault activities taking up as much mental effort as ignoring the *thump thump thump* of Cullen's knuckles against the leather punching bag. The man is shirtless today, his tattoos glistening with sweat as light and shadow sculpt every muscle. Even standing a few yards away, I can remember inhaling his male musk, which is not altogether different from the thick scent of testosterone that seems to saturate the air.

"Reynolds." Liam's low command snatches my gaze back. Apparently, I wasn't as successful at avoiding staring at Cullen as I thought.

My face is hot as I pull my focus back to Liam, his stern, beautiful face making me wonder what he wears when he goes about his other activities. Which in turn makes me think about what Cullen looks like naked. Jesus Fucking Christ on a popsicle stick.

Compared to the last session, the workout passes uneventfully, with Cullen mostly busy with his own work. The few times he walks over to coach me on proper form, the man remains an utter professional. Not to say he goes easy on me—he doesn't—but he doesn't push me beyond my limits. Not today. And I wish I knew why. Wish that I understood the puzzle that is Cullen Hunt a great deal better than I do.

By the end of the morning, all perfectly aloofly professional, I'm starting to doubt whether our little interlude had truly happened. No, of course it happened. It just wasn't anything more than it was. Which is good. After all, I don't *want* it to be any more than it was. Not with a man like Cullen.

"Do I have time for a quick shower?" I ask, seeing Liam pick up his vibrating phone and curse at the screen, his thumb scrolling violently.

Cullen juts his chin toward the locker room, which I take for his usual gruff male uncommunicative acknowledgment. Right. Taking my duffel bag, I disappear behind the wooden door, exchanging the scent of sweat for a soft lavender fragrance Liam's cleaning crew must have put here. Peeling off my purple crop top and yoga pants, I step into a nicely appointed stall and tip my face up to the hot stream.

I've just soaped up my face, my eyes scrunched against the soap, when I hear the soft whisper of an opening door. A moment later, a cool breath invades my steamy stall, cutting across my skin. Snapping open my eyes, I see the flawless tattooed perfection of Cullen's bare frame. Ink-covered biceps and triceps glisten shamelessly with sweat, his wide pectorals and the defined ridges of his obliques more fitting for a sculpture than a man. My gaze dips to the V of muscle below his navel, where a trail of light-blond curls runs to his thick thighs…and other things.

The soap stings my eyes from staring for so long, and I thrust my head back under the spray. That was stupid of me, and it makes me pissy toward him. "Wait your turn."

He doesn't respond. He just closes the distance.

"Cullen—" Blinking through the water, I find myself trapped in his gaze, my body zinging awake to his clean, spicy scent. Despite the steam, my mouth dries, my breath catching as my pulse picks up speed as I crane my neck to look up at him.

Instead of speaking, Cullen lowers his face, licking at the collection of droplets covering my naked shoulders. The lap of his tongue along my skin sends jolts of need through me, my sex clenching hungrily before my thoughts can catch up to reality.

Pushing me backward until my knees bump into the bench here in the stall, he envelopes me in his arms, protecting my back and shoulder blades as he sits me down hard onto the smooth, high tile seat. Cullen's green eyes, the same ones that barely acknowledged my existence for the whole morning, now flash with a possessiveness that sends arousal and indignation through my blood in equal, furious measure.

"Who do you think you—" I start to protest, but his mouth takes mine before I can finish.

I taste toothpaste and heat and everything that is Cullen Hunt. Feebly, I try again to push him away, only to feel my whole core flame with desire as he turns the kiss hard in retaliation. The demanding, unyielding intensity of the connection becomes some wild, living thing that drives away my better reason.

Dropping his hand beneath my thighs, Cullen reaches up from below and impertinently grazes the inside of my sex. Bringing out his hand, now thickly coated in my betraying glistening wetness, Cullen lets out a predatory growl.

I forget to demand answers as to why he's in here. Forget the objections that have been swirling on an endless loop through my mind these past days. Forget any rebuff or argument I know I'll fool neither one of us with.

ALEX LIDELL

Whatever magic Cullen Hunt has over my body, it's started, and I can't stop the ride. Don't want to.

With me seated on the high bench, Cullen fills all of my vision as he looms over me, his calloused hands sliding across my wet stomach and rib cage to fondle my breasts. Teasing my nipples into hard points, Cullen pinches them just to the edge of pain that has me writhing against him, the moisture dripping from my core having nothing to do with the spewing showerhead.

An uncontainable moan rises through me, only Cullen's suckling on my tongue keeping the sound from carrying across the entire gym.

The guys. Shit. Pulling my face away from Cullen's, I glance frantically at the locker room door. The *women's* locker room door.

"Mmm," he says, the devious self-satisfaction on his face flickering through the steam. "Better keep your voice down if you don't want them to hear."

Smirking, I reach over to cup his balls in my hand, the thick sac heavy against my hand, the shaft already hard and pulsing. Gripping my wrist, Cullen pulls me away from his vulnerable cock and—grabbing my other wrist into his same palm for good measure—pins my hands above my head. The position exposes my breasts, and I gasp as Cullen crouches before me. His mouth descends to my jaw, my neck, nipping and licking his way down my collarbone and cleavage until it's my erect nipple that is fully in his mouth, pulling it inside even farther.

As Cullen draws the flat of his tongue across the sensitive tip, I feel jolts of need shoot from my aching breasts all the way down to my sex. My hips buck, my hands pulling at the restraint that has no give. Somehow, that wrenches the heat inside me another notch and it's all I can do to stay quiet as Cullen switches his attention to my other breast, the tip of his tongue outlining it in perfect pant-inducing circles.

Lowering my hands, he places each on his muscled shoulders and grips my chin between his thumb and index finger. "Keep your hands here." The warning in his raspy tone vibrates deliciously

176

along my nerves. "Or else I'll make use of mine all over that gorgeous ass."

I glower at him, my sex pulsing with need so badly that I can't think straight. Raising a warning brow at me, Cullen trails his thumb down my rib cage and navel, halting just where my panty line normally sits. He caresses me back and forth in horizontal strokes, so, so close to where I want him. Need him. And yet not deigning to actually go there.

My toes curl, my hands digging into his shoulders.

"*Cullen*," I warn him.

He sends me a devious quirk of his lips and backs away.

I release an indignant noise at his retreat, but the man doesn't go far. Instead, his palms skid to my inner thighs right above my knees. Without any subtlety at all, he shoves them wide open and dips his head between them.

I cry out, no longer caring about staying quiet, as he lets his forceful tongue loose all over my folds. It's a good thing my ass is planted on the high shower bench, or I might slide right down to the floor.

"Quiet," Cullen orders, punctuating the command with a tiny bite on the inside of my thigh that nearly has me coming right then and there. My hips buck so intensely that Cullen's grip on my thighs tightens into immobile iron bands, his overpowering strength demanding that I endure every moment of his teasing.

I whimper as his long vertical licks become faster and faster, and just as my pleasure starts to zoom upward, he enters me with two fingers. My channel clamps around him in approval, my nails digging into his shoulders mercilessly as my need ratchets up and up and up toward the inevitable climax.

I realize that he's stopped licking only when I feel his lips close tightly over my swollen clit. Tightening his hold on me, Cullen gives one quick nibble before sucking with so much pressure that it almost hurts. But then, the edge of pain morphs to blazing pleasure, my orgasm driving me up and up before plummeting me into a mind-blowing abyss.

Again. And again. The shock waves of pleasure rake through

me, Cullen extracting each new wave with the plunge of his finger inside me until my core is cinching down and pulsating. As I slump breathless against the cool tiles, Cullen backs out into the locker room, leaving me aching at his departure.

Fortunately, he's not gone for long. When Cullen steps back in a moment later, he already has a condom out of its packaging and is rolling it up his substantial length. Gripping my hips, Cullen lifts me to my feet and props me against the wall of the shower stall. Guiding one of my heavy legs around his waist, the man plunges inside me in one swift motion. Even through the still lingering haze of my climax, I feel myself stretching, widening to accommodate the great length of him inside me.

With Cullen's mouth beside my ear, I hear his breathing accelerate into an almost desperate huff. He judders forward into me, thrusting and advancing with powerful strokes that send shock waves of rising pleasure through me.

Again. Again. Again.

Thrust. Thrust. Thrust.

My breathing grows ragged, my body rousing despite itself as his pulsing cock hits something deep inside. Looking up into Cullen's face, I watch the water frame his powerful square jaw, his tense forehead as he meets my gaze head-on. The desire and need flashing in his eyes send a wave of sensation through me that's as powerful as the one rushing from down below.

My mouth opens, his descending on it savagely. Deeply. I taste myself on his tongue, feel his groan reverberating through every fiber in my body. His cock gives a final throb inside me as if my body is milking him dry. When he reaches between my legs to brush his thumb over my singing clit, I sink my teeth into his shoulder just to keep from keening as the pleasure takes me.

We stand like that for a few moments, his muscles trembling while mine melt against him, his cock still in my channel as we recover.

"Cullen?" Liam's voice cuts through both the bathroom and my haze.

I freeze, my hands tightening on Cullen's shoulders.

Cullen tips his head back. "Yeah?" he calls without a care in the world.

"Need to show you something," Liam yells back.

"In a minute."

Running his thumb along my cheekbone, Cullen opens his mouth as if to say something, but then steps away without speaking. Still mute, he pulls me back under the spray, soaping me up and rinsing off the soap bubbles with typical Cullen-like intensity. Settling me back on the bench, he disposes of the condom and begins to take care of his own shower.

I know I should leave. Should hurry to towel off and get decent, but I don't. Instead, I sit and watch mesmerized as streams of soap run along the grooves of Cullen's chiseled form, the tattoos shifting as the muscles flex beneath glistening wet skin.

I think I should say something. But I don't do that either. And neither does he.

CULLEN

*C*ullen knifed up in his bed, the movement violent enough to send both his king-size pillows careening to the floor. Sweat dripped from his forehead, his chest feeling as if a vise was cinching tighter around it with every rapid breath. Flinging his legs over the side of his mattress, he gulped down air and attempted to swallow. He had to struggle to do it, and the motion alerted him to the rawness of his throat.

Despite knowing exactly what he'd find, Cullen pressed his fingers against the radial pulse and glanced at the clock to count the beats. Yeah. Pounding away at one eighty. He *had* to calm down. Forcing himself to slow his inhales, he focused on the here and now. An empty room. A blank wall. A tick-tock tick-tock of the wall clock. The clean smell of soap wafting from the sheets. A few minutes later, his breathing began to even out, but the feelings of panic and uneasiness remained. He rubbed his breastbone and closed his eyes, only to peel his eyelids right back open again.

Shutting his eyes only made the nightmare images flash in exaggerated technicolor, and even though they'd been mere flickers, they still left him feeling nauseated.

Good fucking morning.

Cullen glanced up for long enough to register that the sun had started to rise, sliding into his room through the slight parting in his curtains. His alarm clock showed that he had at least two hours before he'd need to be in the office, though. Thank God. He stood, feeling vaguely headachy, and headed into his attached bathroom.

Grabbing the plastic cup he used to wash out his mouth after brushing his teeth, he filled it to the brim with cold water and guzzled it down. Then, he did it again, feeling parched. Fuck. He almost felt like he was coming down with something, but he doubted he was so lucky. No, this was just a side effect of waking from a bad dream, something he'd done many, many times.

Too many times to count, really.

Yet, recently, he'd had more than his fair share—as if his mind was making up for the interlude it had taken during the two nights Skylar had shared his bed. His cock twitched as he recalled the different side of Sky he'd taken in the shower three days ago, the way the streams of water slipped around her luscious breasts while her sex clenched with pleasure.

Damn it, apparently it was possible to have a panic attack and an erection at the same bloody time.

Doing his best to clear the mud and *other* things from his brain, Cullen thought back to last night. Did he forget to take his prazosin? It'd become such an automatic habit of his that he had to think hard to recall whether he'd stopped to knock back the pill or not. But he'd gotten a fresh cup from his kitchen last night—the small clear cup he held right now—so he knew he had. He always took his meds.

It was disconcerting to think he might be backsliding. Maybe he needed to get with the doc and look at the dosage again, even if it meant enduring another lecture about shoulder surgery. Prazosin never got rid of his nightmares completely, but the past week was the worst he'd had since getting back stateside. And tonight's... *Jesus*. There'd been the usual bright explosion followed by acrid choking smoke. Shrieks of pain and fear. Lots of blood. A child no longer breathing. Bar had been there, as he often was. Yet this time, Sky had been there too, yanking a little girl from his arms. Yelling that it was all his fault. That he'd killed them. And then she was the one dying.

Which was impossible. That hadn't been how things had gone down at all, but in his unconscious state…

Goddammit.

His heart rate, which had been starting to slow, was pounding too fast again. Dropping his head into his hands, Cullen forced himself to take more deep breaths. Why wasn't he calming down? Concluding that a cold shower might help, he hopped under the punishing ice-cold spray, his gaze catching a golden bottle of shampoo that certainly wasn't his. He must have grabbed it from the shower at Liam's place by accident.

Without thinking through what he was doing, Cullen seized the bottle and flipped open the cap, taking a whiff. Passionflower filled his senses. He knew it was passionflower specifically because it said it there on the side of the bottle. It was funny. He didn't even know what a passionflower was, yet the fragrance suited Sky so well. As did its name. He'd never known any woman as passionate as Skylar Reynolds. And those times she'd shared his bed, he'd awoken peacefully.

Maybe she'd be a better cure for his PTSD than his prescription drugs. He'd certainly never told anyone else about the content of his nightmares. But when Sky asked, it seemed…right. Safe. And it could never happen again. Afghanistan was Cullen's burden to carry, not hers. His father had been right—Cullen dragged violence and destruction with him wherever he stepped. The least he owed Sky was to not expose her to it.

So long as they both enjoyed it, occasional sex was the most he could allow himself. Fortunately, Sky seemed to be of the same mind. At least her body certainly was.

Turning off the shower nozzle, Cullen wrapped a towel around himself and stepped out of the shower just as his phone rang. Snatching the thing from where he'd left it between the two sinks of his vanity, Cullen hit Answer without bothering to look at the caller. "Hunt."

"Cullen?" Catherine. *Shit.* "Is something wrong?"

He should ask the same question of her—if she was calling before he even arrived, that didn't bode well—but he didn't know if he could do it just then without biting his assistant's head off. "What is it, Catherine?" Still too snappish. Dammit.

"I'm afraid I need to take a personal day. I have a family emergency."

"What happened?" he asked, finally sounding more human. "What can I do?"

"You can calm down, for starters," Catherine said sternly. Apparently Cullen hadn't quite schooled his tone as well as he thought. "It's a normal people emergency, not world war three. My daughter is ill and I need to take the grandkids today. I know we're behind—"

"Take all the time off you need," Cullen said. He'd cut her off, but at least he no longer sounded like some pissed-off hothead. Catherine was the most dependable employee on the planet, and the last thing she needed was his problems.

"Thank you," she said. There was a pause, and he braced himself for her to inquire about his shitty attitude. But thankfully, she didn't. "Hopefully, it'll just be for today."

"You take as much time as you want, Catherine." He pinched the bridge of his nose. He needed to say something more lest the woman made herself sick trying to be in two places at once. "In fact, call Skylar Reynolds. She's a quick enough study and may be willing to cover."

"Thank you, Cullen," she said again before disconnecting, her voice infused with more gratitude than he deserved for just doing the right thing.

Tossing the phone back onto the vanity, he reached for his towel, only to have the damn electronic contraption start up again. This time, he had enough sense to check the screen before hitting the answer button. "Yeah?"

"I've got something you want to see," said Liam.

"I highly doubt it."

"It's about Reynolds." Liam paused. "I got her background file back."

Forty-five minutes later, Cullen strode past the bustling reception area toward the elevator, barely saying hello to Rachel before heading into his office.

Liam was already waiting. Seeing Cullen, the former SEAL swung his legs down from where he had them atop Cullen's desk and stood, the leather portfolio in his hand looking ominous.

"Are you about to tell me our little dispatcher is wanted for murder somewhere?" Cullen demanded, taking his seat, the chair reclining slightly beneath the force.

"No. But I will tell you to be careful." Opening the portfolio, Liam spread several sheets over the desk, his finger tapping against the first one. "Skylar Deanna Reynolds, daughter of Grace Reynolds and Sergeant Patton Reynolds, US Marine Corps. Father's military record is sealed, but Lucy, one of my data miners—"

"Your hacker, you mean."

Liam lifted one shoulder. "Eh, potato potahto. Anyway, he lost his shit on some civilians overseas and should have been dishonorably discharged, but the corps ended up sweeping it under the rug and basically sent him quietly home."

Cullen's jaw tightened. "I take it he packed the violence with him?"

"So far as I can tell, she was in every emergency room within a seventy-five-mile radius from her place as a kid. They rotated to try not to go to the same place too many times in a row. The bastard eventually died, but then she hooked up with another asshole who wasn't too unlike Daddy. Jaden Something."

"By hooked up, you mean—"

"That she's engaged, yes. Or was. Until just a few months ago."

Engaged. Cullen tried and failed to feel nothing at that word. Sky had never mentioned being engaged. Not that she owed him an explanation of anything since they weren't even together but...well, it seemed like the kind of thing that might come up.

Unless it was being hidden on purpose.

Cullen tapped a finger on his desk, pulling himself together enough to work through what Liam was saying. An unstable ex-military father. A similar fiancé. "So you're telling me she has a thing for violent military assholes like me."

Liam's eyes flashed. "Not like you, Hunt."

Yeah.

"Anyway, that's not what actually has me worried. It's what finally happened at the *Manhattan Post*, where she and Jaden were working. She's there for about a year, new and hungry for a break. And then Fleet Week comes, and she decides that maybe the military owes her for all the trouble. So she gets into a private event at one of the dives, claims some marines assaulted and attempted to rape her, and writes the kind of exposé that would be front-page news and get Fleet Week banned all in one go. Except she gets caught and fired instead. Becomes a persona non grata in journalism. Hence—"

"Hence her working for *Denton Uncovered*." Cullen shook his head. Bullshit. It had to be bullshit. Skylar was tenacious and smart and too damn stubborn and reckless for her own good, but she didn't use people for her own gain, and she certainly wouldn't invent a crime. "If she claimed someone tried to assault and rape her, I fucking believe her. In fact, I'm not sure I like you even implying otherwise."

"Cool the hell off, asshole," Liam snapped. "You want someone to tell you what you want to hear, get a whore. All I have are facts. I don't know what happened, but I know that instead of going to the police with her allegations, she went straight to the editor, nearly destroying four careers of boys with impeccable records. This is what it all looked like."

Liam pulled out a series of photographs showing Sky dancing happily, the guys' hands all over the same ass that Cullen lusted over. And unlike the semifrightened glances Sky gave Cullen, she looked carefree in the pictures. Laughing. Throwing back drinks. Nothing like the Skylar Reynolds that Cullen knew. Or thought he did. The one he'd confided his nightmares to.

Liam leaned his hip against Cullen's desk. "Also, this was a private event no reporter should have had access to. She used her fiancé Jaden—he's a former marine—to get in. Jaden is the one who turned her in, by the way. He'd been there too and contradicted her version of the events. And…there is one other thing."

Cullen felt his whole body tense. "What?"

Liam sighed. "This is the part that's utterly unofficial, and I only have it because of Lucy—the paper did a covert drug test, and Skylar came up positive. They never told her, of course, but it did go to credibility."

"No fucking way." Cullen shoved the papers back at Liam. "Look at me and tell me you believe a word of what you're implying."

"That an ambitious young reporter who couldn't get a break used her fiancé to get into an exclusive venue, partied a bit, and then painted everything with a sensationalist brush? That her story happened to be exactly the kind a newspaper would eat up, while conveniently retaliating against the military types who'd hurt her all her life? That she now feels comfortable working for *Denton Uncovered?*" Liam sighed. "I don't know what to think. But as the head of a security outfit, I'd tell you not to give her access to any files Peterson may have an interest in, lest she decides she doesn't like you either."

Heat rose through Cullen's blood, his already short temper flaring as he slammed his palm on his desk. "I'm telling you, she wouldn't use me or the Rescue to ferret out information for Peterson. I know it in my gut."

Liam leaned in, his dark eyes hard. "You willing to risk Addie on that gut of yours?"

"I don't have to," said Cullen. "Everything to do with Addie goes through my private accounts. As for me, I don't discuss Addie's business."

"Hmm." Liam gave him a hard stare. "Sounds bulletproof."

SKY

*A*fter hanging up the phone, I leaf through the three pages of notes Catherine had dictated to me when she asked me to cover her post for a few days. She truly is a one-man—er, woman—army when it comes to keeping Cullen's admin in order and, though I'm technically doing her a favor, I'm absurdly keen on doing a good job.

Checking the time, I pull myself out of the velvety armchair—it constantly amazes me how much nicer this place is compared to my old flea trap—and eye the coffeemaker. Fifteen minutes before having to leave the apartment gives me just enough time for another cup. I'm just finishing pouring the black goodness into a mug when someone knocks on the door.

"Who is it?" I call.

"It's me, Lar baby. Open the door."

My hand jerks on my coffee cup, the hot liquid scalding my skin and staining the sleeve of my white blouse as I set the cup down on top of the shoe shelf and crack open the door without disengaging the chain. My chest is tight, my pulse jumping at the sight of jet-black hair, tight camo fatigues, and a familiar muscular physique. Our relationship had had its ups and downs from the beginning, but it ended with a bang after he'd cajoled me into going to one of the military parties during Manhattan's Fleet Week. He'd promised me an opportunity for an exclusive story. Instead, he'd gotten drunk with his marine buddies, left me to the wolves, and then got me fired for trying to reveal the truth. "What are you doing here, Jaden?"

The man holds out a pint of Ben and Jerry's Cherry Garcia and two plastic spoons. "Can I come in?"

"I'm going to work." I start pushing the door closed, but Jaden gets his boot-clad foot in the way.

"Then at least let me put the Cherry Garcia safely in the freezer. It's innocent." He gives me one of his patented Jaden grins, the one that used to lull me into just enjoying the moment. Or into forgiving him. Though, for the life of me, I can't figure out why he'd even want to bother now. The engagement is done. We're done. He taps the tough leather toe of his boot almost shyly against the floor. "Five minutes. I promise."

I glance at the clock, doing quick mental gymnastics. I can't wait the bastard out, and if I don't let him in, he'll just accost me in the hallway. At least this way, I'll avoid a scene. "Five minutes."

I open the chain and step aside as Jaden lets himself in, taking his shoes off without me having to ask. When he extends his arms toward me for an embrace, however, I step back and cross my arms. "What do you want?" I demand. "And how did you find me?"

Jaden holds up his hands, the pint of ice cream still in his large left paw. "No hugs. Message received and understood, ma'am." Walking around me, he puts the ice cream in the freezer as if the place were his. "The how first—good old investigative journalism. Between seeing your name on the byline in *Denton Uncovered* and what your mother told me of your sugar daddy, it was easy enough. As for the why…" Jaden slips his hands into his pockets, his head and shoulders curling in a slight *aww shucks* motion. "I miss you. The break we took made me realize a few things. Among them, just how good I had it with you, baby."

I pick up my coffee, my hands tightening around the cup, my heart still pounding in my ears. "First off, we didn't take a break. We broke up after you decided that the reputation of your precious marine corps was more important than the truth. And second, I don't have a sugar daddy." I spit the last two words with venom built throughout the years of my childhood.

Genuine surprise flickers over Jaden's face. "Come on, now, Lar. I might be a jerk, but I'm not an idiot."

No. He isn't. Jaden had always been attractive, with his tan skin and muscled shoulders, but it was his intelligence that had drawn me to him to begin with. Intelligence and a keen, instinctive knack for observation. For asking the right questions.

Jaden sprawls uninvited on my couch. "You're telling me that your salary at *Denton Uncovered* pays enough to cover this three-thousand-dollar-a-month rent?"

I bristle. "Not that it's any of your business," I say, indignation gaining the better of me, "but I have two jobs. And I don't pay three grand a month, because this place is rent controlled. Speaking of my jobs, I've got to get to one of them now. You've had your five minutes, Jaden. Are you going to keep your word and leave?"

Getting up, Jaden tugs down on his camo shirt to straighten it. It shows off his defined chest, but I'm no longer interested. "I'm out as promised." Walking to the door, he grabs a card from his inside pocket and scribbles on the back of it. "Listen. I'm staying in Denton Valley for a week, covering the WorldROCK climbing competition since there's a cash purse prize. Do me a favor—just think about things. Maybe come out with me to interview some climbers. It's your thing more than mine anyway. Here's my cell." He holds out the card, which I make no move to take. Jaden sighs and sets it down on my little marble entry table.

"You know, if I were an investigative journalist worth my salt, I might check out whether Pine Towers even actually has rent control," he adds, already halfway out the door. "I might also ask myself how much this furniture here might cost. Hell, if I were an investigative journalist, I might try to figure out who actually owns the apartment I live in and maybe I'd ask myself what's in it for the owner to have me staying here for next to nothing. But that's me. I work for the *Manhattan Post*, not *Denton Uncovered*."

I wait until Jaden is out of my house before managing to uncurl my fingers from around my coffee mug, my hands shaking. The asshole. The absolute *asshole*. I'm not all that surprised that he found my address—he's a journalist, and I'm not hiding—but the fact that he had the gall to show up here after what happened at Fleet Week? That's low even by his standards.

Beep. Beep. BLEEEEEP.

The alarm on my phone scares me out of my skin. I curse. No matter how much my mind and pulse are currently whirling, I also need to get to work before I'm late. *Focus now, Sky. Meltdown later.*

~

FIRST THINGS FIRST, I tell myself as I weave between a group of employees crossing the lobby and nod my hello to Rachel-the-perfect at reception—I'm *not* Cullen's sugar baby. For one, I work for a living. For two, I'm not now nor would I ever be in my mom's version of a relationship, making my life about some rich jerk's fantasies. And for three, things between Cullen and me are…complicated.

Having not been back to the Trident Medical Group building since my interview, I'm taken in by its grandness all over again. The reflective exterior façade. The expansive airiness of the lobby inside with its marble columns and black tile floors and people moving all about. And yes, the giant mural of children's handprints. The artwork reminds me that whatever else Cullen might be, he also has a kind enough heart to spend a certain portion of his funds on philanthropy. I step aboard the elevator heading for the seventh floor. Cullen's floor. The fact that I'll be working two doors down from Cullen all day doesn't escape my notice either. That, or the other bit about him owning this whole place.

Despite myself, I've been unable to resist cataloguing every behavior of his I notice. The differences in how he speaks to Catherine as opposed to Rachel as opposed to me. How he relaxes with Eli, Kyan, and Liam, but tenses up at the mere mention of Frank. It's a fascinating phenomenon. No one riles Cullen like Frank Peterson does.

In short, the mystery surrounding Cullen calls to me like a siren—which is perhaps a hazard of my profession. I long to learn more about his childhood, his military service, his life. I want to know what makes Cullen tick. But most of all—though I know it's none of my business—I want to smooth Cullen's nightmares away.

And yes, the chance to work in Catherine's office may be a window into the man's life. I've no intention of abusing the position, but anything in plain sight is fair game.

As with the last time I was here, the CEO's suite is much emptier than I expect—though given Cullen's addiction to privacy, I'm not surprised that he prefers his staff to stay behind their own doors. Following Catherine's directions, I go to her door and enter a code into the outside keypad to let myself inside.

Settling behind the computer desk, I pull out my notes and spend a lot more effort than is fair on *not* thinking about what Cullen might be doing in his office just now. Whether he might pop in to say hello. Whether the hello will be anything like the shower—

Shit. I shake my head to cut off that thought before the heat low in my body manages to soak through my panties. So not going there. Especially not now. Firmly taking myself in hand, I take in the clean lines of Catherine's office. The mauve walls are so different from the rest of the building, and so are the myriad plants lining one window. Though her desk is walnut and extremely tidy, there's a row of silver picture frames, all showcasing an auburn-haired woman and her two children. These must be Catherine's daughter and grandkids. It's a unique behind-the-scenes foray into the life of Cullen's number one assistant.

If only I could have the same sort of foray into Cullen's life.

Picking up the next set of bills from Catherine's inbox, I frown at the note in Cullen's writing instructing they not be paid from corporate funds, and marking an alternative account instead. Flipping through the invoices, which cover everything from flower delivery to sizable mortgage payments all to the benefit of Adrianna Peterson, I feel my stomach churn. Having paid at least a dozen different charities on Cullen's behalf this morning, I know the man gives generously, but these bills seem…personal. As does the bank account I'm to pay them from.

All for Adrianna Peterson.

He came back here because of Addie. Bar's Addie. Jaz's words from our climbing day float back to my mind. *They all go way back.*

My stomach twists again, though I know full well it's got no right to. So Cullen came back to where Addie Peterson, his best friend's widow and probably his own longtime friend, was left behind. And he wants to take care of her. What's so wrong about that? It doesn't mean there's anything more to it. And even if it did…Cullen and I aren't a couple. A few hookups give me no claim over the man. Cullen has a full right to see whichever women he wants. Maybe that's what he and Frank are at each other's throats about.

Except why didn't Addie come to Eli's barbeque, then? a small voice inside my mind insists. *Is he hiding her from you, or you from her?*

Stupid. I'm being stupid.

Firing up the computer, I log in to the account and pay the invoices as instructed, the checks for roses and gift cards to Bloomingdales and even utility bills flying off to their recipients in cyberspace. I even get into the rhythm of it—all until I come to a receipt for a special-order engraved heart locket from Tiffany's Forever Love collection and feel bile touch my throat all over again. No matter how I twist it, Forever Love isn't the kind of thing a guy gives to "just a friend." And yes, it's also just too close to the kind of thing my mom likes to brag about.

After living through my teenage years with a mother who fastened herself to well-to-do men as a means of income, I despise the whole setup with a primal hatred that goes well beyond rational thought. My mom might imagine herself a star in her own *Pretty Woman* fantasy, but I see her for what she is: little better than a prostitute hanging on a sugar daddy's elbow.

No, scratch that. My mom has nothing on prostitutes. Prostitutes don't lie to themselves about what they're selling.

Is that what Addie Peterson is? Cullen's kept woman? Or is she just one of a bunch he keeps around, primed with trinkets from Tiffany's, for when the need strikes him?

Unable to help myself, I scroll down Cullen's account history, not even sure what I'm looking for. What smoking gun. And then my heart stops, my fingers clicking the mouse dumbly as I stare at the six-hundred-thousand-dollar check written out to Pine Towers, my apartment number right in the memo. No. No, no, *no*.

Clicking out of the bank account, I rest my forehead on my hands, my mind racing to work out what I've just seen. What to do about it. Jaden had been right, my apartment is no more rent controlled than my expensive furniture or the designer clothes Cullen's handed me. All because I'm...what? The most indispensable temp he's ever had?

I straighten my back, forcing myself to take deep breaths despite the heat now filling my blood and rushing to my face. Whatever else, I owe it to Cullen and myself both to have a conversation instead of burying myself under a heap of circumstantial demons. Standing, I straighten my blouse as if it were some kind of armor and march myself down the hall.

My pulse thins for a moment as I lift my hand to knock on Cullen's heavy door and stutters again as he opens it, his pressed white shirt and fitted suit making his muscular silhouette into something that belongs on a *GQ* cover. I swallow. I've seen the man naked, for God's sake. Have done a great deal more than look when he accosted me in the shower. And yet, walking into his office, with him fully dressed, the scent of starch from his French-cuffed shirt mixing with his spicy male musk, it feels more intrusive. More intimidating.

"Skylar." Cullen's green eyes are cool. Unreadable. "What can I do for you?"

Well, no better time than the present. "You told me my apartment was rent controlled," I blurt.

"It is." Nothing changes about Cullen's face, not even a flick of a brow.

My gut tightens. "You paid six hundred thousand for it. I saw the check, Cullen."

"Correct. I'm the owner, and I rent control it." He straightens his cuff, paying too great attention to the gold square. "Why were you looking through my personal account?"

I swallow, the air between us vibrating with the same quiet tension that lines Cullen's beautiful face. Despite his seeming to focus on his task, the fabric of his suit shifts over coiling muscles. Though he's made no sudden moves, a shiver runs down my spine.

"Several of the invoices in Catherine's inbox had a note with the name of the account they should be paid out of." I raise my chin. In for a penny, in for a pound. "Adrianna's invoices."

His face darkens. It's the kind of reddish hue I've seen before, the kind that says I'd hit on something he was hoping I wouldn't. He shifts his weight. An off-balance Cullen—now there's a sight I don't remember ever seeing before.

"Is there something I should know about Adrianna?"

"The note with instructions was from me to Catherine—I hadn't realized she'd not taken care of them yet," says Cullen. "Or that you'd imagine detouring into a personal account was within the purview of a temp's duties."

A temp's duties. Right. A reminder of my place. Yeah, I know the trick. A good defense is an offense that grinds you beneath a combat boot. He knows what those receipts are about, what story they tell—and yet, it's *my* fault for finding him out.

It makes sense, really. Hadn't Jaz and I just discussed the fact that Cullen doesn't date? That he's this rich, ridiculously handsome man who's always lived alone? Logic says he satisfied his sexual needs *somehow*, and apparently, I'm the how. Well, me and Addie Peterson and who knows who else.

The worst part isn't even that Cullen keeps sugar babies. It's that instead of seeing the world with eyes wide open, I've been busy blindly dissecting my feelings for this man. Jaz might believe all her speculations about how good Cullen is, and where his heart must be, and how us getting together—really together—would be such a wonderful idea. But me? I should have recognized the script from my mother's playbook. I've certainly seen it enough.

If Cullen is following the playbook, his next move will involve going after me on something unrelated. Diverting the conversation to examine and pound some defect of mine, until it's me who's begging his indulgence and understanding.

At my sides, my hands tighten into fists, my heart pounding hard enough against my ribs that I feel each dull thump as I behold the man I've recently slept with in a whole new—unflattering—light.

Cullen's face lifts, his mossy-green eyes flashing with a fury that makes me back up a step despite myself. "I'm still unclear how you went from paying invoices in an inbox to sifting through my personal finances. I'm quite certain I left no bills for Pine Towers for Catherine to cover." His voice tightens like a spring. "Is this your version of investigative journalism? Get to what you want to know by any means you find convenient? Paint front pages with your version of the truth?"

And there we go.

"What the hell are you talking about?" Red flashes at the sides of my vision, the twist of the conversation giving me whiplash despite my having expected it. "No. Never mind. I don't even want to follow that line of questioning. What is it with you attacking my career and journalistic ethics every five minutes?" The words spill from me in ragged bursts, barely audible over my heart's pounding. "I respect your career choice. Do me the courtesy of respecting mine."

Cullen's hand grips the doorframe, his knuckles blanching. "Why did you leave New York?" he asks. "Why did the *Post*, a well-respected publication, *fire* you outright?"

My eyes widen. Jaden. Apparently, I wasn't the only visit the asshole had made today. What the hell had he said to Cullen? Would Cullen have believed him? My gaze falls on Cullen's wall art, the few pictures reflecting memories of the good old days in uniform. There's a bond between soldiers, my father used to tell me. A bond that's forged in war and that makes everything in the civilian world look like a washed-out shadow by comparison. *Don't imagine yourself in some competition with the Marine Corps*, he'd growl, grabbing me by the front of my shirt, his breath reeking of cheap beer. *The corps long since won.*

"I was fired because military buddies sweep things under the rug for each other." I shake my head. "I don't know what you think you know, but during Fleet Week, I went—"

"I know where you went." Cullen cuts me off before I can finish my sentence. Reaching into his drawer, Cullen pulls out several photos and scatters them over his desk. The same photos that Jaden had produced to the *Post*, though he'd been passed out drunk most of the night. Me dancing with the marines. Bile rises up my throat as Cullen stares at the pictures that tell so little of the truth. "Tell me that you didn't trade on a personal relationship with your *fiancé* to get entry into an exclusive venue, all while intending to write a story about it."

"Of course I wanted to write a story. Why the hell else would I have gone to that shithole dive in Manhattan?" I force myself to not look at the photos. To ignore the emphasis on the word fiancé. To stick only to the truth. "But Jared knew that was why I was going. It was his idea."

"It was his idea to set up his war buddies to be humiliated on the front page of the *Manhattan Post*?" Cullen's voice drops dangerously low. "I don't like being lied to."

"I don't lie, Cullen. Not in person, and sure as hell not in print." I huff. "I obviously danced with the marines. It was a party. What I didn't do was give up my right to stop. I was there for a story, not an orgy. Jaden had—"

"What drugs were you on that night?" Cullen demands, interrupting me.

"What?" I shake my head in bewilderment. "None."

"Stop it, Skylar. You said you don't lie, so tell me the damn truth. *All* of it."

I lean forward toward him. "I. Took. No. Drugs. Not that night, and not any other night."

"You're sure?" he asks quietly. "You don't lie, and you don't take drugs."

"You wanted to know why the *Post* fired me," I say through gritted teeth. "Are you going to listen to the answer, or does throwing random accusations at me scratch the itch enough for you?"

"I already have all the answers I need," he says. "Excuse me." Turning away before I can say a word, he takes out his phone and presses something on his speed dial. Instantly, a picture of a drop-dead-gorgeous brunette with bright, attractive eyes—like a cross between the pretty girl next door and a supermodel—flickers across the screen.

"Fuck you, Cullen Hunt," I whisper, backing away from the door. My eyes sting, my voice threatening to break if Cullen asks whether I really made up allegations of assault and attempted rape just to have a story. But maybe it's worse if he doesn't even bother to ask. If he believes Jaden's version just like the USMC and the *Post* did.

"Addie, glad you picked up," Cullen says, shutting the door in my face before stepping deeper into the office to finish his conversation.

I'm numb as I stand there for one heartbeat after another before finally turning on my heel. Striding back into Catherine's office. Fishing a blank sheet of paper and pen from the drawer.

Then, collecting what's left of my self-respect, I write out the only response Cullen's behavior warrants. Two words only, in short, bold strokes.

I quit.

30

SKY

*S*itting at my desk in *Denton Uncovered*, I stare at my police response time story from hell. The more I dig into the research on crime incidents and police response times, the more variables keep popping up, like the heads of some kind of exotic monster. Yes, crime is higher in the poorer neighborhoods. And yes, responses are scarce. But so are the calls to the police to begin with. In fact, best I can tell, the PD only found out about my own incident the same way Cullen had—from the local news. But *should* they have known? *Should* a vehicle have been stationed somewhere? I don't know. The only definite correlation I've found so far is one between mistrust of police and socioeconomic levels. I read another set of interview notes with contradicting statements and growl in frustration before sticking the whole package into the drawer. This story is too important not to be perfect, and my mind isn't working properly right now.

Pulling up the story Frank is actually paying me to write, I concentrate on finishing the last three paragraphs on WorldROCK without inhaling too deeply. *Uncovered*'s workroom reeks of old coffee and that bug spray Frank wears all the time, the scent permanently clinging to the old checkered couch. I don't remember the smell bothering me so much before, but now, a week after I've walked away from Cullen, I miss the Rescue's caustic antiseptic smell.

"Yoda is at WorldROCK?" Stopping too close to me, Frank leans over my shoulder to peer at the screen.

Shit. I've misspelled yoga three times. No, four. Plunking in the correction, I hunch my shoulders a bit, making sure my red drape-neck shell isn't showing too much cleavage. If there's one thing I seem to attract in my life, it's males who have boundary issues. Or PTSD. Or a controlling nature. Or a bent for dishonesty. Yep. I sure can pick 'em.

Ignoring my attempt to pretend he's not there, Frank walks around to lean a hip against my desk before folding his arms over his suit-clad chest. It still amazes me that he would purchase such an expensive suit—even if it is silver with weird lapels—and not have it tailored to fit him correctly. It looks too tight around his middle and yet gaps awkwardly at the shoulders. He simply doesn't have the body for how this suit has been cut. He needs a more athletic build to pull it off. Broader shoulders and a narrower waist. A build like one of the Trident gods. A build like Cullen's.

Damn it.

"You're working hard, honey," Frank says.

"I am." I always work hard. But that's something few people ever seem to notice.

"Over this past week, especially. You know I don't pay by the hour, right?" The last is said with a touch of something that smells suspiciously of empathy. Apparently, I look pathetic enough to stir even Frank to pity. "Something going on at the Rescue?"

My jaw clenches, my hands furiously typing some bullshit note about the weather. Then I misspell *yoga* again and close my eyes, hoping Frank doesn't fire me on the spot for incompetence. The way my week has gone so far, he just might. "I wouldn't know. I quit last week."

Frank stays silent for a moment, the lack of sardonic remarks making my skin crawl. Then he lowers his voice. "Did that bastard hurt you, Sky?"

"What?" My head jerks up, something inside me protective of

Cullen even as the rest of me wouldn't mind casting a stone or five. "Why would you think that?"

"Because the best indicator of future behavior is past behavior. And Hunt was violent even before he went into the military." Frank shakes his head. "I'm telling you, the armed forces draw those sorts of overbearing personalities like bees to honey. The muscle-bound hotheads who live to work out and blow shit up. Can't say that I understand them, but I've seen plenty of it."

Frank pauses, watching my face too intently for comfort. "The most fucked-up thing I find about dealing with those types is that their mood swings come in bursts. One moment, everything is going fine, and the next, they explode like a grenade." Frank scoffs in that annoyingly condescending way of his, but I find myself unable to really disagree.

It's too close a description to the men I know. My father. Jaden. His friends. Cullen.

"Anyway..." Frank stands, straightening his ill-fitting suit. "I know you and Hunt were...close. If he went haywire, I didn't want you thinking it had anything to do with you. Because it doesn't." His hand brushes my shoulder and stays there. "If you ever need a safe place to stay, or just someone to grab dinner with and talk, I'm here."

Wait, what? I carefully remove Frank's hand from my shoulder, but he doesn't seem to notice my discomfort. In fact, his attention is already on where *Denton Uncovered*'s photographer is going over photos from WorldROCK's opening night, the yoga instructor in her leotard posing prominently against the mountain range backdrop.

"Dyer!" Frank calls, sauntering the photographer's way. "Need to talk to you. First, get rid of that time-stamp gibberish on the shots and second..." The men disappear into Frank's office, their voices muted behind the frosted door while I stay where I am, still staring at the photo on Dyer's screen. The one with the mountain range in the background.

Colorado is beautiful, and I do love climbing. Yet there's no denying it's a dangerous sport. Kind of like fucking your boss. Sometimes the excursions just don't end well.

I tap the pen against my notes. Shit. If I'm getting pep talks from Frank, of all people, it's time to go home. Well, to *the apartment.* I can't think of the place in which Cullen had set me up like a goddamn mistress as "home." I've been doing my damnedest to find another place to live, and maybe this weekend I finally will. I'll miss the view, but it will be nice not to be reminded of Cullen with every swipe of my gaze.

I still can't believe how long it took me to figure out what the Cullen situation was truly all about. I guess better late than never, though.

WITH HIGH HOPES for weekend apartment hunting firmly in my imagination, I set about packing my nonessentials the moment I get back to my place. Since I rarely cook, I begin with my meager amount of cookware, setting my two saucepans and single skillet into one of the handful of boxes I grabbed from beside a dumpster at a local housewares store. I've just discovered a way to make the lids fit—flipping them upside down—when my phone rings from the kitchen counter.

It's such a lovely counter too. A rich tan granite with golden speckles throughout. But as lovely as it is, it's not worth selling my soul to Cullen Hunt. Fuck him and the medical transport he rode in on.

"Hi, Mom," Holding the phone between my shoulder and ear, I retrieve the pint of Ben and Jerry's from the fridge. The one Jaden had brought is long gone, but I've been investing in chilled dairy all week.

"Lary darling," she exclaims way too loudly. "Oh, wait one moment, let me take off this earring. The diamond solitaire is very pretty, but it's just too thick not to hurt my ear with this phone." There are some clunky noises. "There, that's better. How are you?"

Does she care? It's doubtful. I'm already regretting picking up. I have packing and apartment hunting to do. "What do you need, Mom?"

"Who says I need anything? Can't a mother contact her daughter without a reason?" Not in my experience. But then she sighs. "I'm sorry, Lary. I wanted to let you know that Greg and I are home now. I'd love for you to visit. I miss you."

Home. As in the Big Apple. As in the same city where I suffered all my worst memories. "I'm in the middle of an upheaval at the moment. This isn't the best time."

"What sort of upheaval?" she asks, and wow, she even sounds sincerely curious.

"Some employment challenges." What else is new? "And I'm having to look for another place to live." In other words, my life is once again in shambles.

"Oh, Lary, that's perfect." She sounds delighted. "What I mean is, it's a perfect time for you to come home. Move in. I'd love to have you, and Greg has lots of connections. He's already told me that he'd be happy to help you find a job that's right up your alley."

I must be bad off, because the idea actually appeals to me. For a whole minute, I consider it. Not having a rent. Not having to pound the pavement searching for a journalism position where I can showcase my writing skills. Having someone to come home to. All I'd have to do is my part in whatever version of house Greg feels like playing.

"Doing tricks for men's treats is your thing, Mother, not mine." The words come out harsher than I intend, my chest clenching at the silence that comes over the line. I open my mouth to say something, but no words come. Not after one breath. Or two. Or five.

I'm already going to disconnect the line when my mother's voice fills the other end. "First of all, Lary, don't you dare judge me or how I've managed to feed and raise you. Don't you dare say that I'm only allowed to be happy with your approval. And if you must know, things with Greg are different—he wants a family. He wants to meet you. The fact that he happens to come from money doesn't say anything about him as a person. Any so-called journalist would've checked her sources before drawing conclusions."

The line goes dead before I can answer, my gaze resting dumbly on the dimming screen as I tell myself that I'm not a horrible human being. In my defense, we've never exactly had a healthy relationship. Maybe it's because my father was such a goddamn tyrant who beat her into submission any time she dared to defy him, but growing up, all my mother's energy went toward dealing with him rather than raising me. I thought things would improve after my dad passed away, but that's not what happened. There I was, eleven years old and desperate to be loved by the parent who remained, but instead, Mom acted as if I wasn't even there. She started to actively date, treating me like a piece of luggage that got in the way if not put into storage with neighbors or friends or in an empty apartment.

I can't even tell whether her invite home was because she actually missed me or to satisfy some whim Greg the current sugar daddy had. God knows she'd do more than that so long as he supported her. She'd had so many of these men over the years that I lost count. When shit hits the fan, my mother's solution isn't to become stronger or more independent, it's to find a man to sponge off.

And I'd very nearly made the same mistake.

Returning to my—to *the*—kitchen, I cinch up the first box with packing tape, finishing just as my phone rings again. Mom again? Nope. Jaz. It's her third call to me this week, and, the coward that I am, I can't bring myself to face her. Tightening my jaw, I hit the Ignore button as quickly as I can.

A second later, my phone pings with a text message.

If you don't pick up, I'll assume you're in trouble and call Rescue.

Shit. Snatching up the phone, I dial her number before she decides to make good on the threat. Knowing Jaz, she just might.

"Hey, girl!" Jaz's forever cheerful voice fills my ear. "Where the hell have you been? And did it involve booze and sex?"

"No and no." I clear my throat. "Listen, Jaz, this isn't the best—"

"Blah blah blah. Open the door." A knocking sound accompanies the demand, the *rap rap rap* beating out a march against my doorframe.

I open the door, jumping out of the way as the petite force of nature that is Jaz bursts into my place, a six-pack of raspberry beer in hand. Jaz, clad in tight ripped jeans and a very cute bright pink jacket, sets her sights on my boxes, her intelligent gaze putting two and two together. Then her dark eyes jump to mine, her curly hair swinging. "Oh. My. God. You're moving in with Cullen the broody and didn't tell me?"

"No!" I rub my face. I'm not sure what I expected Jaz to know given that I hadn't talked to her or anyone from the Rescue crowd since walking out of Cullen's office a week ago, but I thought she'd at least know we'd parted ways. My face heats, guilt rising inside me. I should have told her myself. Should have bitten the bullet and at least explained what happened, extending her the courtesy of deciding for herself whether she still wanted anything to do with me. Well. Time to face the music. Straightening my spine I turn to face Jaz fully. "I'm not with Cullen. Actually, I'm not with the Rescue anymore at all. I'm sorry, I thought one of the guys would have told you that much."

Jaz's eyes widen, and for the first time since meeting her, I find her speechless. "They didn't," she says finally and quite unnecessarily. Moving as if through sludge, Jaz sets down the raspberry beer on the kitchen counter, pops off the caps, and extends one bottle out to me. "No, in case I haven't mentioned it before, my brother is an utter shithead. I mean, it's one thing to go all radio silent on his personal stuff, but this? I'm going to throttle him in his sleep. Now, tell me what happened. Because if I'm gonna be throttling one Trident god in his sleep, I can do two."

Ignoring the raspberry beer Jaz is still holding out to me, I rush forward and wrap my arms around her, relief filling my blood. I don't know what I did to deserve a friend like her, but I'm more grateful than I've got words to explain. "I'm so sorry," I mutter into her shoulder, my body trembling for a few heartbeats as I will myself not to cry. "I was afraid that…"

"That I'd take the boys' side? Like hell." Jaz gives me a reassuring squeeze before gently pushing me away, her bright face full of concern. "What happened? Did Cullen hurt you?"

I flinch. "He...he was well on his way to a pay-to-play arrangement with me, and I was too stupid to see it until I was paying some personal bills for him and discovered that I'm not the only woman he's got this setup going with. Remember when you said he came back here for Addie? Well, you were right." In quick strokes, I fill Jaz in on what I'd found on the computer and how poorly my attempt to talk to him about it went. "I think that may be one reason he hates me working for Frank Peterson. I mean, if he's shagging both Peterson's sister-in-law and his employee, that's not a good look."

Jaz taps her finger against her beer. "I wouldn't have figured Cullen for the sugar daddy type, to be honest. But he has issues. And from what I've, errr, accidentally overheard, he's been off the past couple of weeks. Has he called you?"

I shrug a shoulder. "I don't know. I blocked his number. The guys' too." I swallow, looking out the window. "I've been in bad relationships before. It's for the best this way. Trust me. I'm moving on. As soon as I find a place, I'm moving out of this golden cage. So, well, boxes."

Jaz sets down her beer with a resounding click. "Then I will help you pack. And move. And unpack somewhere close by. But with all the time I'll now be saving you, you have to come cheer for me at WorldROCK tomorrow. Deal?"

Well, I can't in good conscience say no to that now, can I?

31

SKY

*P*ulling into the parking lot staging area for WorldROCK, I can't help being impressed by the sheer number of people who are already here despite the early hour. There are sponsor tents with everything from trail mix packets and electrolyte mixes to sales booths with high-tech gear. A large tent on my left sports an overhead registration sign, and a smaller one on the right is trying to both hand out press credentials and answer the slew of general information queries from competitors, spectators, and family members. Swerving around the meandering crowds, I wave hello to *Uncovered's* own James Dyer taking a few establishing shots of the bare ridge, and check the listings for Jaz's route.

The haggard girl at information hands me a map of the trails and tells me Jaz has already hiked out to her staging point. Half a mile later, I find Jaz under the wide span of some golden aspen branches that sprawl a few paces away from the rock wall. Jaz is bent over her pack, every inch of her and her gear emblazoned with the Arc'teryx bird skeleton insignia. Leaning against the aspen's white trunk, I tilt my face up to the sky and breathe in the fresh Colorado air. It's beautiful here, all azure heavens above and forestry and craggy mountains spreading before us. Breathtaking. Invigorating.

Peering over at Jaz, I find the same placid look on her face as I'm sure I'm wearing on mine and feel like I've known her forever.

"Next year, you're competing," Jaz informs me.

I'm about to agree when a familiar voice cuts in from behind me, making my mouth dry out on the spot as I turn to see Liam not ten feet away. Dressed in a tight Rescue shirt, tactical pants, and enough rescue gear to stop a train, Liam's beautiful face is hard as stone. "Number 479. Jazmine Keasley," he reads off his clipboard. "Gear safety check."

"Liam. What a lack of pleasure to see you." Striding up to the Trident god, Jaz lays her equipment out for the official safety inspection. Liam goes over each piece of gear. Yes, of course the Tridents would be here. All four of them.

Crap.

I step backward until my back hits the stone, my chest tightening. We aren't in middle school where I could pretend Liam is invisible, but I have nothing I want to say to the man either. Nothing I want to hear him say to me. Pressing my hand into the rock, I wonder idly if perhaps the mountain might turn me invisible if I beg it hard enough.

"All checks out. Good luck on your course." Taking a bright red sticker, Liam initials it before attaching it to Jaz's bib. Then, just when I think I'm safe, his hazel eyes lift toward me. Hard. Unreadable. Demanding. "Skylar."

"Liam." I refuse to flinch away from his gaze, but I have nothing to contribute to the conversation either. Fortunately, I've got Jaz the Incredible by my side.

Stepping right between Liam and me, the petite woman manages to somehow glare down her nose at the former SEAL. "Skylar is not *gear*, asshole. I realize the difference between women and objects might be too difficult for your brain to handle, but just trust me on this one."

Liam gives Jaz the coldest glare I've seen from him yet. "When I need your opinion on something, Jazmine, you'll be the first to know."

"Is this jerk bothering you?" A second familiar voice whips me around, this time to find Jaden striding up in all his broad-shouldered glory, a media badge swaying on a lanyard over his gray shirt. Without waiting for Jaz's answer, he scoffs at Liam's uniform. "Move along, ambulance driver. Can't you see that lady doesn't want you here?"

Liam actually snorts with amusement, though there's a gleam in his eye that promises a very painful end to any escalation. Which is the last thing we need right now.

"Everything is fine, Jaden," I say, stepping away from the stone. "We have everything under control. Liam was just leaving, and you should too."

Jaden's gaze slides to me, his smile broadening in an open boyish grin. "Lar, baby. I didn't expect to see you here." He glances at the mountain. "But I'm glad you are. Though you should be climbing, not watching."

My stomach churns uncomfortably. Jaden is lying about being surprised—I can read it in his face. He knew I was here today. Just as he'd known where I live. Whatever else, the asshole has always been good at getting information and even better at crafting it into an engaging story. It was one of the things that attracted me to him in school. Now, he just seems like a master manipulator.

"I'm *not* your baby," I tell Jaden firmly. "And no one is bothering us except you. Please leave."

Jaz, seeing my reaction, loyally offers Jaden a death glare.

Jaden smiles wider. It's the type of grin that reminds me of a shark, all sharp teeth and dead eyes. "I'm on assignment, babe. You know that. And I'm not about to leave without an interview with last year's female champion." The asshole offers Jaz a half bow. "Jaden Harris, the *Manhattan Post*. Ms. Keasley, what can you tell me about your competition this year? Do you expect another easy win as you had in Memphis at the High Point climb?"

He did his homework.

Jaz looks Jaden up and down as if singularly unimpressed with what she sees, and I have to stifle a laugh. "What I expect, Mr. Harris, is that you leave as my friend asked you to."

"Your friend and I happen to be engaged," Jaden says. "Please accept my apologies for any confusion. It's been a stressful few months. Pre-wedding jitters and all."

My mouth drops open. In the corner of my vision, I see Liam stride away, my mind trying like hell to absorb Jaden's claim. Engaged? What reality did that come from? Probably from the same reality that told him it was okay to lie passed-out drunk while his marine buddies assaulted me, then take *their* side of the story.

Jaz narrows her brows. "Seems to me Sky doesn't agree with that assessment."

"Of course I don't!" I wheel on Jaden. "What the hell are you talking about? We aren't engaged. We aren't together. We're one more word away from a restraining order."

"That's enough." Stepping toward me, Jaden has the audacity to wrap an arm around my shoulders, his posture rigid. "Come on, Lar. It's time for us to leave."

My heart pounds. I go to pry his arm off me, the thick muscles unyielding. "I'm not going anywhere with you," I snarl. My blood rushes into my ears. "Let me go."

Jaden's face goes from hotly furious to cold as ice. "That wasn't a question, Skylar," he says quietly, emphasizing my name in a way that makes my stomach drop. I know that tone of voice. Know the consequences it brings. My body longs to freeze, to do nothing that might provoke him further. As I've always done.

But if training with Cullen and the guys taught me one thing, is that doing *nothing* guarantees only one thing—being knocked none too gently onto my ass. My hand closes into a fist.

Apparently of the same mind, Jaz grabs a quickdraw carabiner off her harness. Holding one end of the quickdraw, the petite climber whips the other end across Jaden's cheek, the metal hitting flesh with a resounding *whack*.

Jaden grunts.

Shoving me away from him, Jaden grabs Jaz's arm, yanking so hard that she screams.

"Jaden, stop!" I shout at him, even though I know he won't. My pulse pounds, Jaz's cry echoing through me. No. *Hell* no. This can't happen. Not again. "Let her go!"

Jaden raises his free arm, ready to backhand Jaz across the face. He isn't even paying attention to me. He knows I'm irrelevant. Or was.

Not letting myself hesitate a moment longer, I push off my toes and jump right on the bastard's back. "Let her go!" I shout again, trying to snake my arm around the asshole's neck and choke him the way I saw the guys do in Liam's training.

Jaden jerks in surprise. Curses. For a second, I think I'm making progress, but Jaden recovers before I can finish the move.

Spinning around violently, he flings me off him and into the trunk of the tree behind me. I hit the unforgiving surface with a dull thud, my vision refocusing to the sight of Jaden looming over me.

"Did you just attack me, bitch?" Reaching down with his great maw of a hand, Jaden grabs me by the neck and forces me upright.

I gag, unable to draw breath, my nails scratching fruitlessly at his muscled forearm. My heart races, my blood rushing so swiftly that I feel dizzy, my whole world narrowing to Jaden. Spots flash before my eyes when suddenly, another very large figure materializes right in front of me. I only have a split second to register the danger in those mossy-green eyes before I'm free. Before Cullen Hunt grabs Jaden and slams his face into the thick, wide bottom of the aspen.

I fall to my knees, gasping for breath.

Cullen yanks Jaden back for a fuller swing, my ex barely managing to save himself from a broken skull by getting his arms up in time. Blood streaks down Jaden's face, staining his gray shirt and cracked press credentials that somehow still swing on the red-spattered lanyard. High-pitched pathetic whimpers that I haven't heard from Jaden before now escape his throat. "What the fuck is wrong with you, man?"

Cullen releases him.

The moment he does, a familiar triumphant sneer grips Jaden's face. He climbs to his feet, either too oblivious or too dismissive of the wild, rage-filled look in Cullen's eyes. It's the same look that the brute at Hannigan's Pub wore just before going berserk.

Jaden scrubs the back of his hand across his face. "You want the whore? Fuck, she isn't worth—"

Cullen moves in faster than I can follow. Grabbing the back of Jaden's head, Cullen slams it against his upraised knee, a cracking sound confirming a broken nose. Jaden sways, staying upright only by virtue of Cullen still gripping him.

With the next breath, Cullen lands a fist into Jaden's middle. His chest, his sides, his legs. *Thump. Thump. Thump.* I open my mouth to yell, but the sheer brutality of the scene paralyzes my voice.

"That's enough, Hunt," Liam shouts, moving toward the fight as I finally absorb that all the Tridents are now calling for Cullen to stop. "Stand down."

"Commander! Stop."

My throat tightens, my hands scraping desperately against the dirt as I pull myself up.

To my relief, Cullen lets Jaden go, the man barely able to stand on wobbly legs.

Turning toward me, Jaden spits a glob of blood. "This is your fault, you—"

Cullen shoots forward again, grabbing Jaden's shoulders and slamming a knee into his ribs. Once. Twice. When Cullen winds up for a third blow, I think he might kill Jaden outright.

As if having come to the same conclusion, Liam and Eli lunge in to pull him bodily off Jaden. Wrenching Cullen's arms behind his back, the Tridents haul him several steps back, Cullen struggling like an enraged bear in his friends' grip. A few yards away, Kyan rises from where he'd been crouching beside Jaz and—after getting a thumbs-up from his sister—walks over to where Jaden lies curled up in a fetal position.

"Hunt! Hunt, look at me, arsehole!" Eli's screaming into Cullen's face snaps my gaze back to the men's struggle.

Liam now has both of Cullen's arms behind him in an iron grip, Cullen yanking so hard against the hold that I think he might dislocate his own shoulders. His eyes, glassy with pain, stare at something that isn't Colorado while his chest heaves with quick breaths.

I gasp, the scene before me suddenly echoing another time and another room. Cullen in his bed, facing an invisible assault as sweat runs down the grooves of his muscled back, his nightmares gripping his soul. Except there, in that room, I didn't need to rip apart his shoulders to bring him back. Gathering myself, I start toward him.

"Reynolds, stay away." Eli snaps at me with a military harshness I've never heard from the easy-going Trident before. It's my father's tone. Jaden's. It's the tone Liam used at the gym when he struck him so hard that Eli fell to his knees. I flinch away, my hand clenching the hem on my jacket, and Eli nods his harsh approval before returning his attention to Cullen.

I want to run. But the Tridents will hurt Cullen if I do. He'll hurt himself. As if to punctuate my realization, Cullen jerks against Liam's hold. No. I can't let this happen. I hate Cullen. But I… I feel something else for him too.

My pulse racing, I take a step back toward him, bracing myself for Eli's yelling—which comes right on schedule.

"Which part of stay away did you have trouble with?" he shouts at me.

"The stay away part!" I can't believe I'm actually shouting back. Standing up to Eli. That despite my sweating palms and thumping heart, I put my hand on his broad shoulder and push. "You're hurting him."

Eli spins, placing himself between Cullen and me. "He's not himself, Sky. You don't understand. But let us deal with it before *you* get hurt."

I meet Eli's slate-gray eyes, the glimpse of vulnerability and fear in them making my chest tighten. I'm not the only one who's scared for Cullen. Who's afraid of things getting worse. That quickly, Eli is Eli again to me, with his unruly hair and all too human feelings beneath the godlike body. Putting my palm on his chest, I feel the pounding of his heart as I push him gently. "He's not going to hurt me, Eli. Trust me."

Eli looks over my shoulder, probably to get Liam's consent, before stepping back.

Swallowing, I lift my eyes and meet Cullen's mossy gaze, my hands up in front of me with my palms open. "Cullen," I call.

He flinches.

I don't. Moving slowly, I ignore Liam's growl of warning and extend my palm until the flat of my hand cups Cullen's scruffy cheek. "Can you feel my skin?" I ask softly. "Look at me. Do you know who I am?"

Cullen's throat bobs as he swallows, his cheek pressing against my palm. I stroke his cheekbone with my thumb, the muscles beneath his skin coiled tight. Then his body tenses, jerking against Liam's hold.

"Let him go," I order Liam. Not ask. Not plead. *Order.*

And to my utter shock, the SEAL obeys.

Cullen steps forward into my arms, his body shaking as I wrap myself around him, the pair of us sinking to the stony ground. Coaxing his head against my shoulder, I rub small circles on his broad back, his powerful body trembling under my touch.

32

CULLEN

*C*ullen sank to the ground, his world narrowing to a set of brilliant blue eyes, to silky strawberry locks framing a beautiful face. Strawberry—not red or blonde. That was important, as was the scent of passionflower shampoo, which Cullen held on to like a lifeline anchoring him to the here and now. He was in Colorado, not Afghanistan, and the men who'd restrained him were his friends, not insurgents. The flashing lights in the distance were from the sun and clouds, not mortar rounds. Yet Cullen's heart still hammered against his ribs, his breaths quick and too shallow to let him think clearly. He inhaled again, drawing in that calming passionflower scent that cleared away the phantom taint of gunpowder.

He was in Colorado. In Sky's arms—which seemed too good to be true and thus took several more breaths to accept as reality.

And then more reality kicked in—the part where he'd utterly lost it on Sky's fiancé. At least that was what Liam's radio transmission said, though nothing about what Cullen witnessed was fiancé-like. Of course, his own behavior had been nothing short of feral. In fact, Cullen still felt like he hadn't fully regained control even now, his mind and emotions like a grenade with the pin pulled despite the explosion. *Shit.*

Blinking, Cullen pulled away from where Sky still held him, the vivid details of what happened hitting him like ice water. A few yards away, Kyan was walking Jaden away to the medical staging area, Liam checked a small cut on Jaz's forehead, and Eli stood back quietly, ensuring that no passersby came too close. That was good. For the past couple of weeks, Cullen had a feeling that someone was watching him. Dogging his steps. As for Sky... She was still there, crouching on the ground beside him after having walked out of his life.

A familiar, clawing pain raked over Cullen's heart. The same ache he'd woken up to every night for the past week, when he'd jerked awake to an empty bed and unanswered calls. She'd never given him a chance to talk about the argument that had her walking out of his life. He still didn't know whether it was his callousness that drove her away, or the fact that he'd uncovered the truth about her past, which she'd worked so hard to keep buried. Did her fiancé's return have something to do with it? Or some story Frank Peterson had told? Maybe if Cullen hadn't kept cutting her off midsentence in his office, if he'd shut his mouth and truly listened to what she'd been trying to say, things would have turned out differently.

She'd always listened to him, hadn't she? Oh, she might argue, or push back, or disagree—the woman's mind was as captivating as her heart—but she never shut the door in his face the way Cullen had done to her.

He scoffed at himself. She'd left because she was too fucking smart to be anywhere near him. It was his own fault that he'd let himself get too close, as if he didn't know his own volatile nature. He'd never been fit for normal company, and given the last two weeks of spiraling nightmares culminating in unrestrained violence, he never would be.

He rose to his feet, grunting at the sharp stabbing pain piercing his left shoulder.

"Cullen." Sky reached for him, the concern on her face telling him exactly how awful he must look just then. He'd hurt her. He'd nearly killed a man before her eyes, for fuck's sake. Any reasonable person would be halfway to Canada by now just to get away from him. But Sky had always had more compassion than reason, hadn't she?

He stepped back, putting himself out of Sky's reach, though his every fiber longed to feel the coolness of her fingers just one more time, to inhale her passionflower shampoo and let the scent wash away the acrid memories pounding against his mind. Every inch of distance hurt, but it was the least he could do for her. She'd been right to walk away from him, and he cared too much for her to let her undo that decision.

"Don't touch me," he told Sky.

Her hand lowered, but the desperate concern painting her beautiful face did not. "Talk to me," Sky whispered. "You aren't all right. This isn't you."

"Oh yes, it is." Cullen snorted. "If you haven't figured that out by now, then you're either stupid or a liar." Turning his back so he didn't have to watch his words hit her, he walked away from the scene, all his self-control engaged to keep from breaking into a sprint until Skylar Reynolds and the others were out of sight. Once they were, however, once Cullen had only the full range of nature sprawling before him, he *ran*.

Five miles later, the rage inside him still hadn't dissipated. So when he came across a thick, gnarled tree three times wider than him, Cullen reared back and punched it with all his strength. Agony spiraled up his arm, but it wasn't enough to keep him from doing it with his other hand. Only when he'd bloodied both sets of knuckles and the pain had become prohibitive did he cease his attack.

Shaking, he peered at the damage he'd done to himself, both with the tree and when struggling against Liam's hold. Cullen's heart hammered against his ribs, the scent of pine filling his lungs not holding a candle to the calming tang of passionflower that he'd never again inhale without thinking of Sky. His left shoulder wasn't moving correctly, but at least the fury had burned itself out like a fire started with an accelerant, leaving fatigue washing over him.

He hadn't felt steady ever since finding Sky's "I quit" note, but making someone bleed in front of her was a new level of damage. Rubbing his face, he surveyed his position for landmarks and slowly made his way toward Denton Valley. Once he made it back to a paved road, he dialed an Uber, giving the driver directions to get him the hell out of town.

The clerk at the hole-in-the-wall motel off Interstate 25 gave Cullen a wide berth, watching him with an eagle eye as Cullen collected his door key and requested extra towels for the room.

"The police patrol this here place every day," she said, looking over her brown-rimmed glasses, her tone that of a displeased nun. "We may not be a large chain, but we don't stand for any poppycock around here. I thought you should know."

"No poppycock, yes, ma'am," Cullen said, starting to give the woman a mock salute with his left hand. Twelve inches into the movement, the blazing pain that had eased in the car ride returned with bazooka-level vengeance, Cullen's knees buckling beneath him. *The piece of shrapnel. Shit.*

"Sir?" the clerk's tone shifted from condescension to concern. "Sir, do you want me to call an ambulance for you? You're very pale."

Swallowing, Cullen shook his head. "Thank you for the towels," he managed to say without his voice cracking before he headed into his room. It was surprisingly homey. Double beds with matching quilts in a block pattern. Simple maple headboards. A stack of three extra pillows on the table next to the old CRT television set. The place smelled comfortingly like fabric softener. It might not be the Ritz, but it was a hell of a lot better than the stony wasteland he'd slept on overseas.

After taking a quick shower, Cullen sat on the closest bed and wrapped a makeshift sling over his arm, the room swaying gently around him. He'd done it. Exactly what Dr. Yarborough warned him about. But the thought of going into surgery scared him nearly as much as facing Sky ever again did.

Arranging himself as comfortably as he could on the bed, Cullen attempted to get some shut-eye—which refused to come despite his deep exhaustion. Moving on to plan B, Cullen sank into the slightly lumpy mattress and attempted to empty his mind. Bar had been into this meditation crap—had sworn by it, in fact, despite the hazing he took for it—and at this point, Cullen was willing to try anything to get ahold of himself. Staying in this fucked-up state wasn't an option.

That all ended fifteen minutes later when some trucker used his Jake Brakes right in front of the motel. Cullen startled out of his meditative state—not that he'd been in much of one in the first place—his gaze snagging on his lit-up phone. He had it on do not disturb, but that didn't mean anyone had quit calling him. Eli. Liam. Kyan. Even Jaz. Yeah. He wasn't answering any of them. Life would just have to go on without him for a while.

Sky hadn't called. Not that he'd wanted her to.

The phone lit up again just as Cullen had put it away, and he straightened his spine to see who it was this time. Whether it might be Sky, though he didn't want her to call. It wasn't. But it was Addie. Shit. He couldn't ignore her, not with Frank Peterson on her heels.

"Hey, Addie," Cullen answered quickly, before he could reconsider. "You all right?"

"Me?" She sounded incredulous. "Cullen, are *you* all right? What do you need? What the hell happened?"

Fuck. He knew he shouldn't have picked up. "Yes. Nothing. I'd rather not go into it."

"Well, you're going into it whether you like it or not, because I just got a video from Frank that shows you beating the shit out of some guy at WorldROCK. Start talking, Cullen—and don't try to bullshit me. I lived with Bar. I know all the tricks. Did you stop taking—"

Cullen cringed. "No, of course not. I'm fine. An asshole was hurting someone I care about, and that's all it was."

"What are you, twelve?" She sounded exasperated. "You couldn't just restrain him like you usually do and call the police?" She was right, and he had no business arguing the point. Pissed off at himself all over again, Cullen gripped his phone so hard, it hurt his injured hand. On the other end of the phone, Addie sighed. "I also caught sight of Liam holding you back. How's the shoulder?"

"Bye, Addie." Cullen went to hang up the phone, his finger stopping a millimeter from the button. Why would Frank have a video of the fight? More importantly, why would he send the coverage to Addie instead of posting it on *Denton Uncovered*'s channel? Seeing the CEO of Trident Medical Group going berserk was going to hurt share prices. Snapping the phone back to his ear, Cullen heard his tone change. "Adrianna. Did Frank send any instructions along with that video? Did he threaten you with anything?"

"No."

"Addie!"

"Cullen—don't worry about it, okay? I can handle Frank. I'm more concerned about you just now."

"Don't you dare give in to his demands," Cullen growled into the receiver, his pulse picking up all over again. "I'd rather the video go public than negotiate with terrorists. Do you understand me?"

"Did you forget who you're talking to?" Addie's sounded genuinely curious. "Because it will be a cold day in hell before I let you give me orders. You want a say in what happens? Get your ass back here, get your shoulder checked out, and go talk to that girl of yours. Then you can call me."

Cullen opened his mouth to reply, but Addie—being Addie—disconnected the line.

33

SKY

"*A*re you all right?" Eli asks, drawing my attention away from where Cullen's back had disappeared from view a few moments ago. To my right, Jaz is quietly telling Liam off, Kyan having taken Jaden somewhere. A dark ditch, hopefully.

I swallow, Cullen's phantom green eyes still staring into mine, so much vulnerability lurking behind that steely gaze. No matter what he'd said, the pain raking through his body had been too real and too overwhelming for anyone to have to deal with alone. "Is somebody going to go after him?" I ask when I realize none of the men are following after him.

Eli shakes his head. Despite the coolness of the autumn air, perspiration has gathered along his curly hairline. "Not a good idea." His voice is calm but the tightness around his eyes as they flick to the place where Cullen disappeared gives him away. He's worried. "He'll resurface when he's ready."

I snap myself around to face him. "Really? Just like that? You aren't going to help?" I huff a breath, feeling my nostrils flaring in the breeze. Cullen is hurting, has been hurting for a long, long time. "You are going to let him just flounder in the deep end by himself?"

Eli cocks a brow. "You did."

My jaw tightens, Eli's accusation hitting me like a sheet of ice water. He blames me. Of course he does. I don't expect anything different. Bros before hoes and all that.

Guilt rakes through me, tearing at my heart. But I can't, *I won't* apologize for refusing to become my mother. A sugar baby. A pet, bought and paid for, expected to stay blind to other women, to not question the sanctity of the military, to be controlled for the man's peace of mind. Cullen wants me. Sometimes. But he doesn't *need* me. Doesn't trust me with his pain. Or with the truth.

My heart breaks for Cullen Hunt. But my staying with him would eventually tear us both to shreds. I swallow the bile gripping my throat and will my stinging eyes to keep the tears at bay. I... I fell in love with the wrong person. And now, there's no good answer. No solution bar walking away.

I realize Eli's expression has changed just as I hear Liam talking, plainly repeating his question not for the first time.

"I take it you are not, in fact, engaged to Jaden Harris?" Liam says.

"What?" I shudder. "No. I broke up with him before I left New York." A chilly breeze blows over us, rustling the yellow leaves of the nearby aspen as if to help me make my point. "Jaden showed up at my apartment a week ago. Said he wanted me back. I said no and stupidly thought that was the end of it. I was an utter idiot coming here today. I knew he was covering WorldROCK and... Shit, I thought the place was big enough."

"It's not a secret you like rock climbing," says Liam. "If he's the asshole you claim he is, he may have been looking for you all along."

If he's the asshole I claim he is. Brilliant. Even after what just went down, Liam is going to give his fellow soldier the benefit of the doubt, despite the fact that he's a stranger to him. I'm sick to my stomach of my recounts being doubted just because I'm not a penis-carrying member of the military club.

But I guess it is what it is. Turning my back to the Tridents I walk away.

"What happened during Fleet Week, Reynolds?" Liam calls after me. "And don't bullshit me. I run a security company."

I stop and, with my back still to him, smile without any humor. Like a final capstone rounding out the situation, Liam's question falls right into the narrative they all want. And since they do, they can fucking have it.

"I conned my way into an exclusive party, seduced upstanding marines into pawing at me, and then tried to print lies about them to give my career a boost. Got caught, fired, and rightfully blacklisted from the industry." My voice sounds too detached to be mine, but I'm past caring. Past arguing the truth. Whatever Liam thinks he knows about what went on that night, that's what he's going to believe. After walking down this particular road too many times to count, I'm... I'm done. "You run a security company, Liam. Go ask Jaden. He's the one who turned me in. He'll tell you all about it."

This time when I start walking, I don't stop for follow-up questions. Not from Liam and not from Jaz. Not from anyone. Pulling my phone out as I walk, I dial Rush, the cheap-ass phone service provider I'd been using here.

"Rush Wireless," a perky female says on the other end. "Your number has been matched to existing records. How can I help you, Ms. Reynolds?"

"Yes, hello. I'd like to disconnect my service, please."

THE *DENTON UNCOVERED* office is still locked when I get there early the following morning to slip the envelope with my resignation and press credentials under the door. It hurts. Despite the place being an utter sensationalist looney bin, it was still a link in my dream. I thought I could do it, could escape my past and pave a new path for myself. But I was wrong. Because maybe it was never the *Post* or even the Fleet Week fiasco that was the problem, but me. My choices. The people I let myself get close to.

Walking back out to my Corolla, I hunch my shoulders against the drizzling rain, my sneaker-clad feet making slapping sounds in the copious puddles of standing water. It's not a good day to be cold and wet, but the weather cares little for my preferences. Turning on

225

the ignition, I hold my hands in front of the heater to warm them before pulling the throwaway prepaid card I picked up at Walmart.

"Hi, Mom."

"Lary!" My mom sounds too perky considering our last conversation, a television in the background announcing business news that her boyfriend must be watching. New York is two hours ahead of us. "Honey, what number are you calling me from?"

"I—" I swallow a sudden sob. "Mom, I think—"

"Greg," my mom calls out on the other end. "Can you turn the TV down, please? It's Lary."

The noise stops, and this time, I can't contain the sob.

"Lary, what's wrong?" Mom asks.

"You told Greg to turn the news off. Because I called," I say through ragged breaths. "And he did."

Silence reigns on the other end for a moment. "Of course I did. And of course he did. Why is that bad?"

Because you've never done that before, Mom. And you've never been with a man who would care. "Is that offer to come home for a bit still good?" I whisper into the line. "I wouldn't need to stay long—"

"You can stay as long as you like," my mom says firmly. "Oh Lary, we would love to have you. I'm so glad you called. Whatever is happening, we'll get through it. As a family."

A lump forms in my throat, and for the first time in a long time, I want to reach through the phone and hug my mom.

"Do you want Greg to make some inquiries at the local paper? It's not fancy, but—"

"No. No, thank you. Please don't ask me to explain now, but I'm ready for a career change. It'll take me some time to drive over to New York, but I'll try to have some interviews lined up."

"Hold on one moment," Mom says, the muffled sound on the other end telling me she's covering the receiver. A minute later, she returns, clearing her throat. "Listen, honey, Greg is going to send you an email with a contact of his at a physical therapy clinic his friend runs. I remember you used to like medicine before that whole journalism nonsense. Give him a call. Just another name to add to the interviews, okay?"

"Sure, Mom." I force myself to smile at the phone as I say goodbye, trying to tell myself that returning home is not surrendering, but a strategic retreat.

It's ten in the morning by the time I collect all the good boxes I can find from recycle bins and drag them down the hallway toward my apartment. With my hair a mess, my clothes still damp from the sprinkling rain, and cardboard slipping from my hands, I'm the kind of sight that scares off the neighbors. Which makes it especially odd to see a woman still lingering as I approach my door. With her long dark hair and bright blue-green eyes, the woman looks strangely familiar, though I'm certain we've not met before.

"Excuse me, are you Skylar Reynolds, by any chance?" she asks as I stop in front of my door to pull a key from my back pocket. "I'm sorry to accost you like this. I tried calling, but the number I had wasn't connecting. I'm Adrianna Peterson. Do you have a moment?"

SKY

*A*drianna Peterson. For a second, I simply stare at Cullen's gorgeous sugar baby and wait for the red-hot burst of jealousy-infused scorn to descend on me. But nothing comes. It seems that time has passed. I care about Cullen—there's no getting around that no matter how much I want to—but I have too much self-respect to remain in his world any longer. Maybe my mother is right. It's not fair of me to judge other people and their choices. And maybe if I'd been in Adrianna's shoes, I'd act no differently. But I'm not her. And I'm not Cullen. I'm Skylar Reynolds, and I will always fight to stand on my own, no matter how hard the wind blows.

So, as I consider this drop-dead-gorgeous brunette standing at my door requesting entry, I do the only thing that makes sense.

I let her in.

"Excuse the mess." Moving an armload of packing tape and Bubble Wrap from a pair of chairs, I create a small, human-appropriate space in the kitchen. Beyond us, boxes are stacked everywhere around the furniture that will stay here. I'm not taking anything with me that I didn't bring in myself.

"You're leaving." Adrianna's bright blue-green gaze washes over me, and I feel vaguely curious. How much does she know of me? Does she know that we've been sharing Cullen's resources as well as his body?

"Yes," I say.

"Shit." Adrianna bites her lip. "I got it all wrong."

I snort. "I imagine that you got *it* quite correct, actually. But not to worry. As you see, I'm leaving Colorado altogether. Cullen is all yours." *Bank account and all.*

Adrianna frowns at me as if I've grown a third head, managing to look beautiful even doing that. "Cullen is all mine?" she says slowly, tasting each word. "Wait. You seemed familiar with my name, but I'm not sure I am who you think I am."

I rub my eyes with the heels of my hands, too exhausted to play games. "Why don't you start at the beginning. Since you showed up at my door, I expect there's something you wanted to say."

Adrianna nods, gathering herself. "I do. Well, ask, mostly. I'm worried about Cullen. Seriously worried. And from what little I've gathered—the Tridents are a tight-lipped bunch of asses—I thought maybe you had something going with him and might be able to help... But it seems you may not want to touch Cullen with a ten-foot pole right now, so the question is moot." She swallows, wrapping a lock of hair around her finger. "Since I'm really good at jumping to conclusions today, I might as well keep my foot in my mouth. I'm not involved with Cullen. I'm just saying that in case that changes anything for you."

I hold up my hands. "Adrianna, seriously, you don't owe me any explanation or justification. I know Cullen came back to Denton Valley for you. And—good, bad, or indifferent—I saw the bank statements. The flowers and the mortgage payments and the gift cards and all. More to the point, I've seen how his face lights up when he's talking to you. If you want to sleep with Cullen—"

"With *Cullen?*" She looks horrified at the prospect, her forehead marred by three deep creases. "Like have sex with Cullen? *Gross.* Not that he's not attractive, if you like his type, but I'm not into men who are blond and pushy as all hell. I like 'em dark, sweet, and willing to worship the ground I walk on." Her features suddenly become downcast and wistful, and I realize that she's thinking of Bar. "More to the point, sleeping with Cullen would be like incest. He's like a brother to me. A big, overprotective, bullheaded brother whom I love deeply. And who needs my help right now."

She stands and pushes in her chair, squeezing the back of it so tightly, her fingers blanch for a moment. Then, just as quickly, her back straightens, a mask of strength and composure slipping over her features. "I'm sorry. I shouldn't have come. Please be safe wherever you're going."

I stare at her back, my chest tight, my thoughts racing too quickly for me to keep up with. I still don't know what to make of a great deal of Cullen's bullshit, but the journalist in me warns that once a set of facts are torn apart, all others must be examined. More to the point, if Adrianna is right about Cullen being in trouble—

"Wait!" I call, my words hitting her in the back as she reaches for the door. "Can we start over? If Cullen is in trouble and I can help before I leave, I'd like to."

She turns slowly, her features now guarded enough to make heat touch my cheeks. She'd come with nothing but openness, and I didn't exactly present the most trust-inspiring front. The teapot chooses this moment to beep its readiness, and I pull out two mugs and the last pint of Ben and Jerry's from the freezer, waving the ice cream at her like a bribe. "You came all this way, and I have treats."

Her gaze narrows at the Cherry Garcia. "Unfair tactics, not that it makes me immune to them." With a small, hopeful smile, she returns to my kitchen table, pulls out her phone, and hits Play, the familiar fight from WorldROCK filling the screen. The footage starts with Cullen in midswing at Jaden, fading away with Liam and Eli both wrenching Cullen's arms behind his back to keep him from ending the asshole permanently. By the time the video is done, so is Adrianna's hint of a smile. "Something is wrong. The Cullen I know doesn't go off on people for no reason—and he hasn't been home or in the office or anywhere I could find him since. Idiot that I am, I told him about the video. Now I'm afraid that if we don't find him first, he's going to do something he'll very much regret."

My brows narrow as I rewind the video, something about the footage—besides the sight of Cullen half killing Jaden—bothering me. "The part you're not seeing is Jaden having attacked me a few moments before the fight," I say, taking the phone from her hand to force myself to review the horrid scene again. Swallowing down the bile that rises up my throat, I reach for my journalistic objectivity as I study the frames.

There had been hundreds of people milling about the various routes, so in theory, anyone could have happened to be around to capture the footage. Except the photograph here had caught the fight as if the photographer had been right there in the midst of it, which they *couldn't* have been. The onlookers—whom I'd largely ignored—had been on the outskirts. "Whoever took this had a very good zoom lens," I say, freezing the recording in place.

"It's amazing what cell phones today can do," says Adrianna.

I shake my head. "Most cell phones can take high-quality video, but it takes more than a good phone to get this. Look at the lighting. With that aspen tree there, there were hotspots and shadows all over the place, but the colors all look balanced here. Also, look how stable this is. No nauseating movements like most people holding a phone would have, especially when tensions are high. Whoever took this watched this scary, unpredictable moment and stayed as cool as a cucumber."

"So a professional, then?" Adrianna says thoughtfully. "Not out of the realm of possibility given the number of reporters at WorldROCK."

"But rather convenient to have been there at the right time and place. The climb hadn't started yet. There was no reason to expect something to happen."

I pinch my fingers together on her screen and push them outward to enlarge a section at the bottom. Numbers. A date-time stamp and some other nonsense that probably makes sense to whoever took the shot. Just like the type of marker Frank's always on James Dyer's ass about.

I frown at Adrianna, the question that I should have asked first only now coming to mind. "Wait, who sent this to you?"

"Frank Peterson. Bar's brother. He's been after everything Bar left me, and my house is the holy grail for him. The way the legalities are structured, he can only get it if it goes into foreclosure, so he's been trying to get me to skip payments—mostly by ensuring I bleed money somewhere. But Cullen—"

"Cullen has been picking up the tab, hasn't he?" I say, squeezing my eyes together as the pieces from the bank accounts and Cullen's words snap together into a full picture. It wasn't his disrespect for my career choice that made him protest my working for Frank, it was Frank himself.

Adrianna nods. "Frank sent me this today with a threat to make it public if I don't stop accepting Cullen's help. Not that I haven't tried to tell Cullen to stand down, but this takes it to a new level. It's just a house. I'm not letting Cullen get destroyed over it. Not if I can help it."

"How exactly are you going to do that?" I ask. "If I know him, Cullen isn't going to stop making the payments."

"Because I submitted my notice to the bank this morning," says Adrianna, her voice wavering for the first time. "He can't pay for a house that doesn't exist. I know this doesn't take Frank out of the picture, but whatever is going on with him right now, he doesn't need this adding to it. Looking at that video... I think he's hurt too. There's been a piece of shrapnel in his shoulder that he's been delaying surgery on—and I think that fight did a great deal more damage from the inside than the outside. If I'm right, he's hurting like hell right now, and that's not going to make him more agreeable, I can tell you that. I would normally go to the guys, but with something like this, I can't be sure one of them wouldn't go break Frank's skull in on principle. I'm looking for a de-escalation, not an avalanche. This is all my fault."

She tips her face up to the lights, her eyes glistening, and my chest tightens. Reaching out my hand, I place it atop Adrianna's trembling one. "None of it is your fault, Addie," I say, hoping I'm allowed to use the nickname. "Everything about this smells of a setup. A couple of days ago, Frank mentions Cullen's violent tendencies to me. Which means they were on his mind for some reason. Then a pro photographer, just like the one who works for Frank, happens to be there right when Cullen loses his shit. Frank gets the video within hours. It's almost like he knew to send his guy there."

Addie scrubs her face dry. "You think this Jaden is working for Frank too? That he provoked the fight?"

"I don't think they know each other, but I've been wrong before." I pinch the bridge of my nose. "Either way, this flaming disaster we're in, it's not a natural fire. It's one where someone has poured gasoline all over the place. We need to find Cullen."

"Any ideas?"

"No, but…" I tap my finger on the table. "I'm about to suggest something that I would totally kill him for doing to me—but I'm rather sure that if the situation were reversed, he'd do the same thing without a second thought."

Addie leans forward, her eyes sparking. "Please tell me you've implanted a tracker in his ass."

"No. But I do remember his bank account log-in. Wherever Cullen is, I bet he used his credit card." My fingers run across the keyboard, my heartbeat picking up speed with each stroke. Finally, something about today feels right. After all, turnabout is fair play, and I'm no more leaving Cullen alone than he'd left me when I headed to that house on Lincoln Drive.

Cullen and I may be destined to be apart, but I'll be damned before I leave him in pain.

"Hey, Addie," I call over my shoulder, copying down the motel address. "Can you drive? I need to do some research on the way."

35

CULLEN

*C*ullen sat behind the large table that passed for the Motel Colorado's writing desk, his laptop screen flashing with unread emails. Knowing his lack of fitness for human company, he'd paid last night's off-duty maintenance guy to pick up a laptop, clothes, medical supplies, and a few other things for him at the large box store a few miles down the road. Once Cullen got online, though, he'd wished he hadn't. Hell, he'd wished he'd dropped his phone down the toilet and had a few more hours without learning that Sky had broken her lease and was moving out.

He'd already known he'd lost her from his life, so why did this news hurt so fucking much? He scrubbed his face, irritated at finding prickly stubble covering his cheeks. It was his own fault for allowing himself to imagine her stabilizing presence, that oasis with her strawberry-blonde hair scented with passionflower shampoo, was anything but fleeting. He opened the next email in the queue.

According to Kyan, Sky had given papers to the leasing office sometime yesterday, and even Jaz didn't know what Sky was doing. Not that she'd tell them anything if she did, but she might have at least let him know whether Sky was all right. Instead, all Cullen knew was that she'd disconnected her number altogether. Fuck.

ALEX LIDELL

Of course she wasn't all right. Getting attacked did no one any
favors, and Sky had been traumatized in the past—that much had
been clear from her reaction to simply watching Eli take a few shots
in a friendly sparring match. And if that wasn't enough, Cullen had
lost it right before her eyes. No wonder she was packing.

"You're damaged fucking goods, Cullen." Cullen heard his father's
phantom voice in his memories, spitting out the words. *"If you have
any care for your mother at all, stay the hell away. That's the biggest Mother's
Day gift you can offer."*

Cullen scrubbed his face again, this time with more vigor. He
needed to get ahold of himself. Sky wasn't his. But he could at least
ensure that wherever she was going, she was all right. After
everything he'd put her through, it was the least he could do. The
least he *should* do.

Opening a fresh email, he put Liam on the line.

What do we know about the asshole who attacked Reynolds?

Unsurprisingly, the answer came within minutes. Liam had
plainly anticipated the question and was just waiting for Cullen to
ask. The bastard knew him too well. Just as he knew not to press
Cullen for a location.

Jaden Harris. Investigative reporter for the Post *and Reynolds's ex-fiancé.
He was the one to report her for allegedly falsifying the Fleet Week story. Made
some calls. He did a stint in the marines and called in a bunch of favors to keep
his ass from getting a dishonorable discharge for—you guessed it—assault. At
least two women have filed restraining orders against him now. One of those
during Reynolds's engagement period, which I don't imagine she knew about. He
went after one of the ER nurses, btw, was on some meds and thought the woman
was Reynolds.*

Cullen's hands curled around the edge of the table. Harris
seemed to think Sky was some kind of property of his. He'd keep
going after her unless something was done. A rush of fury hit his
nerves in a cascade that made his breath halt, every instinct inside
him demanding he find the fucker and put him down. Permanently.

Yeah.

Once he could breathe again, he forced himself to hit Reply
instead of smashing the motel mirror.

Look more into Fleet Week?

This time, the answer came within moments. Liam was already on it.

Meanwhile, Jaden Harris needed to be watched. Dialing the hospital administrator directly—being the CEO had its perks—Cullen had a clerk check which ER the man was in.

"None, sir," the young woman on the other line reported. "He checked out against medical advice early this morning. Did you—"

Cullen hung up, his heart pounding. He knew Harris's type. The bastard would be looking for Sky, and with her phone disconnected, there was no way to even call her. Shooting a text with the news off to the Tridents, Cullen got to his feet, a sting of pain zapping through his shoulder despite the sling. The guys would help, but it would be a cold day in hell before Cullen sat this out on the sidelines, hoping that nothing bad happened to Sky. That someone else would do something. No. One way or another, he was finding either Sky or Harris.

Grabbing a button-up shirt from the pile the maintenance guy had picked up for him, Cullen braced himself to plunge his bad arm into the sleeve just as a knock sounded at the door. The image of the bespectacled clerk from last night popped into his head, the one who didn't know whether to call the police or an ambulance for him and probably wanted to ensure he'd not carried the TV out the window to the nearest antique shop. Housekeeping was more likely, but he didn't need them either—as the DO NOT DISTURB sign on his door indicated.

The knock came again.

"Not a good time," Cullen snapped.

"No kidding," a female snapped right back at him. Addie? Pinching the bridge of his nose, Cullen walked over to the door and pulled it open to discover not one, but two women staring at him.

Well…fuck.

For the first time in a long time, he didn't know what to do or what to say. Adrianna's features showed her ferocity as she stood there with her hands on her hips, but Sky looked conflicted, every line of her beautiful face intently focused on him. Cullen's heart stuttered like a damn schoolboy's before starting into the kind of gallop he could usually control even in the midst of a firefight. Yet he had no defense against this woman, standing there in dark-wash jeans and a soft white jacket.

"Have you done anything stupid yet?" Addie asked, letting herself inside. "Or did we get here in time?"

Cullen didn't answer. Didn't even move beyond shifting his weight to let the women by. With his focus pinned on Sky's brilliant blue eyes, he feared that something he might do would make her turn and leave. And that scared him shitless.

"Going somewhere?" Addie called from behind him, her silhouette picking up his shirt in his peripheral vision. "Say, to see Dr. Yarborough?"

Cullen couldn't turn toward her. Couldn't look away from Sky. "Jaden Harris signed out of the ER," he said quietly. "I'm *not* going to let him hurt you, Sky. I promise you that. I know you don't want to be anywhere near me, but—"

"Shut up, Cullen." Swallowing, Sky stepped into his room, her eyes narrowing on his sling. On the blood pooling beneath his skin where the shrapnel had been dislodged. Slender fingers with light pink polish extended toward the bruising, Cullen making himself stand rock still as Sky's hand hovered just above his flesh. His heart beat hard enough to make his pulse echo in his ears. "What happened?" she asked.

"Nothing of consequence."

"He brought a piece of shrapnel with him back from Afghanistan," Addie declared impertinently. "Apparently, the metal shard didn't much like its residence disturbed."

"Does it hurt?" she asked.

Cullen shook his head.

Sky pulled her hand back, a flash of hurt in her eyes over the tiny lie.

Fuck. Cullen tipped his face to the ceiling, his throat closing. It shouldn't be so very hard to say yes, but it was. He was supposed to be protecting her. How the hell could she trust him to do that if he was whining about a bit of bruising? And yet, Sky wanted the unedited truth. Demanded it.

"It hurts like a bitch," he whispered. "I'm not all right, Sky. Something is wrong."

Her teeth grazed over her lush lower lip for a moment, and then her arms were around him, pulling him into her, her warm body folding perfectly into his. The scent of passionflower filled his lungs, the shooting pain in his shoulder a distant pulsing irrelevance. Wrapping his good arm around the one woman in the world who could enter his soul and chase away the demons lurking inside, Cullen held her tightly.

"I don't like who I am without you," he said into her hair, the truth spilling uncontrolled from his lips. "I need you."

"I need you too," she whispered so quietly that he could barely make out the words, as if she were admitting some colossal secret. Somewhere in the background, the sound of Addie's footsteps approached the door, which opened and closed with a soft click. Sky turned her face up toward him, all big blue eyes and vulnerable uncertainty.

It was all Cullen could do to keep himself from pressing his mouth over hers, but one twitch of his shoulder was enough to remind him what happened when wounds festered. A shudder of fear ran through him, the thought of losing Sky just moments after getting her back making his heart race, but he made himself speak anyway. "Please tell me what happened in New York. I need to hear it from you."

Sky pulled back, but he wouldn't let her go. Not even an inch. His thumb grazed her neck in gentle encouragement.

The story came, starting innocently enough, but ending with Cullen shaking in rage. She'd been assaulted, betrayed, drugged—a fact that she still didn't know—and thrown to the curb to let a bunch of misogynistic assholes keep their cocks happy.

"I'm sorry," Cullen said. And damn it, he was. Sorry for not having listened. For not having been there to stop it. Sorry he hadn't killed Jaden when he'd had the chance. "I can't change what

239

happened, Sky, but I promise there will never be a time I don't listen. Not again. Not ever."

A cautious smile touched Sky's face, lighting the room. "That sounds almost docile," she whispered, her fingers sliding tentatively along his face.

"I promised to listen," said Cullen. "Not to *agree*."

She snorted softly. Wonderfully. Then paused, biting her lip. "While we're on apologies... I'm sorry about looking through the account. Everything pointed so strongly to you being with Addie that I —"

"With Addie?" Cullen paused for a second, looking at the door to the motel room through which Adrianna had shown herself out as he tried to work out what Sky might mean. "She's family. Like a sister."

"I know." Sky drew a short breath. "She told me. I'm sorry to have assumed without asking."

"We'll both do better next time," Cullen said. Because there would be a next time. Many, many next times, if he had his way. Now that he had Sky in his arms, he wasn't letting her go.

"There is one other thing." Reaching into her purse, Sky pulled out a packet of stapled papers, the motel's logo at the top suggesting they'd just been printed at the business center downstairs.

"What is it?" Cullen blinked at the small text, images and graphs filling the pages with complicated-looking research into military tactics.

"A postaction analysis on the effects of field medical hospitals for indigenous populations in the Middle East and Central Asian theaters," Sky said primly, then softened her tone. "What all that gobbledygook says is that even though the Taliban and other bastards attacked field hospitals, the medical mission saved lives. You saved lives, Cullen Hunt. More lives than you know."

His breath stilled. He'd said no more than a few words to Sky about his nightmare, but she'd *listened* to every one.

"Anyway..." Sky swallowed. "I wanted to leave this with you."

"Leave?" the word escaped him. He couldn't help it. Did she

mean leave the paper or *leave*? Fuck. He didn't think he could bear it. "I... I don't want you to."

Sky bit her lip. "I don't either. But I can't do this halfway. You have to let me in, Cullen. No holds barred."

"You might not like what you see," Cullen whispered. "I don't."

"I'll take my chances." Reaching forward, Sky put her palm against his cheek. "I know research studies won't chase away the dreams, but *we* will. One night at a time."

Cullen released his breath slowly, his face leaning into Sky's touch. The woman saw so deeply into him that it scared him shitless. But if there was anyone in the world he wanted at his side as he took the steps to healing, it was her.

Sliding his grip to cup the back of Sky's head, Cullen sealed his mouth over her lips, the energy of the connection blasting through him like a lightning strike. Like a billion volts of electricity cascading across every synapse of his brain, every nerve in his system. This was how it always was with Sky. Powerful. Magnetic. Soul-wrenchingly raw.

SKY

*H*eat rushes through me, my mouth yielding to Cullen's claiming kiss. The powerful taste of him fills my senses, rousing a deep primal need for more. More connection. More power. More *him*.

My breath quickening, I meet his tongue with mine and feel the rumble of approval vibrating through his chest. My hands come up, gripping either side of his thick torso, the skin smooth over hard chiseled muscles beneath.

As soon as my fingers close around him, Cullen takes over, not only with his mouth but with his entire massive frame. He steps into me, his hips pressing into mine, his chest brushing against the tips of my bunching nipples. Sizzles of heat and need spiral from my aching chest, heading all the way down to my sex, moisture already slicking my folds.

"Your shoulder," I rasp, pulling away from the kiss, my mind struggling to get a grip on reality.

"My cock hurts a great deal more just now," Cullen punctuates his words with a crass grunt in my ear, grinding his pulsing hardness against me in undeniable proof. His finger slides beneath my jacket and sweater, the rough skin of his calloused fingers sliding along my bare flesh as he takes my mouth again with renewed force.

His palms skim my stomach and slide backward along my hips and spine, dragging upward until, with a single deft flick, Cullen unhooks my bra. The lacey material slides down beneath my clothes, teasing my skin and making my sex clench hungrily at the promise of what's to come.

Something about the bra's fall feels decadent to me, wanton. As hot as the erection bruising my hipbone. Cullen runs his cheek along my neck, his stubble grazing my skin, and God, I want more.

I want everything.

I run my tongue along Cullen's clavicle, inhaling his male musk before nipping the delicate skin right over the bone.

Cullen lets out a noise that's something between a gasp and a grunt. Sliding his hands from my back to my head, he grips the sides of my face firmly, holding my seeking jaw in tantalizing control of how much of him I can reach. His next kiss isn't a kiss at all. It's a wild possession of my mouth, deep and punishing and so hot that my sex drips moisture along my thighs. As Cullen sucks on my tongue, his hands holding my head firmly, I feel myself gladly returning the reins back to him as if I'd never attempted to seize them in the first place.

Cullen marches into me, forcing me back until he's plastered my body between himself and the cool metal door, his hips pinning mine in place. Unzipping my fleece jacket, Cullen slips it down to the floor, pulling my sweater and undershirt over my head in a smooth, sure motion that leaves me feeling undeniably wanted.

With me naked from the waist up, Cullen pauses, the corner of his mouth lifting as he takes me in.

"W-what is it?" I ask, my befuddled mind trying to work out the reason for this halt in the action, my breathing quickening.

Cullen smirks, flicking a lock of hair from my bare shoulder— hair that used to be tucked into a presentable ponytail before his undressing. At the sides of my vision, I see other strands running untamed on either side of my face.

"Your hair," says Cullen.

"What about it?" My voice comes out too high, too needy. Too lost in my want for him.

Cullen chuckles into my mouth. "I just messed it up. And FYI, it's going to get worse before it gets better."

Before I can respond, Cullen's teeth graze my lips, his hands dipping into the waistline of my pants. Strong fingers lower toward the wetness I know they'll find, as Cullen's hardness grinds into me with rhythmic thrusts.

Lower. *Lower.* My pulse quickens, and I wriggle against Cullen's hold as his callused fingers find the top of my sex. The slit of my labia. As his hand slides across my soggy panties with a righteous possession that makes me whimper against his mouth.

Then, with a single determined thrust, Cullen has his finger up inside me, his other hand cupping my right breast at the same time. The sensations link together like a dizzying constellation, my channel and my mouth and my breast all taken with the man's demand. Zings of pleasure and intensity meld together, and I rise on my toes, writhing and searching for relief from the sheer force of his maleness.

Instead of giving quarter, Cullen slides a second finger inside me and pumps.

Again. *Again.*

A noise escapes me, my hands dropping desperately onto Cullen's shoulders. As he pulls his mouth away from mine, his thumb stroking my bunching nipple, it's all I can do to stay upright. Not that I have a choice. Not with Cullen taking charge of my body in a way that's so wrong and so intoxicatingly right that I can barely draw breath quickly enough to gulp oxygen.

My fingers curl desperately into him, and Cullen jerks, a shock of pain plainly jolting down his body. There's a wince on his face as he grabs hold of my wrist, but when he speaks, his voice is filled with low gravelly command.

"Take off my jeans."

My hands are at his waistline at once, my fingers flipping open the fly to let his engorged cock spring free. My mouth waters as I stare at the pulsating shaft, the tantalizing bead of moisture at the very tip of the head begging to be licked. Suckled.

Drawing a shuddering breath, I lower Cullen's jeans and boxers the rest of the way to the floor, and he steps out of them with the confidence of a warrior utterly in charge of his muscular body. Gripping my eyes with his moss-green gaze, Cullen brushes a knuckle from my lips down my midline. I shiver as he snakes too slowly between my breasts and stops at the top of my waistline, as if he'd not invaded it and more moments ago.

"Yours too," he says and, damn him, crosses his arms as he watches me strip.

Heat rises to my cheeks, and I don't know what's more absurd— that after everything we've done, the simple act of baring my body for him still makes me blush, or that my treacherous body is aroused by it. Whatever it is, by the time I stand naked before him, my thighs are glistening with moisture, my nipples hard and aching for relief.

The man nods in a mix of approval and admiration. "You have a gorgeous body," he says, his hands going to the crests of my hips as he leans to whisper into my ear. "Now let's take it for a ride."

Before I can protest, Cullen lifts me off my feet and lays me on his bed, my backside right at the edge of the tall mattress. The bedsprings squawk, the noise a contrast to my rapid breath. Taking my left leg, Cullen lifts it onto his good shoulder and drags the pads of two of his fingers through my wetness, making me moan. Rather than watching what he's doing, he stares into my eyes, and I'm completely consumed by all the fire and emotion I detect in his gaze.

Emotion that goes beyond the passion of our previous coupling to something more. Something so, so much deeper.

For several agonizing minutes, Cullen explores my core, never once taking his scrutiny off my face. Every motion he makes elicits noises from me, and every time a sound escapes my mouth, he changes his pace. Faster. Slower. Trailing along my folds. Swirling in my wetness. Dipping his fingers inside me before sucking my taste off his fingertips. But not once—not fucking once—does the bastard graze my clit.

"*Cullen.*" I whimper out my plea, but he ignores me, continuing the torment until my hips are jutting, jolting up and down automatically without my conscious permission.

CULLEN

*C*hrist, she looked gorgeous. With Sky's face flushed with need and her body singing with need beneath his touch, Cullen feared he might come right then and there. His body vibrated with the longing to plunge inside her, to make her scream his name as he brought her to climax over and over and fucking over.

But he wanted more than that now. Wanted to discover all the secrets of Sky's body—what she liked, what drove her crazy, what scared her spitless in that paradoxical way that drove arousal to new heights. Cullen wanted to take her there. Because that was what she deserved.

"I'm on birth control," she said suddenly, her hips wiggling beneath his hold. Her beautiful soprano was raspy, her breathing coming in short delicious gasps that hitched when Cullen lifted her hips to his mouth and traced her hood with the tip of his tongue. Sky's fingers curled against the sheets. "Cullen, did you—"

"I heard you." He breathed out slowly, savoring Sky's scent as his own pulse hammered against his chest. No condom. No barrier. He'd known Sky was on the pill back from that hospital visit when he'd scanned her chart for any medications that might interfere with each other, but it wasn't just pregnancy that the thin latex had always protected Cullen from. It was…everything.

A symbolic barrier between Cullen and any woman he'd ever taken. A shield that somehow protected them from the dangerous mess of the half-cocked grenade that was him. His breath still, Cullen waited for the rush of panic, the internal alarm that warned him to get the hell away before he did something stupid. Before he hurt someone. Before he let someone rake nails down his own soul.

A wave of heat and need and trust, all heralded by Sky's bright blue eyes, washed over him instead. He didn't just love Skylar Reynolds, he trusted her. He trusted her to trust him.

Placing the aching head of his cock against Sky's tight entrance, he thrust into her hard, holding still for a moment to let her adjust to the intrusion. Then, heedless of his shoulder's protest, Cullen lifted Sky into his arms. Holding her against him, Cullen turned them both to lay his back down on the bed with Sky straddling him, her silky strawberry hair waving around her bare shoulders.

"Fuck me," Cullen said, tightening every muscle in his body to keep the show from being over when it had just barely started. He wasn't in the habit of letting a woman ride on top, but there was nothing typical about anything Sky did. "Now." The words had left him as a curse rather than a command, but Sky smirked at him and gave a sarcastic salute.

"Yes, sir," she drawled, almost purring her response. And damn it if that *sir* didn't send his cock pulsing all the way to his head like a desperate schoolboy.

With her hands braced on his abdomen, Sky thrust herself along the length of him, her channel gripping Cullen's cock, sliding tightly up and down his engorged shaft. As she looked down at him, Sky's eyes were blue whorls of crystalline brilliance. Jesus fucking Christ. Filling her like this made Cullen's head spin.

A ball of anticipation tightened at the base of his spine, his sac firming and drawing up toward his throbbing hardness. He'd never let a woman ride him before, and something about having Sky do it made it even more enticing. Or maybe that was Sky herself. He craved her, and not only for the sublime perfection of her body.

Still, having her straddling him like this was wreaking havoc on Cullen's restraint.

"Hold on to the headboard with everything you've got," Cullen demanded, his voice hoarse as his hips undulated beneath her. "I want to see the imprints of your fingernails left behind."

Sky looped her hands around the maple edge above him, and Cullen bucked up into her at once. He felt himself penetrate deeper with each thrust, Sky's small gasps confirming his cock's report. Continuing to piston into her from below, he scooted his fingers along her silky skin and latched on to her right nipple with his mouth.

Suckling, he thrust faster and faster, the whole bed trembling from the punishing rhythm. Sky moaned with each bump and grind, the sound driving Cullen's thrust harder still, feeding the escalating tension between them. The motion made her breasts bounce delectably right in his face, and he ceased suckling on her nipple just so he could watch.

Lacing his right hand into her strawberry tresses, he pulled her down and branded his mouth to hers. She offered him her tongue, and he took it, suckling it into his own mouth until she fell forward and had to brace herself with one hand on his pillow while the other connected with his good shoulder. He inhaled her passionflower fragrance as it blended with the fabric softener scent already prevalent in the room, and decided the combination was the best smell ever.

Lowering his hand to her clit, Cullen rubbed the swollen bud as he still held her mouth with his, his cock raking through her channel. Sky moaned against his mouth, her body jerking wildly at the triple assault. Fire roared through Cullen's blood, his sac so tight that the lines between pressure and pain and ecstasy had long become blurred.

Giving her one more carefully aimed flick, he felt her walls clamp down on his pulsating cock, stronger and fiercer than ever. At the same time, cascading pleasure rippled through Cullen, the feeling of Sky's legs and channel and mouth all holding on to him desperately magnifying each sensation.

Sky shrieked into his mouth, and he drank in her orgasm, twining it inseparably with his own release.

As their throbs and quakes blended and coalesced into pure shared bliss, he felt something calm inside him. He'd taken Sky prior to this, but today, in this motel room alongside the noisy interstate, it had been different. Intimate. And now, lying there under her, their limbs and bodies still tangled together, Cullen felt his heart change rhythm to beat alongside hers.

SKY

*H*aving showered off, Cullen and I remake the room with the hurry of naughty school kids, finishing just in time to avoid me turning lobster red as Addie returns—bags of Chinese food takeout in tow. Giving me a knowing grin, the woman sets out boxes of lo mein and General Tso's chicken on the motel's tiny coffee table, rapping Cullen's knuckles with a pair of chopsticks when he reaches for a wonton.

"You. Shirt off," she orders.

Cullen gives her a dark look. "Thanks, Addie, but I'm a one-woman kind of guy." His hand slides dangerously to the inside of my thigh in an illustration that has Addie glaring.

"Let me put it another way," she says, her voice honey sweet. "You let me see your shoulder, or I call Dr. Yarborough right now and just tell him what I *think* is happening inside. And then I'm calling all the Tridents with the diagnosis and giving them this address. In my professional estimation, that will have you in surgery by..." She glances at the alarm clock, where 11:26 is just shifting to the next minute, "two p.m. is my best guess."

Cullen growls like an enraged German shepherd, but obediently unbuttons the shirt we'd just put on him, his smooth tattooed skin on delicious display once more. Tightening my thighs, because Cullen's hard body is the last thing I need to be thinking about just now, I impertinently take the very wonton Cullen was deprived of and drudge back to our actual reason for coming here.

"We think yesterday's fight was a setup," I tell Cullen, drawing his attention away from where Addie is peering professionally at his shoulder. "The video sent to Addie was taken by one of the *Denton Uncovered* photographers using a damn good telephoto zoom lens. For Frank's guy to be there at just the right time to get blackmail material is entirely too convenient."

Addie blows out a short sigh. "Except Cullen wasn't there when the problem started. Just guessing that it would be Cullen who'd happen to intervene is rather inefficient."

I swallow. "I don't think Jaden ever expected me to resist his orders. He only got physical when I refused to follow along with him and he lost his temper. His instructions could have been to maneuver me toward Cullen. Except he got carried away."

Cullen's eyes flash in fury, and he makes a visible effort to rein himself in, his chest expanding in deep even breaths.

"And the photographer?" asks Addie.

Cullen taps his good hand on his knee, wincing slightly as Addie probes the joint. "I've had a feeling that someone has been watching me the entire week at WorldROCK. I'd dismissed it as a..." He hesitates, and I suddenly know what he was going to say. Why is he afraid to say it?

"A flare-up of PTSD?" I finish for him, touching his knee when he nods. "It's been bad lately?"

"The worst since I've returned."

I wait for the instinctual wave of fear to hit me at Cullen's admission, but nothing comes. I'm not afraid of him, I realize. PTSD or not, the man isn't going to hurt me. Not now, not ever. I slide closer to him and feel some of the tension seep out of his rigid body as I press up against him. "Frank was just talking up your *violent tendencies* to me recently. And he has his photographer dog you on just the right week. It's almost as if he somehow knew you'd be having a hard time."

Cullen pulls away from Addie and turns to face me, his eyes intent on mine. "It does, doesn't it? And it sounds a bit familiar. Sky. Remember I asked you about taking drugs during that Fleet Week incident?"

Seriously? Now? I pull back from Cullen, but his hand tightens on my knee, his head shaking. "Do you know why it was that specifically I asked about?"

I puff a bit of hair from my face. "Because you were looking at all possibilities of—"

"Because you tested positive for ecstasy."

I freeze, feeling my eyes widen. I've never taken drugs. *Ever.*

"I had Liam dig into your file at the *Post.* They had you take a drug test, but they never shared the results with you. You had it in your system."

A chill brushes over me. "I know how this sounds, Cullen, but I swear—"

"I believe you." His eyes never waver from mine. "I imagine Jaden has something to do with that. But the fact that you had a drug in your system and didn't know about it made me think that maybe I do as well. Or don't, as the case may be." He shifts his weight to look at Addie, whose hand on his shoulder now lies still, her face tight. "I'll make you a deal, Therapist Peterson. You can call Yarborough and put him on notice, but he isn't to sedate me and drag me into surgery the moment I walk into the ER. I'll surrender voluntarily once I have this settled."

CULLEN and I enter the hospital two hours later, his muscles tightening as we step through the whooshing automatic doors. It's a small motion, one I wouldn't have noticed before—one I'm certain no one looking at his stoic features would ever guess—but that's all too clear to me now. Sliding closer, I twine my fingers with his.

Instead of letting go, Cullen squeezes my hand, his grip tight.

"Addie said she extracted a promise," I murmur under my breath.

Cullen gives me a dark look. "I'm sure she did. But I'm not sure *you* know Yarborough very well. He didn't get the note that I own this fucking hospital."

From another man, the words would sound conceited. Hell, when I first met Cullen, I would have taken them exactly the wrong way too. But I'm no longer the same woman who barged in on a traffic accident and made assumptions about a tattooed, too-beautiful medic. "I'll ask Catherine to send him a memo," I promise.

He snorts. "I'm not sure Catherine knows either." Nodding briskly to the man at reception, Cullen uses his key card to open the ER door, unleashing the smell of disinfectant that always clings to medical offices. At the center of the large rectangular room, Michelle rises from behind the nurses station and frowns at the sling on Cullen's left arm. I'm glad she's here, because Cullen's tight grip slackens by a marginal degree.

"How's the baby?" Cullen asks.

Michelle brushes her hand over her no-longer bulging belly. "Started displaying his admirable lung capacity the moment we brought him home from the hospital. And thank you for the thoughtful gift, Cullen, though you really shouldn't have." Her voice softens, her hands fingering a heart-shaped silver locket around her neck, the baby's name engraved on the outside. Tiffany's Forever Love. Yeah. I was an idiot. Michelle shakes her head. "I'll argue that point another time, however. What do you need?"

He draws a breath. "Blood work. On me. I need you to do it personally and mark it stat for the lab."

Her face tightens, but instead of asking the question clearly running behind her intelligent eyes, she pulls a pair of gloves from a box and jerks her chin toward an empty treatment room. "What are we testing for?" she asks, pulling out a butterfly needle and stopping with her hand hovering above the tube choices.

"Draw the whole set, Michelle," a man in a thigh-length white coat says from the entranceway. "I've already put in the order."

"Of course, Dr. Yarborough," Michelle says, her gaze cutting from the test tubes to where Cullen has seated himself on the treatment table. "It wasn't me this time, Cullen. I promise."

Saying nothing, Cullen offers his arm, wincing slightly as she taps the vein with expert precision. I wonder whether I should leave the room when she does, but Cullen motions for me to stay. "Addie called you. I imagine that blood work has pre-op orders already in the computer?"

"Would you have preferred to be stuck twice?" Yarborough retorts, utterly unfazed as he strides forward. Stopping about a foot away, he gives me a measuring glance before returning his attention to Cullen's ruggedly perfect face. "I didn't come to give you an I-told-you-so speech. I came to tell you to worry about your mission and to leave the shoulder worrying to me. I'm very good at what I do, son. You be good at what you do, all right?"

A muscle twitches alongside Cullen's jaw, his posture managing to relax without moving. "Yes, sir."

Yarborough nods and strides out of the treatment room.

Cullen snorts softly. "You know, sometimes I wonder if this place doesn't have me under surveillance."

I lean forward in my chair. "I'm guessing the surveillance here is more the word-of-mouth kind, but Cullen—speaking of surveillance, don't you have a system set up at your house?"

"A security system, you mean?" He nods. "Of course I do. Liam's people run it. Why?"

"Because if you're right and someone altered your medication, wouldn't they need to get into your house to do it?"

Pulling out his phone, Cullen starts dialing.

The Tridents arrive before the lab results do, Eli, Liam, and Kyan striding into the ER like an attack squad and scaring off the technicians. The men's shrewd and calculating gazes assess everything they touch, from Cullen's torn-up knuckles and slinged arm to the stiff set of his shoulders—the most Cullen shows in deference to the pain. Then their eyes turn on me, locking in trained unison. Hard, beautiful faces, all as open as stones.

Right. I don't belong here, amidst the Tridents. A girl who's never worn a uniform, who caused Cullen so much grief. One of the Tridents' own is hurt, and they don't want me here. When I walked into the hospital at Cullen's side, I should have known I was just a placeholder.

Getting to my feet, I lay a course for the door, the space between Eli and Kyan looking like my best option. If I'm lucky and neither man moves, I can blade my body and be gone without touching them. Without meeting anyone's eye.

"Reynolds." Moving faster than anyone has a right to, Cullen hops off the exam table and bars my path, his wide chest blocking out the room. Mossy-green eyes meet mine, every line of his face focused on me with heart-stopping intensity. Reaching out with all the self-assurance in the world, Cullen brushes a lock of hair away from my face, his touch gentle but so very deliberate. My pulse stutters, my body caught between Cullen's touch and the knowledge that three men who very likely want me gone are watching every move I make. *Bros before hoes.*

"It's all right," I whisper. "I'll go. I understand."

Cullen's brow twitches, and, moving with that same patent precision, he lowers his face and seals his lips over mine.

I have one moment to breathe in Cullen's fresh masculine scent before the full force of his mouth on mine sends blazes of heat streaking along every fiber of my body. His tongue plunders me in luscious, possessive strokes that turn my knees to Jell-O. I gasp against Cullen's demanding mouth, the feeling of his strong hand braced against my shoulders grounding me even as my breasts and thighs waken to the touch. Holy freakin' Zeus. If we don't pull apart soon, I'm going to get wet right here in the middle of the exam room. Surely that can't be what Cullen is after just now?

And then I understand.

My heart hammering against my ribs, I rise to his challenge. Wrapping my hand in the fabric of his shirt, I kiss him back just as fiercely as he's taking me and let the Tridents' burning gazes be damned.

I'm breathless by the time he pulls away, tucking me against his side as he pins his focus to each member of his former unit one by one. "Are we clear?" he asks.

Silence.

Then Eli raises his hand. "Actually, sir, I didn't quite catch that. Could you demonstrate again?"

Kyan smacks his knuckles into Eli's diaphragm, the former SEAL grunting at the impact. Still, when he straightens up, Eli's eyes twinkle with welcome, and Kyan's visage relaxes slightly as he gives me a nod. Liam, being Liam, gives no indication of having heard or seen anything, but the tension in the room shifts palpably.

"So what else is going on, mate?" Eli asks, grabbing one of the tourniquets the nurses use for blood draws and wrapping it around his fingers like a toy rubber band.

Before Cullen can answer, Michelle walks in and wordlessly hands Cullen his chart, her face giving nothing away.

"Lab results?" I ask.

"Yeah." Cullen scans the numbers, his jaw tight as he swears under his breath. "The lab is certain."

"I had them run it twice," Michelle confirms. "When you're ready, let me know who you want me to call."

"You pregnant, Cullen?" asks Eli.

"I've no prazosin in my system. Not any."

"Jesus fucking Christ," Liam snarls, making Michelle purse her lips at him for raising his voice in a hospital. He doesn't look repentant, though. He looks pissed off. Still, he must respect Michelle, because he does quiet down as she walks out of the room. "I take it you didn't stop the regimen?"

Cullen's eyes flash. He doesn't miss his doses. He's downright religious about consistency. "You can do a fucking pill count if you want," he says. "I just got a refill about two weeks ago."

"About the amount of time it would take to clear it from your system." Liam's face darkens. "So either there was a mix-up at the pharmacy, which is as damn likely as me learning the violin in my sleep, or someone came into your house and tampered with it."

Without waiting for an answer, Liam yanks his phone from his pocket and hisses orders to someone on the other end of the line. "Get everyone into the damn office. Now. I'm on my way."

"Who's he talking to?" I ask.

"Whichever employee on duty is in charge at his company, probably," Cullen tells me as Liam swishes out like a galloping stallion, barking more orders into his phone. "If someone got into my house, Rowen Security Services will have footage."

Kyan, who has been so quiet I nearly forgot he was there, now pushes off the wall where he'd been lounging. "Sky. Tell me everything you know about this photographer. I want to go have a chat while we wait." There's something so dark and menacing in the way Kyan says *chat* that I step back involuntarily. Cullen's friend or not, Kyan has killed people. They all have.

"It's all right." Cullen pulls me over to stand between his muscled thighs, his amused gaze caressing my face. "You're not about to become an accessory to murder, I promise. Keasley is the most reserved of us when it comes to breaking noses."

Color rises to my face at having been so easy to read. Though maybe it's just Cullen's observations, because Kyan's face flashes with a hit of surprise at my words.

"Make you a deal," Kyan says, his arms crossing a wide chest that strains his button-down shirt. "I won't do anything to get anyone arrested, and you call Jaz. She's worried crazy, and if she learns I saw you and didn't call, it's *my* nose that's getting broken."

SKY

"So what now?" I ask, after Kyan saunters out through the curtain, leaving me, Cullen, and Eli in the treatment room.

"Now we sit tight for a few hours," says Cullen. "Give Liam and Kyan a chance to work while Yarborough gets on the phone with every doc known to man to work out how to best get my drug levels up. Since he fully intends to operate, he's probably interrogating the anesthesia department just now."

I don't realize my hand is squeezing Cullen's shoulder until he covers my fingers with his own. "I'll be all right. Don't get me wrong, I don't much like the idea, but the thought of having both my hands fully available for the things I want to do to you is rather appealing just now."

I do turn bright red at that, especially since Eli grunts in hidden amusement. "Mate, you're so out of practice, you'll need a compass and guidebook just to find south."

It says a lot that Cullen only flips Eli off without ever taking his eyes off me. "I've got a good medical team here. And afterward, with Addie Peterson being the best physical therapist in Colorado, I'll be back on track in no time."

"Addie." My eyes wide, my fingers now dig into Cullen's muscles for a different reason altogether. "Frank sent the video of your fight to blackmail her into letting her house go into foreclosure."

Cullen shakes his head. "I told her I'll take care of her. And one way or another, I will. No one blackmails my friends."

"Have you *met* Adrianna Peterson?" I put my hands on my hips and glare at Cullen. "Does she strike you like the kind of woman who was going to take your 'don't worry, I got it,' and let it go? She surrendered that house to the bank this morning."

"She what?" Cullen is on his feet at once, though I have no idea where he thinks he's going.

"Damn it, Addie. I'm calling the bank now and—"

"No, you're not." Eli stretches his back lazily. "Until we have Frank in a vise, let the bastard think he's winning. Mason Pharmaceuticals is in the middle of a half dozen real estate deals right now, I'll have some subcontractors tie the land up in an assessment. The house won't go anywhere for a while, and we'll deal with it on the back end." Despite Eli's easy tone, the experience and intelligence backing each word are so potent that even Cullen sits his ass right back on the table.

Leaving the men to discuss the details of property law, I wander out to get some food. On my way back, I stop by to greet Michelle, who is typing details from Cullen's chart into a wheeled computer station instead of using the more comfortable seats that make the screen accessible to wandering eyes.

"Did your delivery go okay?" I ask.

"It did," the copper-haired RN says as she shifts her braid behind her, smiling at me. "Baby Henry was my easiest birth yet. My first daughter took seven hours and had to be induced. My second daughter took two hours with no induction, but Henry basically flew out to us once he got off his tuchus and decided to be born. From the onset of contractions to birth, the little booger took one hour, one minute. My husband timed it." Without changing her facial expression, Michelle solicitously slides her eyes toward the treatment room where Cullen and Eli are debating something in hushed tones. "Speaking of men, it's a relief for quite a few of us that Cullen found you. Even with the meds and the shoulder, he's more centered than I've seen him since he came back. I just hope he doesn't do anything to mess it up for himself."

Michelle's words hit my core, melting something that I just realize now was still coiled inside me. Turning my head, I study Cullen's profile as he speaks to Eli, watching as every few seconds, he glances away from his friend to survey the room. To find me.

Yes, Cullen is an overprotective bastard, but he needs me as much as I need him. And that's a whole new level of connection different from any I've ever had in my life. With anyone.

Cullen's posture changes suddenly, and he motions me over as he pulls his phone from his pocket. Making my excuses to Michelle, I hurry back into the room to hear Liam come over the speakerphone.

"No one's been inside the house," Liam reports over the connection. "However, there's a two-hour outage gap on the first of October between ten and noon, the outside footage surveillance. It was entered into the system as routine maintenance, and it would never have been flagged if I hadn't been searching personally—that was the day my maintenance guy had a new kid born, and I sent him the fuck home off the books to take care of family."

"October first?" Cullen looks up at Eli and me. "That's when my new med delivery came in. Do you know who turned off the footage?"

"I'm having his ass dragged in now."

"Not too loudly," Eli says. "Can we please not make a bloody world announcement of all this until we want everyone to know what we know?"

"Roger." Liam comes back at once, all business. "Received and understood."

"When did you start running a PR firm?" I ask Eli as Liam disconnects the line.

Something dark comes over Eli's beautiful features. "You have no idea." He turns to Cullen before I can ask anything further. "Let me talk to Michelle and Yarborough and see if we can get you released for good behavior tonight if we promise to bring you back for surgery after we resolve this mess."

. . .

THAT NIGHT, we gather in Cullen's living room next to his massive gas fireplace, with everyone except Cullen nursing an adult beverage of choice.

"What do we have?" Cullen asks.

"James Dyer, the *Denton Uncovered* photographer, was, in fact, under orders to follow Cullen around and try to capture compromising footage," Kyan reports. "Once I let him know I was displeased at discovering Cullen's video getting emailed about, he was quick enough to point his finger at Frank. Just following orders and all. He'd been at it for a week now."

"And Jaden?" I ask, quite proud of myself for saying the name without flinching. "Was he under Frank's orders as well somehow?"

"Negative. So far as I could tell, Dyer got tired of dogging Cullen, so he was trying to get his new buddy Jaden to start something that could be recorded. Except then Jaden saw Sky and went off script. Photographer is still pissed. Says he barely got the camera lenses changed and had no time to reset the setting."

"In other words, Jaden is mostly just an asshole," I say, a new disgust running through me. That entitled bullshit wasn't an act or setup. It was just the genuine personality of a man I nearly married. Cullen hands me a gin and tonic, and I take a grateful sip just as the doorbell plays a chime of cascading rain. "I'll get it."

Grateful to move around a bit, I peer through the front door peephole and feel my chest flutter at the sight of Jaz with her wrist in a brace.

"Hey!" I pull the door open, hesitating when the normally bouncy Jaz scowls over my shoulder. The championship. The one she had to forfeit because of me. My voice sobers. "Jaz. I'm so, so sorry about—"

She spins on me, her dark eyes flashing. "Don't you dare, Skylar. Don't you dare take responsibility for some other asshole's actions."

"But…" I wave my hand in her direction like some sort of genie. "You're mad about something."

"Of course I am. I had to fucking follow my brother like a damn tween just to find out what's going on. And now *that*."

The "that" in question saunters into the foyer, his arms crossed over a broad chest. "This isn't a social gathering, Jazmine."

"You going to let me in, Sky?" she asks brusquely, and, feeling like a moron, I step aside.

Liam shakes his head and disappears. I've still got no idea what has these two hissing at each other but... "His truck is outside. Did you not figure that he was in here?" I ask Jaz.

"I knew. But I don't have to like it, do I?" she spits out venomously.

At least my friend is consistent. Throwing my arms around Jaz, I pull her along into our makeshift situation room and swear I see her stick her tongue out at Kyan before claiming my gin and tonic for herself.

"So where were we?" Jaz asks.

Liam gives her a look that would smite a lesser being, but turns his attention to Cullen. "Timothy Browning. That was the technician on duty when Cullen's outside camera went dark for bullshit maintenance. Three guesses as to who put him up to manufacturing the malfunction."

"Frank." I don't bother phrasing it as a question, but Cullen nods anyway. I blow out a slow breath.

"The bastard's been conducting illegal activities for years," says Cullen. "But he's so damn slippery, nothing sticks."

"Can we call the police on this?" Jaz asks.

"And say what?" Liam snaps at her. "That because Frank squeezed a weak link in my company, he's somehow responsible for Cullen's meds getting switched? Or that having his photographer dog a top Denton businessman is a smoking gun of anything but gossip? We might as well try to convict the fucking tooth fairy."

"Maybe you should be vetting your own people better," says Jaz. "Are you the head of a security company or Disneyland?"

"Enough, you two." I don't realize I've raised my voice at Liam until the man cocks a brow down at me and my pulse stutters, my muscles bracing for a blow. Cullen's quiet curse says he'd seen my flinch, but before he can say anything, Liam steps back, giving me the floor.

"You were saying?" Liam prompts.

I draw a fortifying breath. "Jaz is right. We do need the police. But like Liam said, we need proof. I think I know how to get it."

And I'm one hundred percent sure Cullen is going to hate every word of it.

SKY

I'm wrong. Cullen doesn't hate my idea at all. He despises it on all grounds. But that doesn't matter. It's the only idea we have, and if I can manage to pull it off, it will work.

Mostly because it has to.

"I don't like that it's you," Cullen says, scrubbing his hands through his closely shorn hair while Liam fits me with a tiny recording device.

Truth be told, I don't like it either. My nerves have become living things, writhing through my intestines like rabid snakes, but I'm not letting that—or Cullen—stop me.

Taking my shoulders, Cullen turns me toward him. I start shaking my head, sure he's about to tell me to call it off, but instead, Cullen levels me with his gaze. "We've got your six, Reynolds."

Cullen's words bore into my core, filling me with warmth and confidence. And yes, they also make me want to strip that shirt off him and burn off some nervous energy just now, but that would mess up the button camera Liam has been so carefully adjusting on me. Standing between Liam and Cullen just now, the pair of muscle-bound men towering over me make me feel like a Lilliputian beside two giant Gullivers.

The Lilliputians got the upper hand on that one.

Holding on to that final thought, I step out from between the men and, with a steady hand, smudge my mascara.

THE SUN HAS BEEN UP for several hours when I slink into *Denton Uncovered*, see his frosted glass office door standing wide, and flinch in Oscar-winning surprise at finding Frank behind his desk. At least I don't have to fake the rapid beat of my heart, which hammers against my ribs. "Frank." I swallow. "I… I just wanted to pick up my things and apologize." I bite my lip, barely lifting my gaze off the floor. "I know it wasn't the best exit but, well, let's just say you were right. About everything."

Frank walks down the aisle separating the various work spaces toward where I'm hurriedly packing my belongings into a haphazard pile and perches his left buttock on my desk, the sweet bug-spray-like scent drifting off him. "Want to tell me what I was right about?" he asks, his voice so gentle, I'd believe it if I didn't know better.

I shrug one shoulder. "Cullen. The… You were right about the temper, Frank. Please don't make me say any more. I…" I look up at the ceiling, imagining the damage that Jaden did to Jaz and finding my eyes watering on cue. "I couldn't do that again. I'm sorry I just slipped my resignation in like a coward, but… It got bad, Frank. Really, really bad."

"Sky, honey." Frank takes the liberty of wrapping an arm over my shoulders, which makes me glad the guys have no visual on me, lest they barge in and ruin everything before it starts. "I understand. The asshole's hurt me too. Like I said, there's a certain type to people like him. But it's all right. I have you now, and I'll stay with you as long as you want. You can even stay with me for a while." Frank's hand snakes down along my spine.

I swallow bile. "You know what I hate the most?" I say, leaning into his shoulder. "I can't *do* anything about it."

"Why in the world not?" Frank rubs a circle between my

shoulders. "You're a journalist, Sky. The one thing you know you can do is write. So start with a statement of what he's done, and we'll go from there."

I stare at the paper Frank slides over to me, a pen following suit.

"We can press charges against him," Frank coos into my ear. "A restraining order. Anything that might help you feel better."

I pick up the pen and see Frank's breath still, satisfaction glimmering in his sweaty face. Holding it just above the paper, I wait a few seconds before deflating his hopes. "There's no point," I say— which happens to be the truth, though not for the reason the asshole thinks. "No matter what I write, nothing will come of it. These damn vets, they're above the law. They do shit, and it's *oh, my meds made me do it*. And before you ask, yes, Cullen is one of those faux PTSD bastards, popping pills as an excuse to do whatever he goddamn pleases."

Frank's fingers halt, my breath stilling with them. Then the man moves his hand, trailing it across my face until my—no longer fake —anxiety-filled face tips up at him. "What if there was a way of proving meds had nothing to do with it?" he asks quietly. "Would you go to the police, then?"

I snort. "Impossible. I've been to Cullen's. He's more religious about those damn pills than most evangelicals are about church."

"Maybe. Maybe not." Frank's smile flickers in concert with the satisfaction in his eyes. "I have it on good authority that Cullen Hunt is off his meds. They'll confirm as much if the docs test him."

Asshole. I freeze. As good as a damn admission. But good enough?

"Keep going, Reynolds," Cullen's iron order sounds through my earpiece, releasing something strange into my blood. Confidence. Resolve. For all his overprotectiveness, when the decision has been made, Cullen is backing me fully. Trusting me fully. A commander used to leading from the front, taking a support role with the same perseverance he does everything else. For the first time, I feel myself part of a unit, and damn it if it doesn't make a world of difference just now.

I give Frank a hopeful gaze, my hand coming up to *almost* touch his cheek before falling away in despair. "It won't. I'm telling you, he pops the pills like candy." I swallow, blinking rapidly in rhythm with Frank's quickening breaths. "Sorry, I was just hopeful there for a moment, but then reality struck. It's no use." I start pulling my things toward me, back into a pile. "I have to leave. It's the only way of keeping safe from him."

He licks his lips, the bulge in the front of his trousers stirring. Unlike my hesitating hand, the pad of his thumb does touch my lip, caressing the skin. "But what if it were true?" he whispers.

I scrape my upper teeth over my lip, worrying the skin where he'd just touched me, my eyes locked on his beady muddy brown ones. "Then I'd say you're the most genius man to walk the earth. But please, don't tease me." I touch the tips of my fingers to his knuckles, his skin covered with a thin sheen of perspiration. "I don't think I can stand another broken hope."

"All raw truth, Sky." He leans closer to me, his face inches from mine. "I replaced his prazosin with a placebo two weeks back."

Did you now? Like personally? I lay my palm on his cheek. "If that's the truth, you're a damn genius. It means that all Cullen's antics, all the violence, that's the true him. Not some meds. Not on paper, not anywhere."

"Oh, it's true, sweetheart. I knew Hunt was a ticking time bomb. It was my responsibility to show the world that too."

"That's brilliant," I breathe, letting the tease of my open mouth hover between us for a moment before speaking. "But dangerous as hell. What were you thinking, breaking into his house? He could have hurt you."

"Didn't have to, sweetie." He gives me a triumphant grin. "He's too lazy to pick up his stuff, so it was just a matter of switching it out of his mailbox. I did him a favor, if you ask me. What kind of entitled ass leaves drugs in a mailbox?"

"The kind who doesn't care what happens to other people," I tell him. "I mean, there are kids who live on that street. What if one of them had grabbed the bottle?"

"Exactly." He moves closer to me, his fingers tucking a lock of hair behind my ear and sending my pulse into a gallop. "We have to look out for each other. Sticking together is the only way to deal with these commandos."

"Good enough," Liam says over my earbud. *"Get out of there."*

Frank's fingers grip my chin, the hold tightening when I try to pull back. I draw a quick breath, my mind racing my heart.

"It's all right," Frank whispers. "I know you've wanted this since you walked into *Denton Uncovered*. There's no reason to fight it any longer."

"If you want us to come in, clear your throat," Liam says over the earbud.

Frank's breath tickles my skin, his bug-spray scent making bile climb up my throat. But I don't clear it. Because the last thing I need is more flying fists and splattering blood—and that is exactly how the Tridents' version of backup is going to play out if I let them in here just now. Pinching the corner of my eye with two fingers, I wipe some black smudge along the bottom lid and jerk back hard, holding the makeup toward Frank's face like garlic before a vampire. "Oh my God! I must look like a hot mess. I don't want you to see me like this."

Frank blinks, indecision playing across his face.

"Do you mind helping me construct my statement after I get cleaned up?" I press on, getting to my feet. "I'm not up for doing it myself just now. I know it's an imposition."

"Of course." By the time Frank finds his voice, I'm already halfway to the washroom. More importantly, I'm yards away from the man. "I'm here to help."

"Thank you, Frank." For once, there's nothing fake about the sincerity in my tone, because I mean every word. "Thank you so much for talking me through this."

"Yes, I appreciate it as well," Chief Arnie Jackson booms, walking in as if he owns the place, his salt-and-pepper mustache defining a strong upper lip. Frank, who was still leaning against the table from which I escaped, stares at the chief like a deer caught in the headlights, blinking only when the door opens again, this time to admit Cullen and Liam.

Cullen holds his arm out to me, and I walk gratefully into his embrace, while Liam holds up a cell phone—a recorder app already pulled up. A flick of Liam's finger, and Frank's voice fills the newsroom once more.

"All raw truth, Sky." Frank's breathing on the recording sounds even more intrusive than it had in real life. *"I replaced his prazosin with a placebo two weeks back."*

Liam throws the recording onto what passes for a conference room table in *Denton Uncovered*'s newsroom, the chief pulling a chair out for himself. "Take a seat, Frank."

Moving with impressive self-possession, Frank walks over to his desk, stows away the blank sheet he'd handed me for my "statement," and reaches for something deeper inside the drawer. For one insane second, I imagine he's somehow planted a gun inside the drawer, but what he retrieves is nothing more hazardous than a sheaf of papers.

"Good morning, Arnie." Ignoring the Tridents altogether, my editor pulls a chair out for himself beside the chief. Settling in, Frank motions me to a free seat as if I'd walked in on a companionable chat instead of having just set him up for criminal charges.

My stomach tightens. Frank is sleazy and two-faced and vindictive. But he's also a coward. Which does not at all jive with the self-possession oozing from him now.

I glance at Cullen, but the man's stony face gives away nothing of his thoughts.

"Frank," says Arnie. "I'm pretty disturbed by what I just heard. Trespassing, theft of a controlled substance, mail tampering. We're talking federal offenses here—and I haven't even talked to the prosecutor yet to get a comprehensive list. I'll level with you—it's a bad situation. But I've known you for a long time. I think maybe you had your reasons. You don't have to talk to me just now, and you can get on the horn with your lawyer, if you'd like, but I wouldn't sleep right if I didn't at least offer you a chance to help yourself out of this mess."

"Help myself out?" Frank parrots. His eyes narrow on me and Cullen for a moment, but then return to the chief with too great an inner confidence. "What did you have in mind, Arnie?"

Arnie reaches between his legs to adjust his chair, then leans forward. "Accept responsibility, give me some names, and we can talk about a plea deal."

"Mmmmm. I see," my editor drawls. "I had something different in mind, though. I'm an extraordinarily careful man, you see. And I like information. It's what keeps the world moving. You want to know things, I want to know things, the public wants to know things."

"What are you blathering on about?" Palm on the edge of the table opposite Frank, Liam manages to loom over everyone without even trying.

Frank holds up the papers he pulled from his drawer. "I'll let Arnie here tell you."

As he slides the papers over to the chief, I glimpse the front page of notes and feel the blood drain from my face. These are *my* papers. The story I've been working on for weeks about the response times of the Denton Valley PD by neighborhood. I'd gone through several drafts of the piece, and the copy in the police chief's possession is an early version exploring a possible corruption angle. Since gathering more data, I'd started a second piece that cast doubt on my original assumptions, but that's not what's on the table now.

It's not what Chief Arnie Jackson is reading, his face darkening with every word.

Every word that *I* wrote, dragging his whole department through the mud. *Shit.* I can't look at Cullen, can't even think of any of the Tridents. In two minutes' time, I've just plummeted from being a star evidence collector to becoming a Denton PD persona non grata. That has to be a damn record. More to the point, it makes everything I touch radioactive. Including that recording Liam tossed onto that table.

"I like the idea of helping each other out, Arnie," Frank says, leaning back in his chair as the chief leafs through one page after another. "I personally think the DVPD is doing the best it can with the resources it has. There's only so much 'more with less' that anyone can do. But you know how the public likes to rush to conclusions. Still, maybe there's a way we can help each other, like you said. A win-win."

SKY

"Ms. Reynolds." The chief of the Denton PD turns his stern pale eyes to me, making the heat of mortification surge to my face. "Were you planning to print this?"

"No, sir," I stutter out.

He raises a brow. "Your name is on the byline. Is this a forgery?"

My hand closes around the edge of the table, but there's nothing I can do except tell the truth. It's who I am. As a person and as a journalist. "It's my first draft, sir. Based on preliminary statistics and interviews. But those don't form a complete picture. I like having an angle when I draft, but then assumptions often get disproven. That isn't a finished draft, sir. It isn't even the most up-to-date draft that takes into account actual calls made to the police."

"We'd be sure to mention that *Denton Uncovered*'s investigation into the situation is ongoing," Frank coos on the tail of my words. "But facts are facts. And, headlines."

"These aren't the facts," I snap, my eyes flashing at Frank.

He waves a copy of the crime report. "Seems factual to me."

"Context matters, Frank. It—"

"It's the story I intend to run," Frank says, cutting me off.

"That's all there is to it. Arnie can argue context from the podium all he likes. Unless, of course, he'd like to get ahead of the issue."

Drawing a breath, I shore up the guts to check the other men's faces, finding carefully closed expressions across the board. If I had any doubts before, they're gone now. Frank has us over a barrel. All of us. Not only me and the Tridents, but Arnie Jackson too. Every one of us is fucked. Royally.

Brazenly, Frank turns to look at the police chief. "I assume we have an understanding. Isn't that right, Arnie?"

"You could say that," the chief says evenly, with a type of dignity I wish I had. I've sunk this ship for us, but for some reason, the chief is still maintaining his ground.

Frank smiles and gets to his feet.

"Sit your ass down, Peterson," the chief says. "To start with, I'd like to point out that it's very difficult to run any headline from a jail cell. More to the point, your last three months of headlines included proposals of *Natural Foods Mart Adds Minced Rat to Angus Beef*, *Local Vet Hospital Hosts Illegal Dog Fights*, and *Police Wiretap Couple to Listen to Shower Nookie Sessions*."

I glance at Cullen at this last reference, the word *shower* bringing up all sorts of delightful memories. Cullen snorts and, without having the decency to even blush, quickly hides his amusement behind a trained stony façade, while the chief of police continues unperturbed.

"So you'll understand if my concern for Denton PD's reputation is less tied to your paper than to the facts." Twisting his chair to get a better line of sight to me, the chief leans forward, bracing his forearms on the edge of the table. "You said your investigation is not yet complete, Ms. Reynolds?"

"Yes, sir. I mean no, sir. I mean, yes, it's not complete."

"Would it help your accuracy if you had unfiltered access to all our call logs, records, and mileage reports?"

Wait, what? I open my mouth, close it, then finally find my words. "It would, of course. But I don't understand."

The chief taps his finger on the stack of papers. "This is important work, Ms. Reynolds. Either my officers are not

276

responding as they should, in which case there's going to be a readjustment of my force to stamp out this nonsense, or else they're doing the right thing but an important segment of our community is unaware of the facts. Either way, the situation needs to be corrected, and I cannot think of a better writer to get to the bottom of this."

Frank's jaw slackens.

Getting to his feet, the chief claps Cullen's good shoulder. "I can see why you like this one, Hunt. We're responsible to the people we protect—and journalistic integrity helps get us there. Thank you for what you do, Ms. Reynolds." Pulling out a set of handcuffs, the chief walks around to seize Frank's arm. "I've changed my mind about wanting to help you out, Peterson. We're done here."

"REMIND me again why I'm having to don this fancy nightmare?" I ask Cullen from the gleaming white marble bathroom of New York's Carlyle Hotel. I may not be moving back to the Big Apple anymore, but that hasn't stopped my mother's—and Greg's—insistence that I visit. Padding to the doorway, I scrutinize Cullen from his place in front of the double mirrors, and—unlike me—what I see is a sight to behold.

Cullen's blond buzzcut and mossy-green eyes are set off by the simple black lines of his tux, the formal white shirt beneath it a dazzling contrast. I'm so lost in the stunning handsomeness, I forget my own question until he walks over and takes the dress out of my hands.

"Because Dr. Greg Andrews, also known as your stepfather-to-be, is opening up a new hospital with a couple of his heart surgeon buddies on the Upper East Side. Showing up to dinner and ribbon cutting in rock-climbing gear tends to be frowned upon."

Right. Turns out Mom's latest sugar daddy may actually be, well, just a good man in love. One who truly cares about my mother —enough to have proposed to her last weekend. Apparently, his insistence on my visiting was part of his romantic plans, but he finally couldn't wait. Sometimes, miracles do happen.

"Plus," Cullen adds, holding up the velvety black-and-azure

gown with a crisscross design which dips low in the front and even lower in the back, "I need to know how this looks on you. I fear this isn't the last high-profile event you'll be forced to attend." Leaning down, Cullen presses his mouth over mine, the demands of his lips lifting me to my toes and leaving me wanting as he breaks it off. "It's the hazard of being with me."

I shift my tingling thighs to relieve the sudden tension.

He gives me a wolfish grin. "Before you do that, though, do you know how to tie this damn thing?" He waves at his bowtie, not wincing at all as he moves his shoulder. Dr. Yarborough removed his shrapnel four weeks ago today, and the incision and internal damage is largely healed now. "Catherine usually does this for me."

I bat his hands away and rescue the expensive cloth from his grip. "In fact, I do. You'll find I'm full of surprise talents. Wearing dresses not being one of them."

"Mmm. Nothing that can't be trained." Before I can bat at him the same way I did at his hands, Cullen wraps an arm around my waist, pulling me down and to the side as if doing the tango.

I can never seem to get over how easy this is with him now. How easy we've become over the past month since getting together. Truly and genuinely together. While Cullen may always be a hard man in some respects, with me, he's softer. Especially when it counts. Even returning here to New York City, the location of my greatest humiliation and trauma, feels different with him. *I* feel different. Confident. Grounded.

And, at the moment, half naked. Realizing that it's either the dress going on or my underclothes coming off, I glower at the clock and let Cullen hold the zipper open for me.

Twenty minutes later, I loop my arm through Cullen's elbow as he leads me down to the reception Greg and his colleagues are holding below the twenty-four-karat gold ceiling at the iconic hotel's Bemelmans Bar.

"When Greg finds out you own a hospital network, he may try to corner you," I warn Cullen, doing my best not to trip in this ridiculously tight skirt. It's something Jaz referred to as a mermaid cut, which means I have to take teeny tiny footsteps to walk in the stupid thing. "Also, there will be press here, so please don't do anything you wouldn't want on the front page. No, scratch that. Don't do anything Trident Medical's board of directors wouldn't want on the front page."

Cullen scoffs. "Greg will want nothing to do with me, Reynolds. I'm no heart surgeon. That would have been my father. They have a very different notion of success, trust me."

There's a flicker of tightness in Cullen's voice, but before I have a chance to ask about it, we pass through the double doors into the heart of the reception. Renowned murals decorate the bar's walls, scenes of various pleasures depicted by an artist's vibrant brush. The slowly milling groups of people are dressed as formally as Cullen and me, which at least means I'm not alone in my suffering. Or maybe I am. Cullen certainly seems as much at ease in his tuxedo as he does in his rescue gear. I guess he's right. When you run a hospital network, you learn to camouflage yourself in the environment.

Spotting my mother and Greg over by the baby grand piano, I steer us that way, nearly tripping over my heels as I catch sight of two men in tuxedos with press credentials clipped to their lapels. Jaden Harris and Martin Bainbridge, the *Manhattan Post* editor who fired me.

"What manner of Murphy's Law has Jaden here?" I murmur to Cullen under my breath. "The bastard doesn't even cover medical news."

Cullen brushes his thumb slowly over my hand. "I made a special request to the *Post.*"

I jerk my head toward Cullen's, but before I can demand what the heck he was thinking, my mother and Greg walk over with champagne in hand.

"Lary, honey, don't you just look wonderful." Leaning toward me, my mother touches her cheek to mine, kissing the air the way they do in movies set in Paris. "Let me finally introduce you to Greg Andrews. Greg, this is my daughter, Skylar. Lary, Greg."

"A pleasure to finally meet you." Greg shakes my hand, his grip strong without being crushing. In a tux similar to Cullen's, he looks like the textbook doctor with graying hair, intelligent eyes, and diamond cuff links in the shape of the star of life. Turning his gaze to Cullen, Greg holds out his hand. "And you must be the Cullen Hunt responsible for keeping Skylar in Colorado?"

"I've learned that no one keeps Skylar anywhere, sir," Cullen says, returning that handshake. "But I'm grateful she's decided to stay."

Greg frowns at the clasped hands. "Are you injured, Mr. Hunt?"

Cullen blinks. "Sir?"

"My grandmother has a firmer handshake, son."

Cullen withdraws his hand, placing it behind his back into a parade rest position. "I've been told that it's disrespectful to put pressure on a cardiac surgeon's fingers, sir."

Greg blinks. "What blathering self-pompous idiot gave you that notion?"

Cullen's other hand joins its partner in the small of his back. "My father."

Uncomfortable silence fills the air between the men, creeping to encompass my mother and me. I rack my brain for something to say and almost laugh when I find the same lost bewilderment shaping her face. If my mother and I have been on the same side of anything in the last two decades, I don't remember it.

Suddenly, Greg snaps his finger. "Hunt. Your father wouldn't have been Henry Hunt the third, would he?"

"He was." Cullen's voice is utterly void of emotion.

Greg's is not. "I knew him. I mean, it's all been many years ago, but we crossed paths a couple of times over business matters. Now it all makes sense." Greg grins, clapping Cullen's shoulder. "Good God, man, I know who you are now. In fact, I've always wondered how any offspring of Henry's could land so far from the tree to do *good* for a change. Not just for your hometown, but for our country as well. I hope you don't mind my forwardness, son. It's always been my way. Now, how do I talk you into giving me a tour of Trident Medical?"

Seeing the spark of interest in Cullen's gaze, I step away a couple of paces to let the men talk while I catch up with my mother.

"I take it you won't be returning to New York, Lary?" she asks wistfully.

"I've been offered a position at Denton Valley PD in their internal investigations unit. But it looks like you may be visiting us soon." I point my chin toward the men and see my mother's face soften as she watches Greg talk enthusiastically about something.

"Sometimes you go looking for one thing and something else finds you instead." Her voice tightens. "Back straight, Lary. There's a pair of reporters coming our way. Please tell me that is not Jaden I see."

My stomach tightens. "It is."

"*The* Jaden?"

"Mr. Hunt." Bainbridge stops beside Cullen and Greg, Jaden hanging a few feet behind. "Martin Bainbridge, *Post.* Can you tell us what brings the CEO of Trident Medical Group all the way to New York City? Is there a merger being discussed?"

"This is a personal trip, actually," Cullen tells the editor, holding his arm out to me. "But I imagine the person you really want to speak to is Skylar Reynolds."

What the hell are you doing, Cullen? I plaster on a fake smile that matches the one on Bainbridge's face as Cullen folds me against his body.

"Ms. Reynolds," Bainbridge says tightly. "What an…unexpected time to see you again."

A smirk slides over Jaden's face, lighting up his eyes. "Mr. Hunt, did your lady friend not mention that she had departed the *Post* under some unfortunate circumstances? Fortunately, Denton Valley seems much more lax when it comes to journalistic integrity, so I'm happy to hear that Skylar found a place more suitable for her… creative writing needs. Ms. Reynolds." Jaden turns toward me, all but preening at the exclusive drama he's drumming up for the *Post*'s front page. "Wasn't your editor at *Denton Uncovered* arrested for multiple charges a few weeks back? Blackmail and possession of controlled substances, I believe?"

Undiluted fury-filled heat fills my face, Jaden's loud speech now drawing a crowd. I reach for my voice and find nothing but rage filling my lungs. With so many eyes on us now, maybe that's for the best.

Seeming to suffer no such handicap, Cullen releases me and blades his body to stand halfway between my ex and me. Not to protect me from Jaden, I realize, but to keep me from tearing the bastard limb from limb in the middle of a ritzy bar.

"It's a pleasure to meet you again under better circumstances, Mr. Harris," Cullen says, the look of surprise on Jaden's face at Cullen's choice to reference their prior incident mirroring my own confusion. Cullen, however, presses on, this time addressing my former editor. "Mr. Bainbridge, I'm a big fan of the *Manhattan Post*, especially your coverage of the military. In fact, I just referred Major Lovvit to your office. Did you have a chance to speak with him?"

Bainbridge frowns. "He must have called after we'd already departed today."

"No problem. Let me share the lead with you directly." Reaching into his tux pocket, Cullen pulls out a neatly folded sheet of paper, Rowen Security's logo visible at the corner. Around us, other members of the press close in, cameras and notepads at the ready. My heart pounds, and I hope to God, Cullen knows what he's doing, because I sure don't. "Approximately eight months ago, a *Post* reporter had intended to write an exposé on several marines whose partying turned to assault."

Jaden literally scoffs, huffing out a burst of air through his front teeth. "That's old news. Ancient history." He deliberately eyes me. "The report and *reporter* were shown to be hacks, and the story was never printed."

"Yes, well, according to a security firm I work with, those very marines have continued their *unsubstantiated* activities to the tune of gang rape. Once the victim, Gloria Redman, retained the law firm of Hite, Hite, and Wellesley to represent her, several other women came forward with similar instances. I believe the attorneys are now doing a thorough investigation into the marines' previous conduct, so I would highly recommend you locate all your records of that particular investigation, as I'm sure a subpoena is forthcoming."

Bainbridge's face—which went bone white at Cullen's mention of gang rape—now slackens altogether. Hite, Hite, and Wellesley are some of the sharpest attorneys in Manhattan, known for leaving no stone unturned. "Thank you for the heads-up, Mr. Hunt," he breathes finally, finding his voice for the other media that are watching. "The *Post* will, of course, cooperate fully with the investigation."

A warm trickle of satisfaction spills into my blood. Bainbridge isn't a bad sort, and I'm certain that the thought of having gotten it wrong scares him as much as the pending lawsuit. Gathering himself, my former editor turns to me. "Ms. Reynolds, would—"

"Bitch. Fucking slut of a bitch." Cutting his editor off midsentence, Jaden comes at me with nostrils flaring, his eyes flashing with a wild rage. "This is all your doing. All your lies. How many good people are you going to destroy?"

Beside me, Cullen tenses. And then…then steps back, leaving me to face Jaden one on one. The confidence in Cullen's eyes ground my bubbling panic.

My pulse settles, my thoughts returning to me as I see Jaden for what he is. Not some fierce warrior, but a hack unable to control his basic impulses. "Mr. Harris. I'm so glad to have run into you today." My saccharine-sweet tone makes Jaden's face turn a new shade of burgundy. "I'm in the middle of a freelance story myself. Are you aware that WorldROCK former champion Jazmine Keasley's sponsors—that's Arc'teryx, and now prAna and SCARPA—are filing charges against the *Manhattan Post* reporter who assaulted her before this year's competition? She was unable to participate due to her injuries, and, well, I imagine some more subpoenas are coming to the *Post*'s legal department."

"Do you know something about this, Harris?" Bainbridge asks in the gruff way that all newspaper editors seem to have in their genes.

"Just slander from a known liar, sir," Jaden hisses, his hands curling into fists.

"Mr. Bainbridge." A woman in high heels a few paces away raises her recorder, her press credentials swaying as she reads from her phone. "WorldROCK's media roster lists only a single reporter from the *Post*: Jaden Harris. Is that, in fact, the man you sent to cover the event? And if so, how are you unaware of a physical confrontation between him and one of the competitors?"

"Mr. Bainbridge, over here, sir," another reporter chimes in. "Have there been any previous accusations of misconduct against Mr. Harris?"

Feeling Cullen's hand in the middle of my back, I realize he's come up to my side again and is now guiding me out of the feeding frenzy surrounding the *Post*. "I didn't know you were covering the lawsuit," he murmurs appreciatively into my ear as we come to stand next to my mom and Greg.

"Neither did I," I tell him. "But I never said *when* I started covering it. It just happened to be about five minutes ago."

Greg chuckles, and I suddenly feel my face heating all over again. "Oh my God. I'm so, so sorry," I say, my hands covering my mouth. "I've upstaged your dinner with this nonsense and—"

"On the contrary, you did me a favor. I get press coverage *and* I don't have to be in the middle of the reporters myself. Plus"— Greg's face grows serious—"I did not have the honor to serve my country the way Cullen did, but I do what I can. If I helped in some small way to open the right eyes to injustice, I'm grateful for the opportunity."

Greg turns to Cullen. "Now, Mr. Hunt, is there anything else you have up your sleeve that I might want to know about?"

I expect Cullen to give Greg one of his rare smiles, but for the first time since I met him, Cullen looks…frightened. "Actually, sir, I have one more thing, if you don't mind. I was going to wait, but—"

Greg cocks a brow. "Whatever it is, son, you may wish to reconsider the waiting lest you tachycardia yourself into my professional services."

Cullen nods, then reaches again into his inside pocket, and, with his hand still inside his jacket, turns smartly toward me.

My chest tightens. Before I can speak, though, Cullen lowers to one knee, his gaze flickering to my hand before finding my eyes.

"Skylar Reynolds. Since I've met you, you opened my eyes to a different world. One with kindness and decency. You taught me to be a better man. Hell, just loving you makes me a better man. And I do. More than I ever thought possible. Would you be my wife?"

I want to speak, but there's a lump lodged in my throat.

"*Honey,*" my mom prods. "This isn't a one-way conversation."

"Let the woman think, Grace," Greg says. "There are many things to consider. Maybe he snores. Or—"

"Yes." The word comes not from my brain, but from my soul. "Yes."

"Thank fucking God," Cullen murmurs. Rising to his feet, he slides a gleaming ring onto my finger, the pear-shaped solitaire sparkling from a diamond-encased band. I've never seen anything so beautiful in my life, with the exception of the Trident now looming over me, his fresh, spicy scent filling my lungs. Everything around me goes blurry, and I realize that I'm teary-eyed as my fingers press into Cullen's muscled shoulders, unable to pull my gaze away from his tantalizing moss-green eyes.

"A kiss for the camera?" someone calls out.

And before I can blink, Cullen's mouth seals over mine, his strong hand gripping the back of my head in a vise that sends tendrils of heat all the way to my sex. I gasp against Cullen's mouth, my world narrowing to the soft yet unyielding feel of him as he plunders my mouth. Fully. Unapologetically. With a primal desire that wakes each of my senses, making me drunk on him. On us.

There's nothing like it in the world. There's nothing like *him* in the world. And he's mine. So very *mine*.

As I kiss Cullen back, I'm aware of someone starting to clap, then the whole world erupts in a cheer that echoes the joyful pounding of my heart. Cullen's arms tighten around me, holding me proudly. Assuredly. I know he always will.

Now and forevermore.

~

REVIEWS ARE A BOOK'S LIFEBLOOD. If you enjoyed ENEMY ZONE, please consider reviewing it on Amazon. Also be sure to look for Eli's story in ENEMY CONTACT, coming in 2021. If you are reading an ebook version of this book, please continue for a FREE preview of Alex Lidell's best-selling reverse harem fantasy romance, POWER OF FIVE.

ALSO BY ALEX LIDELL

TRIDENT RESCUE
Contemporary Romance
ENEMY ZONE
ENEMY CONTACT

POWER OF FIVE (7 books)
Reverse Harem Fantasy Romance

POWER OF FIVE (Audiobook available)
MISTAKE OF MAGIC (Audiobook available)
TRIAL OF THREE (Audiobook available)
LERA OF LUNOS (Audiobook available)
GREAT FALLS CADET (Audiobook available)
GREAT FALLS ROGUE
GREAT FALLS PROTECTOR

IMMORTALS OF TALONSWOOD (4 books)
Reverse Harem Paranormal Romance
LAST CHANCE ACADEMY (Audiobook available)
LAST CHANCE REFORM (Audiobook available)
LAST CHANCE WITCH
LAST CHANCE WORLD

Young Adult Fantasy Novels
TIDES

FIRST COMMAND (Audiobook available)

AIR AND ASH (Audiobook available)

WAR AND WIND (Audiobook available)

SEA AND SAND (Audiobook available)

SCOUT

TRACING SHADOWS (Audiobook available)

UNRAVELING DARKNESS (Audiobook available)

TILDOR

THE CADET OF TILDOR

SIGN UP FOR NEW RELEASE NOTIFICATIONS at https://links.
alexlidell.com/News

ABOUT THE AUTHOR

Alex Lidell is an Amazon KU All Star Top 50 Author Awards winner (July, 2018). Her debut novel, THE CADET OF TILDOR (Penguin, 2013) was an Amazon Breakout Novel Awards finalist. Her Reverse Harem romances, POWER OF FIVE and MISTAKE OF MAGIC, both received Amazon KU Top 100 awards for individual titles.

Alex is an avid horseback rider, a (bad) hockey player, and an ice-cream addict. Born in Russia, Alex learned English in elementary school, where a thoughtful librarian placed a copy of Tamora Pierce's ALANNA in Alex's hands. In addition to becoming the first English book Alex read for fun, ALANNA started Alex's life long love for fantasy books. Alex lives in Washington, DC.

Join Alex's newsletter for news, special offers and sneak peeks: https://links.alexlidell.com/News

Find out more on Alex's website: www.alexlidell.com

SIGN UP FOR NEWS AND RELEASE NOTIFICATIONS

Connect with Alex!
www.alexlidell.com
alex@alexlidell.com

Lightning Source UK Ltd.
Milton Keynes UK
UKHW010240090223
416650UK00001B/55

9 781949 347197